Satan
Burger

an anti-novel
by <u>Carlton Mellick III</u>

ERASERHEAD PRESS

 THE ERASERHEAD COLLECTIVE

ISBN 0-9713572-3-4

Eraserhead Press
16455 E. Fairlynn Dr,
Fountain Hills, AZ 85268
email: publisher@eraserheadpress.com
website: www.eraserheadpress.com

Carlton's website: www.angelfire.com/az2/mellick

FROM THE AUTHOR

I wrote this book when I was 20 years old and on the verge of self-murder. Not sure if my verge was due to a fascination with an unknown afterlife or due to utter boredom. Most likely the latter. The world becomes clearer and clearer the older we become, much less mysterious/exciting and all of its appeal we experienced during childhood turns logical, and *logic* is a dirty and boring word. This story is from the viewpoint of the rebel, who I am still deeply in love with, who refuses to accept the beliefs (the *logic*) that have been issued to him like a uniform. Some simple rebelious attitudes: I refuse to be a slave to money, I refuse to accept clarification of the afterlife, or the beliefs others might swear to be fact, I refuse to speak/write proper language, I refuse to make up my mind, I refuse to remember all that I've learned, I refuse that one plus one always equals two, I refuse to compromise my happiness, I refuse to agree with popular opinion, I refuse to be good, because we are not sure about the definition of good just yet, and I refuse to become blind, lose my hearing, misplace my legs . . .

Satan was a rebel too. The bible teaches you to hate rebels.

- Carlton Mellick III, 3/10/01 1:58 pm

Dedicated to Food Fortunata,
a genius in his own retarded little way.

"I want God to see me."
- Doug Rice, *A Good Cuntboy is Hard to Find*

ACT ONE
Hero Accepting his Journey

Scene 1
Acid Ocean Eyes

☺

The world is still new.

It is still developing/mutating like it is sludgeling through its puberty moments, within the tricky awkward stages of physical and emotional development, just finding hair where it did not have hair before. It seems old to us, but it only *seems* because our lives are so short. Not to mention that time goes faster for planets than it does for us humans. Just how time goes faster for humans compared to small sandwich bugs, which *need* to live at a slow pace in order to get a good view of the world before their scheduled expire, since the life span of a sandwich bug is only 2.51 days.

To the rest of the universe, Earth is just an adolescent boy, whine-crying around the legs of the aged worlds in the universe. His older brothers and sister - Jupiter and Venus as example - are also considered immature, but compared to Earth they are the top of sophistication, and Child Earth looks up-up to them all day long. Since the elder worlds prefer not to probe into the matters of brat-hooligan planets, the universe doesn't recognize our solar system on a regular basis.

And our human race has been around for such a brief amount of time that the universe hasn't had the chance to detect us yet. One blink is all it needs to miss our dance through actuality.

☺

In contrast, there are many other worlds inside and outside our galaxy that are considerably older than ours. They are like hundred-or-so-year-old humans, crippled and drooling all over their selves - drool being the ocean water spilling onto the coast, which is a tidal wave, sometimes called a tsunami – and because of their senility they forget all about the laws of nature and accidentally kill their parasites, which we call living beings. Forgetting to spin on its axle is the most common mistake of a senile planet, which splits the world into endless day and endless night, both of which are life-ending positions.

Another way a world kills its parasites is journeying too close to the sun, from sleep-strolling or mindless-wandering. This gives the world a nice brown suntan – or sunburn, depending on how long it bathes – and in less than a week its crab-red skin flakes and peels away; along with its burnt animals, vegetation, and most of its water supply – revealing a fresh surface to build on.

Earth won't grow senile enough to do this, at least not in our generation, and not in a thousand to come. It will most likely die long before it goes old, when the sun grows and grows up into a red giant, swallowing the Earth into its fire stomach. Unless Earth figures a way to detach itself from its orbit and find another system to live in, which in turn will destroy living kind anyway.

☺

So God (who called Earth the spoiled brat of his nine planets) gave him the dinosaurs. Dinosaurs were Earth's first toys, fun and BIG and cute for infant games, but they got boring rather quickly, just as stuffed animals get boring to aging human children. They were fun in a physical sense, but they were lacking imagination and the ability to form a society, so Earth wiped them out.

Then God gave Earth a being which was capable of forming a society – which was mankind.

Child Earth putter-played with us, watching us build up civilization and grow and flourish, then every once in awhile he'd wreck us with earthquakes and hurricanes. Though cruel to the human society, Earth found destruction quite amusing. It was much more fun than watching dinosaurs eat each other.

Now the human race isn't enough. There's only so much entertainment you can get out of a single brand of toy before it gets boring.

Recently, Earth approached the idea of trade. He wanted to swap his toys with the ones owned by his friend worlds. This idea came to him by watching human children in little schoolyards, who had action figures quite like the ones Earth has. The only difference between human beings and action figures is that action figures come with rocket packs and laser guns.

God was the being that made it possible for Earth to swap action figures. He set up a door called a *walm,* which gives our Earth access to beings from other worlds, times, and dimensions. Now Earth can pluck any creature from any place in the universe and put them into his personal collection, and he's been doing it all decade.

So God is keeping Child Earth clear from boredom. But as children always are, boredom only stays away for a little piece of a while.

☺

The walm is located in Rippington, which is now the most populated city in the world. About five years ago, it wasn't that large at all and was being recognized only as the capital of New Canada. The walm changed all that.

A young man named Leaf was born in this town, before the walm was born. He came into place the same year they re-elected Pat Paulsen for his second term as president of the United States of America, in 1976.

☺

Over-populating Rippington created a difficult lifestyle for the Rippingtonians. A sick-hard struggle. It also made life a jumble-confusing subsistence, with the majority of the population consisting of foreign action figures, who rarely learn to speak the native language, Canadian.

Once the rest of the citizens of the world found out about the walm causing an overpopulation problem, they just stared at their walls and shrugged.

Nobody cared then, nobody cares now, not even the New Canadians care and they are the victims of this situation.

Nobody cares in the least bit about *anything* anymore. It's like there is a drug in the air that makes everything seem unimportant, no matter how important anything is. A mother will witness her own child convulse and die, right in her chubby lap, and all she will do is stare at her wall and shrug.

Then she'll say, "Guess I'll have to make another one."

☺

Actually, I am exaggerating. *Some* people still care, especially the younger people. But *most* of the population is lame/untrue to their human emotions and nobody has found out exactly why.

I can only think of one man who even tried to uncover this problem's cause. It was an Alaskan psychologist who called it a *disease*, but he could not figure out why so many were so numb in the spirit. Even after several years of research, the only thing he came up with was that the world and its population had come into a plain state of endless *boredom*.

After the fourth year, he put his notes and books down.

And said, "oh well."

Staring at his wall, shrugging.

☺

The people of Rippington are not quite as *bored* as the rest of the world for one reason or another. I suspect it's because of the walm, but I'm not sure. Nor do I care.

Leaf is on the border between emotionful and emotionless. He cares a lot about some things and a little about others. Maybe it's because some things are boring and some things haven't bored him yet.

☺

Let me correct myself:

I am Leaf.

☺

I apologize for speaking in the third person when explaining myself, but that's just how I seem to be. I catch myself doing this quite often. It's because I can *see* in the third person. Anywhere in the world I want to go, my eyes will go. They will pop out of their sockets and wander the countryside. Just as a god or a movie camera would go. Even *myself* is just another character to me, hovering over my body from *God's Eyes*, watching someone else moving and talking to my commands, my own living corpse.

I call my body a corpse sometimes. It is because I don't like it at all. It bores me. I'd much rather live inside a strong man's body. Then maybe I'd have more self-esteem and I wouldn't need to look at myself in the third person. My body is all dangle-lanky and weak. It whines when I ask it to move, and the bones creak and complain as they labor.

My last name is no longer in use. I am just plain *Leaf*. It was Cable in the beginning, if I remember correctly, but Cable is retired now. I am just a Leaf. And I don't feel that I need to have a last name.

I feel pathetic sometimes, and I think that it is funny.

☺

My parents were Mr. and Mrs. Cable. I don't care to remember their first names. I'm sure they don't care to remember mine either. Actually, they *better* remember my name. They gave this weak-wretched title to me.

They said to me, "Leaf is also a name for a person and not just the vegetation that grows on trees and plants."

However, they meant *Leif*. Leif is the person and Leaf is just a leaf.

Great, eh? I'm a leaf, not a human being like my parents once told me.

☺

People always took my parents for hippies for naming me Leaf.
I would respond: "No, take them for idiots."

☺

I would not capitalize my name if I hadn't been named Leaf. My personality calls for a spelling in all lowercase letters, like mike or bobby or stephen or joey. Spelling your name like this shows that you feel inferior to the rest of the world, as I certainly do.

But if I were to spell my name *leaf*, then someone might suspect that I really am the vegetation that grows on trees and plants instead of a person. Maybe even God would believe that. And during autumn, when all the leaves crumple and fall from their branches to die, I too would curl into a crispy ball and drop from the surface of the planet, to suffocate in the breathless areas of the universe.

☺

I'm not very good at talking either. I am utterly confused, sometimes. This is because I took too many drugs when I was in high school. Actually, I wasn't in high school during this period. I was dropped out. When I say something like "back when I was in high school," I usually mean: "back when I was *supposed to be* in high school."

Anyway, I did a lot of Felix back then, and snoopies and cucumber seeds and slur corn – this was back when I had the money for such high society drugs – I also did a lot of opie, but that was usually free from friends. Nobody really sells Opie thinking there's a market for the stuff. It's basically dirt, the chemical version of Groo.

☺

After my parents, Mr. and Mrs. Cable, figured out - it did take them a while to figure anything out - that I replaced doing homework with doing expensive, mind-altering drugs, they decided it would be best for their selves to not have a child anymore.

So I left my parents, off on my own, working at corner shops and thinking they'd miss me. But they didn't, and to hell with them.

One day, I called up Mrs. Cable (mother) to ask if she missed me. After I asked, there was a long pause. I'm sure she was just staring at her wall, shrugging. So I never called again.

☺

After I was on my own, I resorted to drugs that were easier to come by. Actually, I can't relate them to *real* drugs. They were just chemicals, household products that you can buy in any/every store. Air-fresh was the first product I tried. It was invigorating, like taking a bubble bath with your brain. Cough-away was good too, but your vision strobe-battered and made you sick. Later, I experimented/gambled with anything that had toxic ingredients inside. Some things made me gorefully sick. Some things could have killed me.

I hate to think back on those days.

☺

About fifteen months after I left home, I found myself permanently deranged by these drugs. And I haven't been cured.

Because of my drugging experiments, I can no longer communicate like the rest of the world can. My mind is locked away from reality somewhere; the thinking is perfect/straight, but my voice doesn't come out right when I speak my thoughts. I have a stutter, and it takes time for my thoughts to process into words people can understand. Maybe that is my problem, I think in thoughts instead of in words.

I have a bad attention span too.

Speaking eventually became so difficult to me that I gave it up, almost entirely, and I have loads and loads of free time to think now, which I actually enjoy. Who needs a voice anyway? I stay silent during the whiles, usually talking in my head, speaking only to my best good friend and those who are blessed with patience. I do partake in conversations with people, in a way, but my opinions are only expressed to myself, within my brain, and nobody gets to hear them.

I *do* have friends, plenty of friends. This is an odd thing, now that I think about it, since I'm so antisocial and mind-screwed and all. They think I'm funny for being the way I am, the *silent* character of the group. Every group has one. I guess. Somebody has to be in the back of the crowd, following. They say I appear and disappear without any of them noticing. Sometimes they say I'm a ghost. Sometimes they say I have magic powers.

Since I don't speak so much, I write words on my shirts to express myself to the world. I wrote *ghost* on one of them. *Slave* on another. The most descriptive shirt says *crippled*.

Other shirts tell people: *I am a sandwich, I am a dildo*, and *I am the drunk driver that killed your kid* - an attempt at being mean.

☺

But my voice is only one thing that the drugs screwed up. The worst part is what happened to my vision. It is all cracked up, kind of like acid-drug. Everything I see is always shifting and melting, like the world is made of water, streaming down and around and up again.

It's like schizophrenia, I guess, but my thoughts are completely normal. Maybe it's half schizophrenia; my thoughts are sane, but my vision is insane. Maybe it really is schizophrenia and I just *think* I am sane. I don't know. I just know I have to go through this alone.

I call the watery world, *Rolling World.*

My friends call it, *Acid Ocean Eyes.*

☺

But - I can see in the third person without everything rolling, thank Yahweh (or whatever God likes to be called), so I don't miss my old eyes so much.

Sometimes I believe that I'm *blessed* with my God's Eyes, just like the people on TV that say they are blessed with psychic powers. God's sympathy is why I can see this way, even though I have never been a BIG fan of God's. Someday I'll figure out why He gave them to me.

Maybe I am His son, like Jesus Christ, but regarded as the fuck-up of his two children. Who knows . . .

☺

Occasionally I enjoy my rolling world. It can put me into a peaceful hum that relaxes every twitchy nerve in my body. Sure, it's hard to get around when you can't see straight, but sometimes it is pacific-beauty.

☺

Once I asked a doctor, "What is wrong with me?"

I figured he wouldn't believe me. Even *I* don't believe me. Who has ever heard of acid ocean eyes?

But the doctor was just staring at his wall, paying no compassion. Then he shrugged.

He said, "There is always something wrong with someone."

Scene 2
The Warehouse Between

☺

I live in a warehouse with three friends and two strangers.

My highest of the three friends is named Christian. He has a speaking problem caused by drug abuse as well — maybe that's why we became friends — but it is quite the opposite of mine. His problem is that he never shuts up, like he's naturally cranked up on snoopies, the dippy-fun guy. He talks and talks and talks, even when there's nothing to talk about, even when he's alone. Over and over, the same subjects, annoying mostly everyone he comes into contact with. Most of the time all his talking gets on my nerves as well, but I'm sure that all my silence is a pester to him.

But it isn't like that all the time. When I'm alone with him, we communicate differently than with a crowd. I speak more and he speaks less, so that it all evens out to a medium speed somehow. Besides the small people in my wall, he is the only person that I enjoy talking to.

Nobody knows that Christian and I speak differently when we are alone. They say that Leaf is as silent as a leaf, and Christian is as obnoxious as a Christian.

☺

I don't remember Christians being obnoxious, but my friends tell me they all were at one point. So they say. There are no more Christians today, at least not the Christ-worshipping kind, and there aren't any religions either.

The religions were the first things that everyone became bored with. People stopped praying and going to church, holy water went unblessed, crosses and candles were no longer being purchased. The whole religious phenomenon just vanished, like *snap*, besides the few who considered their religion's ways of living too routine to stop.

- 15 -

Routine is an important word today, because it is the only thing left that makes the world go around.

The people of Rippington are excluded from this statement, since the walm is the opposite of routine. And the walm brings out odd feelings in the beings that surround it. These feelings are the natural reaction to the foreign energy that fuels the walm, the stuff that makes it go. We call the energy *sillygo*, but that's not the scientific term. The name the scientists gave it was *the stuff that makes it go*, because the scientists didn't care much to give it a proper scientific name.

We call it sillygo because it makes you go silly. Nobody knows any more about it than that. Probably because everyone in Rippington went silly, and I'm sure everyone outside of Rippington could care less.

As for the people that come out of the walm, they could give a pig's twat about the native Rippingtonians. They are Earth's *new* toys, and the only things Child Earth pays attention to these days are the new toys. No longer does he enjoy watching the lives of us outdated action figures as he did with my ancestors. New toys are now higher classed citizens as far as Earth is concerned, even if the old toys have more money and better living arrangements.

The new people live on the streets in small settlements. Two settlements are nearby the warehouse where I live. One is a medieval tent village by the train tracks. The other is a colony of midgets that dress up like past U.S. presidents. (The word *midget*, by the way, is no longer an offensive term since no one is offended by anything anymore.)

I think I've seen an Ulysses S. Grant midget once, but I'm not for sure. Grant was the closest president that popped into my head at that time, so I guessed it was him. How many were fat and bearded anyway? Most of the midgets are not very good at impersonating. Maybe they like it that way.

I am sitting in the warehouse with my cello right now.

It's not a very healthy cello. I found it in an abandoned apartment house all crippled and warped. But I'm not a very good cello player, so it all evens out. I like to make scratch-crazy noises on it, defacing it with the bow. I'm very good at this. Getting more and more obnoxious every day. And I am very proud of myself.

The cello is also the soundtrack to my rolling world vision. Right now, I'm scratching at the strings, creating a sound similar to a saw cutting wood, ogling at a group of steel sculptures, very sharp-spiked and crude, and they roll around like lardy belly dancers.

The warehouse was once used for producing hundreds of steel sculptures by a female artist known as *The Lady of Steel*. The works are awe-interesting in my roll-woggy eyes, but none of my roommates appreciate them, spitting candy-phlegm on the ground sometimes. The outside world has probably lost *all* interest in art by now. Not even the citizens of Rippington care for it. Not even my friends.

After The Lady of Steel lost all her money, she gave us her warehouse and all of her sculptures. She said she was going to go through the walm to find a less boring place to live in, one with an appreciation for fine art. She was the only person I can think of who wanted to go through that horrible walm door, into another dimension-world.

I look down at my forearm:

The arm hairs are fanning without wind, crawling like creeper-weeds, wire-spiders, pulsating soup skin.

I look to the window: a malformed wave of water, coming to crash over me, the drool of a senile planet. My stomach turns with the wave. My breath vibrating. I can no longer keep up with the rolling world, so my eyes close drunk.

Whenever my visions get me dizzy from an overdose of movement, I either shut myself off from the outside world or look through my God's Eyes. I've chosen the latter.

☺

God's Eyes:

I go to my best friend, Mr. Christian, looking down at him through the cloud's chin-hair, as he walks up the train track carrying a steel drum. Christian is wearing a polyester suit; he *always* wears a polyester suit. We call him a wannabe rude boy, smoking on his cheap cigars. There aren't any more rude boys. There aren't any more wannabe rude boys either. The term I am speaking of is a Jamaican slang word for *gangster*.

In the sixties, Jamaicans would pretend to be rude boys. They would dress up classy in zoot suits, porkpie hats, cold eyebrows, smooth words. They were influenced by ska music, which often glorified the lifestyles of rude boys and made everyone want to be one. Years later, the same thing

happened with rap music. Glorifying gangsters (sometimes spelled/pro-
nounced *gangstas*) in music usually creates wannabes.

   Christian does not consider himself a rude boy, and he doesn't care
for the jazz-like music that rude boys listened to. He considers himself *punk*
and wears his suits just to be unusual.

   In other words: UNUSUAL = PUNK.

☺

   Two medieval knights are sword-fighting in Christian's path, going
clink-clink and *arr-arr!* He doesn't mind to them, passing by with hardly a
flinch when their swords collide. We are accustomed to walking through
battles in our front rail yard. It is so common that we don't care enough to
use our dodging skills anymore – too lazy. Charging right through is the
quickest way.

   Nobody is afraid of dying these days either.

   "Death isn't as bad as everyone thinks," Christian always says. "It's
just one step away from being alive again."

   He's believed in reincarnation ever since he was a child. He swears
that his little sister was reincarnated into his pet ferret five years after her
death. Then his pet ferret was reincarnated into a wolf spider, and then an
autocar, and then a rock. It's always an animal or object, never another
person that can say *hi, I'm a reincarnation of his sister*, so he's hard to argue
against. Nobody believes him, but he'll punch your face off your head if
you tell him he's wrong.

   Somebody said that Christian was responsible for his sister's death,
leaving her all alone in the kitchen when he was supposed to be watching
her. But it was probably his parents' fault or, more likely, God's fault.

☺

   When Christian arrives at the warehouse and trips over my corpse,
only half a thumb of a cigar left, he yells out my name and I awake inside of
my rolling world.

   His face melts out twitchy-fast words: "Figured your punk ass'd be
here, always locked away, never doing anything anymore, you look like a
pile of dick."

   He's right about one thing. I'm always indoors. Everyone calls me
agoraphobic, but you'd be too if you had eyes like mine. I pause, continuing
with the wood-sawing sounds, staring at the sculpture-dancers.

I respond, "You'd be too if you had eyes like mine." It's my usual response.

Christian goes to the toilet in the center of the room. We use this toilet for crapping and as a television stand since it is situated in the middle of a room instead of a bathroom. He has to take the television off the seat before he tinkers into the tinker pot.

"You're always bummed about that shit, guy," he spurts. "Get on with your life. If I could trip all day without needing any drugs, I'd be cumming in my pants."

He always says that.

And I always say this:

"You get stressed of it quick." I scratch my shirt that says *Brain Disease.*

"Yeah, yeah, always complaining." Christian grumbles the toilet water down. "Complaining, complaining, whining, complaining."

"What's wrong with you?" I say in a shaky, tiny-girl voice.

"The usual," he responds, placing the television back on the toilet seat. "Overwhelmed with boredom."

He turns the channels on the TV, most of which seem to be cooking shows and game shows.

"I think Battlestar Galactica's going to be on soon," I say grubulous.

Christian complies with a squint and corrects the channel, pulling up a milk crate. I hate sitting on milk crates, but they're our only chairs.

I continue, "If I had to choose only one show to watch forever . . . it'd be Battlestar Galactica."

I go into my God's Eyes and wander the room, move around to the back of the television set and watch us as we watch television.

Behind Christian and my corpse, I see a bald, fat, middle-aged man staring at us through the window, puckering his lips, making perverted expressions.

"I thought you only liked the theme song, guy," Christian says. "Nobody seriously likes that stupid show."

I am actually offended by this, but nobody shows offense anymore so I don't make a BIG deal out of it.

"No, I *seriously* like it." The words leave my brain and come out of my corpse in the distance, almost like ventriloquism. "The theme song is good, but I like everything about it. You're thinking of Hawaii Five-O. That's the one that has a super Mr. T song, but nobody likes the show."

The fat man begins licking the glass in our direction with a fat spongy tongue. He is John, one of the two strangers that live in the back of the warehouse who have no connection to the inside of our home, who we do not speak to, who we collect rent from and don't like. One of his hands is sweating a palmprint into the window, but I think he has the other one inside his pants. I don't feel disturbed by him, even though he is jerking off to my own picture. I pretend not to notice.

But I begin to wonder how many perverted old men have masturbated to my picture in the past. It is quite possible that this performance took place very many times. Before I had God's Eyes, it could have happened all the time. Like there are perverted old men everywhere, behind tinted glass, in public bathrooms, on balconies or behind holes drilled into walls, watching, masturbating, fantasizing about you. I wonder if anyone else ever thinks about this.

"I like the Greatest American Hero song the best," says Christian. He hasn't seen the perverted man.

"That's a groobly one too. We should cover that song at the show tonight."

"That'd be killer, guy. I'll work on it."

Battlestar Galactica really is my favorite show. I worship it. There's something about science-fiction from the seventies that turns me dippy, something about the mixture of disco and futurism and sexy spandex space suits.

☺

A figure, too fast for my God's Eyes, passes John from the outside, John still licking the glass, saliva running the dust-window scent up a nostril. The figure enters.

It is Mort, another roommate. Christian's best friend besides myself. He's Japanese but never speaks his birth language. But he still carries the accent with him.

I enter my natural eyes and we turn to his attention.

Christian's greetings: "Mortician, where have you been all day? I thought we were supposed to be playing a show here tonight."

"I was getting a new distortion pedal," Mort replies. "The one we have's bust, and I looked all over town for one. Eventually, I got one from Lenny."

"How good is it?"

"Not great, but it'll do, me matey."

Mort says *me matey* because he is obsessed with pirates, or the old-fashioned stereotype of pirates. He always dresses up pirate-like with a skull hat and eye-patch. And he speaks with a mock-pirate accent, which doesn't work very well since his Japanese accent is so strong. The combination of Japanese and Pirate form a new accent of Mort's own. It's difficult to understand him at times, but Christian seems to catch his words clearly.

Mort turns to me:

"Arr, did you tell him, Leaf?" he asks me, motioning to Christian. A tremor shoots through my body. I heard him ask me the question, but I can't come up with an answer.

"What?" I respond, unsteady.

"Did you tell him the news?"

I shrug.

"Tell me what?" Christian saves me from speaking.

"We rented out the other room."

"Really? T'who?" Christian asks.

"To Satan," Mort answers.

Christian pauses, his eyes bobbing. "There's a guy nicknamed *Satan*?"

"No, that's his real name."

"Someone named their kid *Satan*?"

"No, it *is* Satan. *The* Satan. You know, the devil. And you're not going to believe this, but he's a fairy."

"A fairy?"

"You know, a tart, a full-flaming homosexual. And he was even coming onto me. Who'd of thought the Lord of Darkness would be the Queen of Darkness?"

Christian laughs. "Mortician, you're the biggest weirdo in the world, guy."

I barge in with a soft yell, halfway upset. "I'm trying to watch Battlestar Galactica."

"You can't watch that there tele-rubish. We gotta get the place ready for the bastard show tonight."

"I can't help you," I say, pointing to my eyes. "I'm disabled."

"So am I," Christian giggle-says. "I'm quadriplegic."

Mort explodes at Christian. "Why am I the only person who does anything around here? I've been out searching for a damn distortion pedal all day to replace the one that you broke last week, and you're probably going to break this one again tonight, and you won't even help me set up the stage!"

"The last time I helped you, all you did was bitch at my sloppiness. I'll help if I don't have to do orders."

"Arr, ye glimey bastards! Get the bloody hell out if ye be lazy arses," Mort whines, turning the television off. "I don't want you getting in me way."

Mortician hates laziness. Maybe it's a Japanese stereotype, but I think he's just sick of being around groo-heads all the time. I ignore him, because I have no choice but to be lazy.

"Fine with me," Christian says, and we get up to leave.

"Be back before eight," Mort hiss-spurts.

Christian seems happy to get out of work, but now I don't get to watch Battlestar Galactica.

And the room turns into a huge churn-wheeling machine as I stand. Thunder-shrieking into the ground and around my face, buzzing – as if I am polluted with bees, my hair honey-eaten. The ground absorbs me as I grossly to the door, rushing billow-rollers inside my head knocking me off balance. This always happens when I stand up from a long sit.

John is still licking the glass at Mort as we pass the window. I would tell him to go away, but I've forgotten how to talk.

Scene 3
The Effects of Sillygo

☺

They have put shaggy carpeting down on the sidewalks, so now I can walk barefoot up the way, gleaming at caterpillar-kaleidoscope, squishy the fibers between my toes. I cough and put some phlegm onto the shag, cold on my heel when I massage it between threads.

Christian does not take off his shoes. I don't mean just at this particular time. I mean he *never* takes off his shoes. I've known him for seven years and not for a second did I ever catch him without something on his feet, whether it be socks, boots, animal skins, plastic bags, towels, bandages, or small boxes. I'm thinking he has some deformity on his feet that he refuses to show anyone, or maybe he just hates going without shoes like the skin is too sensitive for the ground, or maybe he feels naked with bare feet. Personally, I find shoes to be crude customers and try to wear them as seldom as possible. That's why I'm glad there is carpeting on sidewalks now.

Christian has been drinking from a bottle of *Fool's Gold* – a secondary brand of gold cinnamon schnapps – for the past five minutes. Actually, he has been drinking it every day for the past five years. It contains flakes of gold that dazzle-flutter through the liqueur if shaken, and they continue to dance in your stomach bag after you swallow them. I wonder if the gold flakes are bad for your digestive system.

I tell him: "I bet your entire stomach is gold-coated by now."

He tells me: "You can bet your penis on that one."

☺

We head to Baja-Style Mexican Food Stand that is up in the tower shops – which are shops that are stacked and stacked and stacked on top of each other, like the autocars in the autocar junkyard. The shops all lofty and weaky, constructed by amateurs, ready to collapse at any day. Several ladders and splinter-rickety spiral stairs go from shop to shop to shop to shop.

- 23 -

We go up a ladder for three shops to a ledge, take another ladder through the floor of a sewing store, then through a wood shop, then through a small school for autistic children. The roof of the tower owns the food shops; one food shop being the Mexican burrito store that we always-always eat at. And it's very surprising that the best Mexican food in the entire world is in Rippington, New Canada.

☺

Up here, there's a large cage with a female baboon inside, the baboon squawking and slapping at herself, eye-goobers sliming into her facial fur, sticking. We always eat where we can see the baboon, watching her sit there all miserable and squawking, slapping, rolling in my swirl-vision.

People keep female baboons at the tops of tall Rippington buildings to scare away scorpion flies. It all started last year, when a swarm of them migrated through the walm and took up residence in our sky.

Along with the prowler beast, a scorpion fly is one of the most dangerous species to come out of the walm. The scorpion fly looks half dragonfly and half scorpion, but is about two feet long. You'll never find one by itself, only the mass, like a violent cloud in the distance. They feed off of whatever animal they can find, but humans are the most common meat besides bird. And, since they're allergic to the ground, they live, sleep, and breed in the air.

A common warning in Rippington is: "Be cautious in high air."

I've heard they are silent, stalking very furtively, sneaking up on you from above without your notice. Then they use their stinger in the back of your neck, and the poison is enough to paralyze you for a good three hours. During that time, the swarm devours you with limbs that resemble tridents made of corn-patterned bone. And they secrete digestive fluids from glands on their faces, to make your meat soft and easy. Nobody survives an attack from the swarm, unless in a large crowd with plenty of luck. They are too many to dodge or kill and they are too quick to run away from, but their victims are usually unaware of the scorpion flies and do not own time enough to react.

The only defense against them is a female baboon with nyminits, which are parasites that live within their female sex organs, and are fatal to the scorpion fly if ingested. Since the scorpion fly has no predators and is immune to almost every disease, the nyminits brought an unusual scare into its beady intellect. Now scorpion flies are too frightened to go within a mile radius of any female baboon.

Of course, they'll eat the baboon's husband if she isn't nearby. And I bet the wife baboon thinks that this is funny sometimes, because if they get into a fight she can threaten to leave. Then the male baboon has to apologize immediately.

She says, "I'll let the scorpion flies get you then."

☺

Into my God's Eyes:

I see Christian and Leaf munching greasy burritos at a crispy table. Staring down from the pole which holds a tower shops flag – patchworked together from scraps of cloth. Slobbering and smacking sounds orchestrate their environment before a word is spoken.

The baboon squawks and slaps at herself.

Christian gorges into his burrito, squeezing green sauce into his throat, and some leftover gravy, washing it all down with Fool's Gold.

"These are always Mr. T, guy," Christian says with his mouth full. He always speaks with food in his mouth, and not just because he has lousy table manners, but because he thinks talking is much more fun when you can taste the words. "I wish they'd hire me as a fulltime burrito-eater."

"That'd be a super Mr. T job," I say.

Mr. T is the word that replaced *cool* and *dudical*. It's based on the guy from the television show called the A-Team and the movie Rocky III (getting the role by winning a bouncer contest, which included a midget toss). Back in the eighties, Mr. T was the epitome of cool and dudical.

Christian continues, "Even though they make them out of dog meat."

My head is shaking *no*. "I bet it's only cat meat."

"It's gotta be dog. Cats wouldn't taste this good."

"What have you got against cats?"

"They suck. I fucking hate them."

"Doesn't mean they taste bad . . ."

"I don't care. They fucking suck."

Leaf says, "I bet the carne asada is the dog and the carnitas is the cat."

"No, carnitas is pork."

"No way. I tried making a burrito with pork at home and it tastes nothing like the carnitas meat here."

"Was it good at all?"

"It blew."

The baboon squawks.

Christian asks, "Well, if carnitas is cat and carne asada is dog, what do you think chorizo is?"

"Guts and intestines and all that good stuff."

"Really?"

"Sure. The man who invented it was a damn genius."

"Well, you'd have to be a genius to make intestines and tongues taste good."

"And rectums too."

The baboon slaps.

☺

I let God's Eyes wander:

They go to a small bookstore at the bottom of the Tower Shops where the only popular author in the world is signing books. Yes, people still read books. But only out of *habit*. And they'll only read the one extremely popular writer. Nobody cares to look for new ones, because they think: "He *must* be good if ten billion copies were printed and the cover says *bestseller*."

Even if the book is terrible, they'll buy it. Because people must read something for every last hour of every day, right before going to sleep. It doesn't have to be good reading. It doesn't have to be educational or enlightening. It doesn't have to be imaginative or even entertaining. It just has to be common to the rest of the world – a book by an author everyone has heard of, so novel conversations can be more convenient.

Everyone who reads artistic novels – and there are very-very few – calls this BIG author the *mega-sellout*. This is what I call him too, but I don't read novels. My eyes roll so much that I can only read comic books.

Eventually, reading altogether will be forgotten as a habit and then become nonexistent to the human world.

Writing is not an art, it is a business. It doesn't matter what the author writes, as long as it is written quickly and is something everyone can relate to. Actually, the mega-sellout can be long-long dead already and some twice-as-terrible author can be writing books under his name, and the world will still buy the imposter's books, even if it is completely obvious that he's a fake.

And nobody cares. Not even me.

There is a line that goes from down the street, through the store, to the mega-sellout's table. He's signing a book for a nerdy wearing magnifying glasses. The nerdy doesn't actually need glasses, but since he's a *nerdy* it is his obligation to wear thick-thick glasses, even if they are fake. The author hands the book back to him.

"Thanks," says Nerdy. "You're the best author in the whole world."

"Of course," says Mega-Sellout.

Nan is the next in line. She wears dark long-limbed clothes and she's bald with the words *blonde hair* tattooed on her head where the hair should have been. She drops a red book onto the table.

"This isn't my book," says Mega-Sellout.

"So?" Nan replies. The author bearing a suffer-dazed face. "This is a book signing, isn't it?"

"Yes, but for *my* book. Not . . ." he glances at the cover, "Mark Amerika's."

"But I didn't like your book. This one's *way* better. Sign it."

"Why should I? It's not mine."

"You always sign your own books. Why can't you sign someone else's for a change?"

"Go away you weird person."

"R. Kelly signed my Ratt CD."

"GET OUT!"

☺

Nan leaves the store.

She's a friend of mine. Well, sort of. She is the girlfriend of one of my friend/roommates besides Mort and Christian. She never talks to me, probably because I never talk to her, but I still consider her a friend. Christian doesn't really get along with her either, but they consider each other friends too. Girls find Christian disgusting and creepy, probably because he is.

We meet her outside the tower shops, Christian still drinking gold flakes. The proper greetings are exchanged and we get down to business. I call it *business*, but what I'm really meaning to is: *finding a way to fight boredom*. It's hard to find anything interesting to do in a world that has gone boring, but every day we try to do something exciting, always keeping busy, so that we don't end up like the world outside of Rippington. It is necessary.

"So what's going on tonight?" Nan asks, scratching at a hole in the armpit of her shirt.

"We got the show," Christian says, "but there's not much else to do."

"There's always something to do. You just got to figure out what that something is."

"We could go drink . . ." Christian says. "I'm already buzzing, but I can get you something."

"I don't have that much money." Nan squeezes her face inward like she always does. I think it's her poor attempt at being cute. Nan is rather attractive, even though she's a skinhead girl, but she's too much of a tough guy to be cute.

"Are you kidding?" Christian chuckles. "You're the richest bitch I know."

She punches him. A common thing for Nan to do and Christian never punches her back.

I decide to speak. "We could go see Satan."

Nan sneers at me as if I did something wrong.

I continue, word-staggering, "He moved into the empty room . . . behind the warehouse . . . by John's."

"I thought Mortician was just joking about that, guy." Christian drinks some gold.

"No, it's really Satan, the devil."

"What is he doing here? Trying to lay the world to waste?"

"He's opening a chain of fast food restaurants called *Satan Burger*, home of the deep-fried hamburger."

"Sounds good," Christian says.

"Sounds disgusting," Nan says.

I say, "The first one opened up in the village. I want to go."

Christian complains, "We can't do that now. We just ate. Not to mention the village is too far to walk to. Maybe after the show."

Then the three of us realize the boredom sinking in.

I stare down at the jambling carpet-sidewalk, warding off a shrug.

This is what I can see with my other eyes:

Mort is with the third of my roommates, who is Gin – a rattle-lofty fellow with hippie dreadlocks and shoes that don't match, and he wears a shirt that says *Nan's Boyfriend*. Mort is trying to set up the stage, getting little help from Gin as he never gets help from anyone. Gin just stands there, watching Mort set up the drums, drinking from his mega-drink.

"Arr, help me ye glimey bastard!" Mort says.

"I'm on break," Gin responds.

"Hand me that cymbal."

Gin slurps his mega-drink.

"Oi!"

The cymbal is tossed near Mort, crash-smashing.

There are five taps at the door.

"There he is," Gin says.

"There *who* is?" Mort asks.

"Didn't Nan tell you?"

Mort shrugs. Five more taps.

"I finally got you a piper."

"Your brother's back from Germany?"

"Yeah." Five more taps. "The psycho looks like a techno-goth now. He says he's ready to release his soul into the body and shaft of the music or some weird shit like that."

Taptaptaptaptap.

They stare at each other. Gin slurps his mega-drink.

"Aren't you going to answer it?" Mort asks.

Gin slurps his drink.

Pause.

Taptaptaptaptap.

Slurp.

"I'm on break," Gin says.

"You tit."

Taptaptap . . .

Mort staggers from the drum pieces, across to the door and opens to the tapper, who is Vod – a depression-faced, robot vampire of a man, dark clothes, pale skin, and . . . a bagpipe.

"Hello. I am Vodka." His voice an emotionless, fake German accent. "But people do not call me Vodka. They call me Vod."

"I'm Mort."

"Yes, but people do not call you Mort. They call you Mortician. That is very amusing."

"Come in then." Mort swells with boredom in Vod's immediate presence.

Vodka creeps into the warehouse with his fingers stretched out like batwings. Dracula-eyes scoping the details of the warehouse. Then he freezes in mid-step when he sees the toilet situated in the middle of the room. He turns to Gin and raises an eyebrow, then glances back at the toilet.

"I find your toilet most delectable," he says. "It beckons me to sit upon it."

Without asking permission, he sits, slowly, preparing for ultimate gratification . . . and a satisfying smile cracks the corners of his face. "Wonderful."

Pause.

Mort says, "So you're the lad with the bagpipes?"

"Ja," Vod says, "and I'm so excited to release my soul into their shafts, and to become one with my music, that I cannot resist an erection."

Mort's face contorts, turning to Gin. "Wanna come with me to get the rent from John?"

"Get it yourself," Gin says.

"I'm not going to John's by myself. He's . . . old."

"Then take Vodka."

Vod exclaims, "I DO NOT WISH TO LEAVE THE TOILET SEAT."

☺

Gin, sipping at the mega-drink, scratching a soft spot on his hip, and Mort, swinging a saber, pass an Abraham Lincoln midget as they stroll behind the warehouse.

They get to a fire engine red door in the back of the warehouse. A BIG doggie door covers half the entrance, with a sign reading, "Beware of Doggie."

A questioning face emerges from Mort's neck.

"That's a big doggie door," Gin says. "I didn't think there were doggies that size."

"Thought I told John he's not allowed to have pets," Mort says. "Arr."

Mort hums the door buzzer.

Gin says, "Maybe it's to scare away burglars and Mormons."

Mort buzzes again. "He's not answering."

"But he's always here." Gin buzzes.

Pause.

Gin rubs his neck, sipping the mega-drink. "Look through the doggie door."

"No, thanks," says Mort, "I don't want to see the doggie that needs a door that big."

Gin laughs. "Afraid?"

"Arr!" Mort flips him off. "You do it."

"I'll do it."

"Go ahead then."

"I will."

"Then do it."

"I will."

Gin bends down, scratching a breast.

"Then do it."

"Shut up, I'm doing it." Gin throws open the doggie door and looks inside.

But first:

Spin-feelings rush into Gin, giving form to a large orange structure in Gin's head which is a living being quite like the cross between a tapeworm and an apartment building. This creature is the offspring of Gin's hangover, and Gin's head is the incubator, pulsating warmth. It takes twenty-four hours before it will leave into the outside world, and Gin will have to bear its pain until then. He gets this infant in his head many times a week from drinking too much hard alcohol – which, of course, is gin.

And with the infant/creature handing him a blood-rushing of the head, Gin doesn't realize the doggie on the inside of the doggie door. The doggie being of a certain breed that no one has ever seen before. It is the *John* breed. Well, it is actually just John himself, naked and on all fours, growling with foam. A fat, bald, middle-aged man that thinks he is an attack doggie.

Then, just as an attack doggie would, John flies toward the intruder, splashing the mega-drink between them. And Gin screams out, flap-dashing down the street with the human doggie chasing him, barking.

And Mort bends down to pick up the rent money settled on the ground just within the door, inside of an envelope with two flowers and a pencil and four paper clips and some breakfast, and the bills have little smiles drawn onto the president faces in blue ink.

The naked doggie springs at Gin's legs, thumping him to the ground, handing him a large number of claw-scratchings.

The Abraham Lincoln midget comes to save the young man from further injuries, rapping John-doggie on the scalp with a rolled-up newspaper, which angers the wannabe doggie, turning to Lincoln midget and biting his pant leg, thrashing it about.

Gin darts away.

Mort, from a distance, gives a cluttered face – a confused spectator watching John chase Lincoln down the street, barking and biting at his ankles.

☺

Back to me:

I find myself reading a Mutilation Man comic book at a corner store/liquor store, and I'm not positive how I got here. Mutilation Man swirls off the page and hides under the magazine rack, which looks more like a transformer in my eyes.

Christian and Nan are searching the shelves for nice cheap liquor.

"What you want?" Christian asks, swarming his arm around Nan's stomach.

"I don't know. They're all too expensive."

"Just pick one. You can afford it."

"Well, you're hasty all of a sudden."

"Bite me."

She bites him on the chubby part of his shoulder and he screams a laugh. Then she grabs a bottle of Fork's Gum for him.

"Whiskey?" amazed at her choice. She usually drinks butter almond rum.

Christian takes it to the cashier, a brown-haired, blond mustache-bearing man, who has never slept with a woman under the age of forty, who is now reading a newspaper.

Christian puts the bottle and his ID onto the counter.

The cashier looks up from his paper. "Eight even," he says.

Nan throws some crumpled bills. The cashier glances at the cash and then tosses them back. "Sorry, I can't accept this." He goes back to his paper.

"Why not?"

"I don't accept American money."

Christian and Nan stare at him for a few minutes.

"How can you not accept American money in an American store?" Christian asks.

"For your information, this store isn't in America. It's in New Zealand."

"No, it's not. It's in America."

The cashier slams the newspaper. "Didn't you read the sign?"

"What sign?"

The cashier jumps over the counter to the glass of the door and picks up a small piece of notebook paper with four words written in magic marker.

It reads:

The he tapes it back to the glass.

"Real funny," Christian groans.

"I'm not joking. The dirt underneath this store is owned by New Zealand."

"Sure it is."

"Hawaii's not attached to the U.S., but it's still considered part of the country."

"Yeah, but Hawaii's surrounded by water, not another country."

"Hey, Mr. Man, I own this store and it's going to be in whichever country I want it to be in! Actually, I don't want it to be in New Zealand anymore." He crosses out New Zealand and writes in another country.

Now it reads:

WELCOME TO VENEZUELA

The cashier is proud of himself. "There. Now we're in Venezuela and you can't buy that whiskey unless you have Venezuelan money."

Nan comes in. Her expression says *I'm sick of this.*

She punches the cashier in the face. He screams straight to the ground.

"My tongue is broken," the Cashier cries.

Nan takes the money and the whiskey, walking toward the door. "What are you going to do, call the Venezuelan police?"

The cashier bleeds.

As we leave the store, we discover that the sun is ready to go in for the night, heading back home to his wife and kiddies, who are all sit-waiting for him to come down to them with crab sticks and dinner rolls perched on their flowery kitchen counter.

On his way over the horizon, the sun accidentally brushes against a mountain range and catches the landscape on fire.

And as the sunset becomes a forest of flames and red-orange swirls with smoky demons crawling their way to the cloud people, and as the abstracted vegetation and forest creatures fall over in disgust, all that Mr. Sun says about his action is this:

"Sorry about catching you on fire. I'll try to be more careful tomorrow."

Scene 4
History Comes Alive

    The warehouse spits a wad of throat-snot onto a passerby and then goes about its daily routine of sulking in its foundation. When the passerby insists the warehouse explain itself, the warehouse waves him away with a little wooden finger and calls him a log of boob poop.

    The warehouse doesn't realize, however, that there is a group of Gorguals nearby. Gorguals are an alien race that excrete food-waste from their breasts, which work like buttocks. And there's a hole – the breast hole – between both mounds, which lean forward over a toilet for defecation. In other words, their boobs poop. The Gorguals don't take offense to the warehouse's *boob poop* comment since they do not speak English or the language that warehouses speak; and even if they did speak English or Warehouse they would not have taken offense because crapping (an informal term) is accepted socially within their culture. Translated from Gordual tongue, the term *crapping* is referred to as *stool liberation*.

     ☺

    The sun is gone, eating dinner with his family, and the warehouse is taken by old Earth-toys, all punks and skinheads mauling each other and skreaking, which makes the warehouse very bitter and inclined to spit at passing ones on its carpet walkway.

    Inside of the warehouse's guts, a concert is in session. A legion of color shuffles soundly, merrily around and round-a-go. I am behind the stage, muzzy from the round-a-go crowd movements and all the shifty colors, ticking sick.

    My band is playing already, but I am not yet onstage, liquor-inhaling.

    Christian is running the performance, rape-screeching and scratching sheet metal with Mortician, who plays his distorted bass with a knife and a cellular phone. We are an electronic noise band, which is a very popular Japanese food creation. Actually, I didn't mean to say electronic noise is *a very popular Japanese food creation*, though it is a genre of music invented by the Japanese music underground.

This is what I meant to say: the name of our band is *A Very Popular Japanese Food Creation.*

Very few people in the room enjoy our style of music, even though they mosh and punch each other as if dancing to it. They're all waiting for the headlining brutal oi!/punk skinhead band to play, and that will be the start of a large kicking/punching/fork-through-the-skull festival I assure you.

Within the center of the room, there are two things: one is Vod, who is sitting on the toilet playing his bagpipes to the electronic noise, and the other thing is a history book that smells of rotten human.

☺

History books and rotten humans are two things that you'll always find in a graveyard. Long ago, you could only find rotten humans there and never any history books, and this made the cemetery a very boring place to visit. My mother told me, long before I came to hate her, that the whole point of going to the cemetery was to visit gravestones and a plot of dirt, where you were to put flowers if you had the money for them.

Now the whole point of going to the cemetery is to read history books. Let me explain:

It started when all the governments of the world decided that it would be a very neat idea for everyone and everyone to write journals of their lives, including every day, every moment, every thought, every person, every creation, and every thing important to each individual from day to day to day to death, so that everyone will have their memories and their life story written down, to live eternally after department. But only two copies were to be made. One is sewn into the stomach of the deceased and the other is for the public to read.

A Gravestone is not just a stone with a name and a date to another date anymore. It now has a little waterproof/airproof drawer inside that contains the autobiography of the person buried beneath. And ever since I was a child, I've been going to the cemetery and reading the lives of the dead. And every time I read about someone, that someone becomes alive again.

Not too many people care to read history books anymore. Nobody even cares to write them; even I have given them up due to my acid ocean eyes. I still go to the cemetery and look at the pictures and titles, but it's disappointing to know that I can't read them entirely.

They don't let you steal the history books. It's very important that you don't, for history's sake. But they don't have any security guards to stop you, only the gatekeeper, and he doesn't really care. Still, I've never heard of anyone stealing a history book besides myself.

I stole *The Story of Richard Stein.*

It was such a great history that I had to keep it. But I still had respect for the readers of the books of the dead, especially the readers of Richard Stein, so I didn't take the book on display. I thief-slithered onto his grave one night and dug that old corpse up. I stab-cut into his gut with some pizza shears – which was quite the ass painting – and filched the book resting inside. It's just as good, but it has a rotten Richard Stein smell on it. It's the only book that I try to read other than comics. But I already know the majority of it by heart.

His words are called *wisdom* by the critics on the back cover.

Richard Stein has taught me much about the world we live in. His book is my bible. Well, something had to be. The real bible is very boring, being on the level of a bad coffee table magazine. Not that I hate everything the bible says. Personally, I agree with most of the biblical messages, I guess, but I just think the writers weren't any good. Matthew and Mark were okay, but Luke and some others told as drome a story as a ten-hundred-page book about dentistry. (Just in case you didn't know, *drome* means boring and *droll* means interesting, so you don't get confused.)

The Richard Stein Bible is more like a guide to being alive than it is the story of his life. It doesn't seem like *his* story at all, actually, because he wrote it in the third person, which is one reason why I decided to read his book instead of all the other histories. It is next to impossible to read every history book in the cemetery, not to mention it's not worth reading them all since many people live very drome lifestyles. So I had to judge the whole book on reading the first paragraph, hoping it would be an interesting attention-grabber.

Richard Stein's first paragraph was:

"The main thing that keeps the gun away from your head is thirteen hundred bottles of bourbon, eight hundred bottles of vodka, three hundred bottles of gin, two thousand bottles of rum, six cups of everclear, and four hundred twenty-two bottles of southern comfort during the course of a lifetime; but any more than that and you'll be considered an alcoholic. Richard Stein was considered an alcoholic."

☺

Nan is in the round-a-go crowd with a chunky blue-haired woman named Liz, who says she has sex with small mammals. They are at a table, sitting on milk crates, sitting with two Harvey Wallbangers and two walrus-shaped skinhead guys who are trying to take both girls home with them, thinking their red suspenders are attractive enough to surpass walrus-shaped features.

"Your friends are pretty Mr. T, Nan," Liz says, letting one of the skinheads' hands reach around her dimpled thigh. "But I was expecting another punk band."

Nan punches the zit-bearded skinhead, just for looking at her. "Yeah, they suck, but they'd rather have everyone hate them. I think that's the point of being in a noise band."

Zit Beard doesn't leave, finding Nan's violent reactions arousing. He snuggles her shoulder and she punches him in his tits. A smile cats up on his BIG red face, and he does it again, whisper-caressing her stomach this time – not because he wants to turn her on, but because he wants her to punch him again, hopefully harder. She elbows him in the neck. Very stimulating.

"Have you seen Gin lately, Liz?" Nan asks, elbowing Zit Beard once more for a diversion, accepting the fact that administering pain to someone other than herself is a rather enjoyable performance.

But Liz finds the act of allowing a blubber-filled shirtless skinhead rub his hand all over the insides of her clothes a more enjoyable performance. She forgets to reply to Nan's question among all the fat-sweaty sensuality. Instead, she asks another question: "When do you want me to return that Hertzan Chimera book? I haven't finished it, but I don't think I'll be able to."

"What about Gin?" Nan asks.

"What?"

"Gin. Have you seen him?"

"I think he went on a beer run with Lenny and the guy from the first band."

"Thanks." Nan gets up, kicking Zit Beard on the way, and scuffling into a round-a-go crowd.

I appear on stage – swirl-swirl goes the crowd and the color-blooming makes my eyes sizzle – with my cello and my T-shirt that reads *Battlestar Galactica 4 Life*. I play a short slimy cello solo and then the song curdles into a blur of discord before it ends.

The crowd does not seem to notice we are here.

Vodka leaps from the toilet, stampers onto the stage, into our faces. "I WAS SUPPOSED TO DO MY BAGPIPE SOLO AFTER THE CELLO INTRO," he screams, though his scream is non-exclamatory because of his anti-emotional attitude. He shoves Christian, thrashes the sheet metal, and rammer-runs through the warehouse, but his movements still seem robot-like.

The crowd doesn't seem to notice Vodka's outrage.

"This is our last song," Christian says to the crowd. "It's called *The Greatest American Hero Theme Song*."

We play some gak-shrilling noises and squeal, but it sounds nothing like the original theme song. Before the music ends, we are kicked off of our own stage by a band of five skinheads. The singer (Zit Beard) takes the mic from Christian, pushing him into the crowd who beat him up cruel. Zit Beard spits on the crowd and everyone cheers.

In other words: ZIT BEARD = PUNK.

"We're the Oi!s," says Zit Beard. "Our first song is about smashing capitalism and breaking fascism and stomping religion and destroying all the governments of the world. It's called PUNK ROCK!"

This is what he sings:

"PUNK ROCK! PUNK ROCK! OI! OI! OI!"

The punk kids are into songs like this. They cheer and jump and punch each other until the song ends half a minute later.

"Thanks," he says. "Our next song is called ANARCHY!"

Nan gets herself outside to find Gin, but there is no Gin. She meets someone named Lenny instead, scurries over to him, stepping over a flattened little Abraham Lincoln hat.

She calls, "Lenny!"

He mopes around, all drunk and finished, was puking in the back lot, wiping some yellow off his chin. Lenny is a thin little guy, antsy stickman, so it didn't take much beer to make him vomity drunk. He wears old lady glasses and a shirt that says, *Kiss me, I'm Yugoslavian*.

"Where's Gin?" she asks him. "Liz said he went with you."

"Oh yeah," his voice cracks in a drunken sort of way, "Gin told me to tell you he'll be at Stag's place. I would've gone with them, but they wanted to stop off at Satan Burger, and . . . I'm Vegan Hardcore you know."

Her face crimps up all red, squeezing her fists. "That cunt is dead. I told him not to go anywhere without telling me."

Lenny shakes his head at Nan for acting the tough guy and walks away. "Well, I should get going then."

"Lenny," she stops him with her awkward voice, "You have a truck, don't you?"

He turns back around, "Look, Nan, it's not that I don't want to take you . . ."

She grabs him by the wrist and drag-pulls him toward his truck. "Come on. We still might be able to catch him at Satan Burger if we hurry."

Nan has many-many problems besides her tough-guy-dominating-Gin routine. She's also manic-depressive, she's missing half of her right lung, she's an insomniac, and she's always having problems with her sexual identity (An abusive father and three older brothers raised her as a boy). This kind of upbringing could have turned her into a lesbian, but since she is disgusted enough just *being* a woman, there's not even the slightest chance that she would get the desire to have *sex* with one.

Richard Stein said that the only thing children need to do to keep the guns away from their heads is to have pets of their very own. A dog or a cat or a gerbil or even a goldfish would suffice, keeping their fragile little minds on the pets instead of on the nasty juices that society likes to spit at them. Pets may be just small creatures to adults, but they're gifts of good mental health to the kids. Some children are allergic to animals, though, and tend to avoid owning them; and not owning an animal as a child ruins the perfect cure for keeping the gun away from the head once adulthood arrives. This sometimes results in what people call *a bad childhood*, and what *a bad childhood* does is make a person bitter.

Bitter is what we call Nan.

The only pet Nan ever had was a small black duck. She named it Chico and one time her father decided it was food and ate it. He was drunk and thought it would be a funny way to show off to his hairy shirtless friends.

The worst of Nan's problems had nothing to do with visualizing poor Chico digesting inside of her spiteful father's beerbelly. Actually, the worst of her problems had nothing to do with her father at all.

You see, Nan loves Jesus Christ very-very much. She's deeply in love with him. *Obsessively* in love with him. And I don't mean in a good-mannered sense of the word *love*. I mean she's sex-erotically in love with him. She talks about how she wants to strip him to his crown of thorns, whip him until he bleeds salty red and the blood dribbles down his body until her nipples get hard and her sauce starts bubbling. Then she envisions screwing him violent-sinful, while he is nailed to the cross, dying-dying. And she fantasizes about fucking him until he's dead on the cross, and then fucking him until he resurrects.

It all started when she was eleven and going through puberty. All her friends were boys, of course, and would talk about a thing called *masturbation*. (Richard Stein, by the way, said that masturbation is God's gift to ugly people who have trouble finding any other way of obtaining sexual gratification, like myself.) They told her it's all about fantasizing intercourse with the opposite sex. But she always felt she *was* the opposite sex, so she couldn't fantasize about boys without feeling *gay*, and she thought of girls as stupid and disgusting, so both sexes were ruled out. The only person she could think of that she loved was Jesus – let me remind you she didn't know the difference between Jesus-love and sex-love back then - so the savior, Jesus Christ, became her first masturbation fantasy.

Nowadays Nan masturbates to paintings of him all the time.

Around Christmas, you can see a strange glimmer in her eyes, like the spirit of Christmas is generating all kinds of nerve-tinglings on her insides, forcing her squeeze-excited. Even the nativity scenes get her sweat glands drip-drip-dripping.

Gin says that sometimes she'll let out a BIG *Ho! Ho! Ho!* when she climaxes on him. "I think I like that," he says. Christmas is a happy time for Gin too.

The strangest part of Nan's Jesus-sex fantasies is that she gets the most aroused by visualizing Jesus going to the bathroom. She likes to picture him on a toilet, or crouching down in the bushes, or peeing over a balcony onto a crowd of his followers. Sometimes she imagines dropping a log on Jesus while he is being crucified (Richard Stein says that when you drop a log of sexual excrement onto your partner it is called a *Hot Carl* or sometimes a *Dirty Sanchez*, if you were wondering) or even squatting over his face to pee in his mouth.

Richard Stein said that the whole process of digestion and egestion of waste material is considered sexually stimulating to many people, even though it's socially unacceptable to admit. However, *very* few people dare to watch that kind of thing and even less dare to participate in the act.

Nowhere does Stein mention anything about Jesus Christ being actively involved in sexual performances with excrement or being dominated on his crucifix. It's not a very common topic for discussion, I am guessing.

☺

I go to the inside of an autocar:

Stag – a shirtless guy with spiked hair and a tattoo of his own face on his face – is indulging in his favorite pastime: drunk driving. The road is empty and Gin in the passenger seat changing through radio stations and nervous-sweating over it, as if it's dangerous to leave one on for over a second.

"Watch this," Stag says, a grumpy-goof voice.

He lets go of the wheel and begins to slam a beer, with the autocar leaking into the left lanes. But before the autocar goes over any curbs, he finishes the beer, crushes it into his skull, slam-seizes the wheel, and straightens the autocar back out.

"Pretty Mr. T, eh?" he says.

Gin's buzz is wearing him down to sarcasm. "Yeah, great."

"I can do it every time. Never fails."

"Impressive."

"How many beers are left?" Stag asks the back seat.

"One," says the back seat.

"Who drank 'em all?"

The back seat burps. "Sorry."

"You asshole. I paid for twelve of those, not five."

"Sorry," says the back seat.

"Give me the last one." Stag claws his hand over his shoulder.

The back seat reaches the last beer over Stag's neck, but the autocar hits a bump and the beer rolls out the window.

"DAMN IT," Stag cries.

"Sorry." The back seat is too drunk to care.

The brakes slam. "I'm still gonna drink it." And he jumps out of the car to look for his crippled beer. Instead of a beer, Stag finds a dead jogger.

"Whoa . . . Fuck yeah!" he exclaims to the dead person, but the dead person isn't listening.

Gin gets out of the autocar in response to the *whoa . . . fuck yeah*, asking, "What is it?"

"A dead guy."

"Did you kill him?"

"Maybe." Stag daze-smiles, kind of proud. "What should we do with it?"

Gin's gut kinks up. "There's gotta be all sorts of Mr. T stuff we can do with a dead guy."

They pause to think about *all sorts of stuff.*

"We can give it to my uncle," Gin says. "He's a taxidermist. We can get him stuffed and mounted on the front of our stage at the warehouse."

Another pause.

"What I think is . . . we should strap it to the roof of my car and drive around town so we can pick up goth chicks."

"Yeah," Gin says. "Dead bodies turn them on."

☺

The warehouse is asleep now. It was very tired and told all of our guests to leave immediately. Normally, a crowd of tough guy skinheads would not give in to the threats of a warehouse, but *our* particular warehouse can be rather intimidating when it's cranky.

Now I am alone in my own room, watching a Grim Reaper poster jingle-dancing up the walls, striking cello strings like a drum. Grim Reaper and other butt rock bands are very popular these days. Back when they were touring you'd get beaten for listening to them. But now they are funny and everyone loves them.

In other words: BUTT ROCK = PUNK.

My room is nothing more than a janitor's closet that can only hold my body and a mattress. A whole bed couldn't fit inside, so I just put the mattress on the ground. I can't sleep on an entire bed anyway. If I sleep too far away from the ground, I get sucked out of my body and hover in the air above it. And believe me, it's pretty hard to fall asleep when you're floating outside of your body.

Richard Stein said that sleep is the best part of your life. Many people take sleep for granted and don't think to appreciate its beauty, but Richard Stein said his sleep was quite beautiful. If you do not find satisfaction in something as simple as sleep, you might never find satisfaction in something as BIG as life. Being without satisfaction makes you *bitter*, so it is best to obtain it wherever you can.

Also: a man who enjoys sleep never puts a gun to his head, he just sleeps his problems away. This is because death and sleep are very similar states, due to their tranquil conflict-less characteristics. So the suicidal man can trick his brain into thinking he is dead, when he is actually just asleep. However, it can be a very dangerous thing to trick your brain into thinking sleep and death are so related, because if a person is very tired and can't fall asleep at night, he might pick up a gun and shoot his skull across the room. And I'm sure he'd feel pretty stupid the next morning, when he finds out that he traded his brain to the wall for a good night of sleep.

At this time, Christian is entering my room. He doesn't emerge fully, because of his claustrophobia, standing by the doorway instead. I can see Vodka far behind him, on the toilet in a stare, caressing his bagpipes and the porcelain.

"Do you want to go to Satan Burger now?" he asks.

I look up at Grim Reaper joy-tumbling, Christian splashing. Pieces of fish meat falling from the ceiling. "Yeah. How we gonna get there?"

"I didn't think that far." Then Christian yells to Mort, who is putting all of the equipment away and getting no help from anybody, as usual, "Mortician, did you get your bus fixed yet?"

"No," Mort says within working, "I probably won't be able to until next week or next month."

Mort's bus hasn't been working all year. He gets it fixed every month, but it only works for a couple of days before it needs fixing again. It is always polluting the back of the warehouse. If it was a normal autocar I wouldn't care, but this is a bus. Not a VW Bus, I mean a full-sized school bus, laced with graffiti and bullet holes.

I point to Vodka, whispering, "What about him?"

Christian turns to Vodka. "Vod, got a car?"

Vod is in a trance.

"Vodka!"

He snaps hard out and twitches at Christian.

"Do you have a car?"

Vod glimmers down to his bagpipes. "I do." Then up to Christian again. "It is only the most luscious and vigorous piece of machinery UPON THIS INSIGNIFICANT PLANET."

"Well, can you drive us to Satan Burger?"

Silence.

Vodka continues a trance at Christian until his face turns dirty, the toilet seat sweats round pools into his buttocks.

He coldly answers, "Certainly."

Christian claps his hands together. "Great. Let's go then," heading toward his next bottle of liquor, and his polyester jacket.

"NOT YET," Vodka howls at him. "There are rules in my car that must not be taken lightly. If you break any one of them you'll be THROWN OUT INTO THE STREET AND BANNED FROM MY CAR FOREVER."

☺

Vodka's autocar turns out to be an AMC Gremlin, not the usual style of car to be remarked as *luscious* or *vigorous*, but some people seem to like them. It is sparkling black with silver lightning bolts on the doors and large metal wings attached to the back end. Vodka approaches the front and cuddles to it, warming the cold metal.

"It is more powerful than life itself, isn't it?" he says.

A smile cracks Christian's lips, not concerning Vodka though. He has remembered the most essential thing to remember upon entering a vehicle.

He yells, "SHOTGUN," and we all grunt.

Mort argues, "Paper-rock-scissors, ye bastard."

Christian argues, "I already called it."

Vodka barges in, "NONE OF YOU SIT IN FRONT. I get both front seats in my car."

"We can't all fit in the back seat," Mort whines.

"How dreadful," Vod responds.

☺

We pile into the Gremlin, with my corpse squished in the bitch seat. Vod starts up the car and takes a few essence-breaths into his lungs, humming with the engine purrs.

Vodka is one of those people who loves everything that is bizarre and disturbing and dreary and dead. Richard Stein called these people *Black People*, because they always wear black clothes and sometimes listen to black metal. He said that these people become black from hating everything. They only like things that nobody else likes, and that is because they hate everyone else. Once their favorite underground band becomes popular, they won't like it anymore. Not because it isn't good anymore, but because they can't stand to see normal people listening to their favorite band. That is why many of them turn to black metal, because that style of music can only be found in Germany and the Scandinavian countries.

He also went on to say that the leader of the black metal scene was a small troll who could only speak in ancient druidic languages.

After Vod finishes his car-meditation, he blesses the steering wheel. Then we leave for Satan Burger.

Scene 5
Silence Hurts the Eye

☺

Stag and Gin and a corpse strapped to the roof, all drunk-slobbering and bobble-stupid. Up a sideling sludge hill, where crab-thorn trees and scorpion flies live - no female baboons up here, but neither man nor corpse is afraid. Stag's motto is: "Too drunk to fear."

The moon is a white construction paper cutout, the sky and night stars colored with crayon-chalks, which made God's fingers all dust-gritty from the smudging and trying to color between the lines. When God fails to color properly and misses a tiny space, we call it a *ghost*.

Beginning colorists, such as kindergarten students, always finish a picture with many ghosts unaccounted for, but the mistakes are pardoned because they are only five-year-olds and aren't even old enough to buy beer.

Sometimes five-year-olds will go back to their creation and fill the ghosts in with color, and the picture will be fine. But when God creates ghosts while coloring the world, it's not so easy to correct them. They have to be filled in with the souls of people who have recently died. These poor souls are condemned to Earth forever. Instead of going to Heaven, they have to stay here and cover up God's mistakes.

☺

Neither Stag nor Gin believe in Heaven. They believe in a place called *Punk Land*, which is kind of like an amusement park but people can punch each other bloody and none of the security guards seem to care. It is supposed to be a gladful place to live, like Heaven, but only for punks.

Since the punk style of person would not be happy (nor welcome) in Heaven – being surrounded by white colors and angels and God and very *nice* people – he is sent to Punk Land, where he can be punk and talk about punk and listen to nothing but punk rock all day long in a totally anarchist society.

☺

Stag is still very drunk. He is swerving widely about the road, singing an Irish drinking song called *All For Mr. Grog*.

I once knew a man named Mr. Grog. He lived next to my ex-parents and would buy me alcohol when I was underage. He always told me that the world is just a boring place made for rich conservative old men and there's no reason to try to succeed in it unless you're one of them. Best to just get drunk, try to be happy, and screw lots of married women.

Last year, old Mr. Grog was arrested for selling heroin to an twelve-year-old. At that point, he didn't have any emotions left in him at all. When the judge asked for his plea, all he did was stare at his wall and shrug.

The autocar starts faster-faster as Stag's foot goes heavy with intoxicated weight on the gas pedal. Faster-faster. Soon it is *wind*-fast, and since the wind sees the autocar as competition, they begin a race. Autocar vs. the wind, getting me confused to which is which. And they both go faster-faster-faster . . . Stag thinking he can actually beat the wind.

Stag has drunken reflexes and doesn't make the sharp turn at the bottom of the sideling sludge hill. Going full speed on a grass field, out of command, drunk-fast.

He's also blinded by a sharp orange light similar to a lightning flare, coming out of nowhere and electrocuting the horizon. Bright like an atomic explosion, but then gone in an instant.

Then I see the difference between the wind and an autocar. The wind can hit a tree, shift around it, and then keep going, but an autocar becomes crumpled to a wreck. And that's what happens here.

Both of the characters are tossed from the car, through the unforgiving windshield. Stag's face attempts oral sex with the tree's trunk, but since the tree is not attracted to Stag it breaks his skull indoors, and Gin's neck cracks on a large branch as he flies face-leading into the grass field, with dirt and a bug tasting into his mouth.

And as the wind passes, there is *silence*.

☺

However, neither of the two drunkards actually died, because right before the autocar made contact with the tree, something supernatural happened. There was that blinding flash, the sharp orange light similar to a lightning flare.

Richard Stein said that sometimes a god will give his people a mes-
sage, or sign, to alert them of something he has done wrong. The sign can
be a lightning flare, frogs raining from the sky, a long extinct animal found
in a public place, or the ocean turning to fire. If one of these four things
happen, it is safe to say that God is trying to communicate.

What God was trying to tell the world's people with this lightning
flare is that Heaven is full and there's no room for any more souls, so He's
made the decision to discontinue the performance of *dying* to save His home
from overpopulation.

Meaning: death doesn't exist and everyone is immortal, including
Stag and Gin who would've been dead if this had been yesterday or even
minutes prior.

Now Gin's face is in the dirt, tasting some soil and a bug who is
tasting him back. His heart is no longer beating; he thinks he is dead. He
can't feel any of the physical pain that he should be feeling. His thoughts
spark-flicker through his eyes and he can *feel* them moving about inside of
there. It seems the only body part that still has nerves is his left eye. Extremely sensitive, the eye even hurts once his thoughts become nervous,
stabbing through his brain to the eye as they panic.

And the only thing he can hear is the *silence*. Growing so loudly, it
hurts.

My vision shifts into Vodka's autocar:

I find my corpse alone, sleeping there. All of the car doors are
open, letting the lifeless kind of air get a hold of my shivering nerves, totter-
ing breaths.

Hesitating the cold, I don't enter my body right soon. I just stare
at it (me) and explore the flesh. It is without color or muscle, just bags of
grease-goo hanging from the nerves. My facial skin is tight to the bone; I
am sick-ugly, healthless. The God's Eyes go closer into me, to within an
inch of my face.

My eyelids jerk.

It is strange how nobody ever sees their own eyelids jerk. People
go through their whole lives living with jerking eyelids but never get a chance
to really see them jerking. It's only common for someone else to see your
eyelids do this. Even when looking in the mirror, there's no way, because
eyelids only jerk when they are closed, and not a single person out there can

see with closed eyelids. Well, I am seeing this performance now, but I don't actually consider myself a *single person out there,* so I don't count.

It's interesting to see your own eyelids jerk, I tell you, because they are jerking in response to certain thoughts – thoughts that bring out emotions powerful enough to twitch-jerk the lids. And usually when you watch this happen to yourself, the emotional thought hits you twice as hard and makes your entire being twitch-jerk. But this time my entire being did *not* jerk, which means I'm becoming alien to my emotional thoughts. I think this is a bad thing.

I look again and find that my complete body is hardly familiar to me, almost a stranger. So many years of neglect that I've turned sour-soggy and ill without realizing. I can't bear to go back inside of myself anymore. And the worst part is – I know I have to in order to survive.

This will never change.

☺

After a lot of convincing, I go inside my body - back to the rolling world. I touch my stranger flesh and become sick. Best not to think about it; I'm always too aware of my defects. Better to ignore . . . Then I get a sick spell from a giant whirlpool-waver on the autocar's eel-skin interior, so I change to the outside.

I crack my knees to the pavement, cough-cough, choke my vision away . . . My voice croaks . . . a short groan . . . Then I relax. Relaxation is the key. The spell sifts to a mild swirl, all pacific inside.

I am at a gas station, the gas hose still inside of the gas tank, glunking-glunking it full. The emergency lights are going *blink,* questioning their purpose. And their purpose, of course, is to make you ask it questions.

"Where did everyone go?" I ask the emergency lights.

The lights say, "Blink-blink, blink-blink."

Then I notice the whole gas station is empty. The lights are all gone. Only the bright flickers above the gas pumps and the lights that say "Please pay inside" brighten my walk, but it is dark inside the store, *nobody* there, and all the surrounding buildings are dark and empty too. The street lights also seem to be burned out. It's like the whole town is saying, "Sorry, we're out of service."

Coldly *silent.*

The silence is muscular. It is a force that has eaten away all forms of sound, excluding my breath, my footsteps, and the blinkers. Like Mr. Death is creeping, stalking me. All signs of life have been taken away as well, stored inside of Earth's closet beneath the surface, and the dusty *emptiness* that is usually in Earth's closet is here with me now, along with plenty of closet skeletons.

Silence is the first stage of slipping into oblivion, objects just stop making sounds for you. Here are the other four stages: nothing will be smelled or tasted, nothing will be felt, nothing will be seen, and nothing will be thought.

Richard Stein said that oblivion is the worst possible thing that can happen to an individual, worse than going to hell. He said there is little difference between reincarnation and oblivion because in both cases you lose all your memories, and it's better to go into damnation and keep those memories than have them forgotten permanently.

He also goes on to say that Alzheimer's is the worst possible disease you can get since it erases all of your memories, which do not return even after you die. People that go into oblivion are usually the people that have a bad case of Alzheimer's. So, word of advice: if you know you're going to have this disease in the future, it's a good idea to kill yourself now, before it comes. Sure you'll go to hell for committing self-murder, but it's better than *nothing*.

I feel the oblivion all around me. Maybe it has taken my friends and all of the other people in the town to it's home - to *nowhere*. And it has forgotten all about me. Lucky me, all alone in an empty world with no sound, with a spin-wheeling picture.

It's so cold now. There's no wind but it's still freezing, even for New Canada. My teeth start chattering. It scares me at first. I'm not used to having my teeth chatter in me. Maybe they are trying to communicate, to tell me there is something wrong with this place and to leave immediately.

"CHATTER, CHATTER, CHATTER," my teeth scream at me. But I don't seem to leave.

I begin to look for my friends.

☺

All the nearby streets are closets. I do not take them. The buildings behind the gas station look more admitting: a slight light shining from that direction. Once I go, I see all but one of the windows are darkened, still silent. An alley of vacant crabwebs and pallid scraps of plastic dolls.

The only lit building looks like this:

A wood shack structure with one window and one door. It has no sound coming out of it, but there is a dull light. The structure blends in with all the alley garbage. It is moist from rain, malodorous, stodgy. There is a sign that comments, *Humphrey's Pub*, looks to be made from the aluminum of beer cans and black house paint.

I enter to a small room made for no more than ten sitting or eighteen standing. There are four people inside of here, but it still seems as lifeless as the outside. They are bundled up in snow clothes, seem to be Russian. One man is a waxy-faced bartender, polishing his beer steins, and the others are on stools, nodding at their drinks. The only noise they make is a tipping of their mugs.

I pause, waiting for a response to my presence.

No response.

"Has anyone seen three men?" My voice echoes over the silence. The sound seems stale.

Nobody answers.

"One pirate-like Asian, one in a suit, and one vampire-looking wannabe German?"

Nobody even turns around.

"I'm talking here."

Nothing.

Patience . . .

Then I get an answer:

One of the customers speaks without turning to me. His words slip out from under a bushy handlebar mustache, whisper softer than the breath that carries them. "We heard you. Nobody's seen anyone here. Nobody *ever* sees anyone here." His voice has no sensation.

Another one, an old man, whispers, "You should be quiet. Nobody talks here."

"Why doesn't anyone talk here?" I crusty-ask without whispering. I've always been annoyed by whisperers.

"Nobody ever talks in Silence," the third one answers.

My eyes curl about. The bar rolls in my vision.

The bartender remains silent.

I don't understand them. I say, "I don't understand you."

"You're inside of the Silence," he says. "The Silence has eaten you away from your friends and put you in her belly. You are not dead, however. And you will not be dead for as long as you keep quiet. If she doesn't hear any noise inside of her belly, she will think there is no food. She will figure you are part of her and forget about you. Otherwise, she will digest your meat and you'll be excreted as part of the wind."

"I don't understand," I say. "I go to this gas station all the time.

And it has never been quiet here before."

"What gas station?" one asks.

"The one outside. You're all cracked on dippy bobs, aren't you?"

"I've never heard of your gas station, nor dippy bobs," another says.

"All of you, be quiet," whispers the bartender, cop voice.

"You can see the back of it from outside the window," I say.

I try peaking through the window but I see blackness; the glass doesn't seem transparent. Huff-frustrated, I open the door and point to the station's backside.

"See," I say, still pointing.

None of them speak. They ignore me.

"You're all crazy."

☺

I go back to the front of the gas station, afraid that it has disappeared. But it's still there and so is the Gremlin autocar. Mort, Vod, and Christian are back, smoking cigarettes on the pavement, drinking some fresh-bought Creamed Corn Pale Ale.

When they ask me where I've been, I say, "Taking a piss."

When I ask them where they've been, they say, "Smoking a bowl."

The air is still silent as ever, and the surroundings are as dark as before, but I feel safe enough to realize that the old crazies in Humphrey's Pub really were just old crazies. We get back into the autocar and head for Satan Burger, drinking beers and singing *All For Mr. Grog*.

☺

Back at the gas station, Mort asked, "Why is everything dead here?"

Back at the gas station, Christian answered, "Because it's 3:00 in the morning, guy. Nothing stays awake this late anymore."

"Except Satan," I said, back at the gas station.

☺

Nan and Lenny are driving in the silence too. There's no sound coming from the wind. It should be hitting them through the open windows right now. No sound from the outside at all. Like everywhere else, the road is empty-dark. There are streetlights all down the road, but none of them have turned on. Even the lights don't care about anything anymore. They stare at Lenny's autotruck and shrug.

"Have you been to the walm?" Lenny asks Nan.

"No, have you?" Nan seems to care less.

"I went with Stag the other day. It's weird as hell. There are something's going in and somethings coming out – mostly coming out. It's guarded by these fish people with wings and large brains. We also saw this creature that had a blank face: no physical features or any hair. Stag called it a *Dance*, a heavenly creature whose only purpose in life is to dance across eternity. He said he read about them in mythology class."

I've heard of the Dances as well. They are ignorant (innocent) beings similar to humans, but have no mouths or ears or eyes or noses. The only sense they have is *feeling*, so the only thing they can do is dance and screw each other, trying to produce as many Dances as they can populate. Usually, they *over*populate to drive their race as far from extinction as possible, since it is not very hard for a blind and deaf mute to go to its death.

We call them *Dances* because they appear to *dance* in the sun on the mountains - blind, deaf, and mute - but they are not really dancing. They are eating sunlight. The dancing motions are similar to the motions our arms make when eating sausage with a fork and a knife; the only difference is they're eating solar energy. And when the sunlight gets digested and goes through the tubing to the exit, it is dumped as a shadow. In fact, thirty-four percent of the world's shadows are now produced from Dance droppings. Some Arizona businessman used to harvest the energy waste and sell it for BIG profit during the blistering hot Arizona summers. He called his product *Shade in a Can*.

"Sounds boring," Nan says about the walm.

"No, it's great. You should go there sometime."

"Lenny, I'd bash my face into a brick first. Why the hell would I care to go see a bunch of disgusting walm people? You're the only person I know who enjoys learning about other cultures."

"I'm the last anthropologist, you can say."

"I never cared there was a first one," she says.

☺

Lenny's autotruck goes up the scorpion fly hill and down to the scene of an accident, which is shrouded in *silence*. No one has arrived before them.

"Is that Stag's car?" Lenny asks, knowing the answer.

- 53 -

They park next to the wounded autocar. The thing's been torn in half by an aluminum tree which is now leaning out of its roots. Pieces of engine have been sewn into the soils for nature to grow them into new autocars.

Nan darts out of the truck, asking a tree, "Where is Gin?" but the tree is still unconscious. She doesn't bother to ask the jogger that is strapped to the roof, because it is very obvious that he is dead.

Lenny finds Stag on the other side of the autocar covered in black loam and tree sap, with his skull broken indoors and all the blood dried to a film on the outside of his body.

"Stag's dead," Lenny says.

Stag is not dead, as I told you before. He is unconscious without a heartbeat.

But we can't blame Lenny for thinking this, because it is a very common misunderstanding to take a sleeping someone who has no heart-beat for a dead someone. Doctors, coroners, morticians, even grave-diggers all make the same mistake on a daily basis. If you haven't got a heartbeat, I suggest that you don't sleep so much because eventually someone will think you are dead and either cremate you or bury you. And I assure you, waking up to find out that you've been cremated or buried is no way to start your day. I especially stress that you don't sleep in the middle of the street, float-ing in the swimming pool, hanging from a noose, curled up in a bathtub with a toaster, holding an empty cup of liquid plumber, or lying on the kitchen floor with a knife stuck in your back.

In addition to the missing heartbeat, Stag doesn't breathe, feel (other than his left eye), or need to eat. He's a zombie.

Richard Stein said that a zombie is the star of a very low budget horror movie that can't be killed and hates to come out during the day. Its favorite pastimes include the mindlessly gnawing of human brains with a group of companion zombies, moaning really loud, and taking very-very slow nature walks by the graveyard. But Stag is not the same as Richard Stein's zombie. He's just a dead person that is still alive. He's not mindless and doesn't care much for eating human brain.

Nan finds Gin rickety-smoking a cigarette on a nearby pile of gran-ite, trying to straighten out his broken neck. She hears his neck snip-crack a bit, getting a better position; he sighs with relief. The sigh was queer to him, not a normal sigh of relief that comes naturally after fixing a problem. It was a *forced* sigh. This is because he doesn't breathe anymore. He can *force* himself to breathe if he wants to, but he doesn't need to in order to survive. For Gin, breathing is completely voluntary now. He can go weeks without taking a breath and without even realizing that he hasn't taken a breath.

Nan squats next to him on a cardboard log and asks, "What happened?"

"I was killed," he answers.

"What - how could you be killed?"

"Stag and I got in a car accident and died."

She laughs. "What are you? A zombie?"

"Yes." He puts her hand on his heart. "No heartbeat," he says. Ripping her hand back, she shivers a laugh. It is *funny* to her.

"You're cold," her voice giggling-drunk.

"Not completely," he says, serious.

"Does that make me a necrophiliac?"

"Stop."

His hippie-sorrow eyes drool into her, and she feels his hurting. *Please-please*, she senses him say. Nan holds him. All he can hear is her awkwardness.

☺

Lenny arrives to repeat, "Stag's dead," purple-wide face, stutters. Gin answers, "Yeah, so am I."

"How can you be dead if you're walking around?" Lenny asks.

"I don't know. I've never been dead before."

"Stag isn't walking around," Lenny says.

Gin says, "Maybe he is asleep."

"No, he's dead. His skull is broken."

☺

They go back to the autocar to find Stag.

"I'll show you," Zombie Gin says . . . But Stag isn't there once they arrive.

"He *was* here," Lenny says, adjusting his nerdy-wear glasses.

"Are you sure he was, Lenny?" Nan asks, holding onto Gin to warm his blood.

"Of course I am," answers Lenny. "What did he do? Just get up and walk away with a collapsed skull?"

"Yes," Gin says coldly, scratching his left eye.

☺

I go to my body.

A handwritten sign says, "Satan Burger, 2 miles."

"It's a pretty long drive for food," Mort comments.

I look through the windows at the moon. It isn't our *original* moon. We lost the original moon in '72. Well, *we* didn't lose it. The moon lost itself. It forgot its way around the Earth, probably because of its Alzheimer's or maybe it was committing suicide to save itself from the oblivion that Alzheimer's would cause. It strayed from its usual path, breaking from its orbit, sinking into infinite soot, through millions of tiny white dots - pinholes in black construction paper held up to a light. And we never heard from it again.

Now we have a new moon.

We had to build it ourselves out of concrete. It wasn't an easy job. Making colossal molds, miles and miles high – a pain in the ass. It was a titanic ball of white, larger than mountains, but not as BIG as the original. To solve the size difference, it had to be launched into a new orbit, placed closer to the Earth, so that it would appear to be the same size as the original.

Sometimes I look at pictures of the old moon. There's not too many differences, except that the sponsors who paid for the new moon insisted on putting their logos all over the surface. But it's better to have a corporate moon than none at all.

The world was miserable without its moon: that's what my ex-father told me. He said the night skies were empty-dark. So dark that more streetlights had to be made and people owned a dozen flashlights each.

Back then, romance seemed foolish without a moonlit night; not that anyone cares for romance anymore, but I heard it was a BIG thing back then. And the astronauts that went to the original moon felt really stupid for wasting their time on a sphere that no longer exists.

They thought the poetic words, "One giant leap for mankind," should've been used somewhere else.

Scene 6
The Queen of Darkness

☺

It is now the period between day and night where the sky is dark blue and silky cold. Normally, the sky's condition would not be considered strange, but after three minutes of driving, the sky went from pitch night to almost morning. Even though it's only 3 a.m.

I come to the conclusion that this side of town is closer to the sun than our side, so the day here arrives earlier than what I'm used to.

Vodka drives without noticing the sky change. He is within a small cotton ball cloud, which is his *go-away* place. A go-away place is the place where your mind goes when it is tired of being on Earth. Normally, it is a comfortable place where you can sleep and relax and forget all your worries. Sometimes it's a fantasy world that is more interesting than real life. It may not be less laborious, but it is less boring.

It's not hard getting to your go-away place, but coming back can be hard. One side effect of not coming back very often is having difficulty distinguishing fantasy from reality. That's what Richard Stein said. In his history book, he talks about his cousin, Anne, who was committed to an institution because she couldn't tell the difference between fantasy and reality. They called her *insane*. An institution was once a place where they cared for people like this, but nobody cares enough to care for anyone anymore, so insane people are now in the streets and institutions are places where new people find refuge after coming out of the walm.

My go-away place is almost impossible to leave. Luckily, I don't go there often enough to lose touch with my sanity. I call it *Sleepyland*. It's a place where dozens of naked people are piled together inside a moist fruit cellar, doing nothing but sleeping lustfully on top of each other. This doesn't seem like much, but it is complete comfort to me. Sleepyland is so hard to leave because the fruit cellar chemicals make you feel drugged-drowsy and stiff-shanked, so all you do is sleep and dream, which makes it hard to get back to reality.

To get out of Sleepyland you have to: first, get woken up by one of the sleeping nudes who inhabit the sleepy land, and second, you have to be taken out of your head by someone in reality before you fall asleep in Sleepyland again. You can never get out all by yourself. You need to go there when a friend is nearby who has the ability of waking you; and inside of sleepy land, you should sleep next to someone who snores or rolls around a lot. Actually, it's better not to go at all.

☺

We see a BIG sign ahead:

SATAN BURGER:
THE NEW FAMILY RESTAURANTE

The street is no brighter than before, but now it's grayed misty. An early post-rain morning, cold and calm, the whole city asleep. Well, besides one car and one business. It's still around 3:00 a.m. on an *Erdaday* - the eighth day of the week.

They created the eight-day week about ten years ago. Erdaday was put between Saturday and Sunday, to break up the alliteration, kind of like how Wednesday breaks up Tuesday and Thursday. Erdaday means Earth Day. It was invented by TES - The Environmentalist Society - who thought that we were messing the planet up much-much more than we were cleaning it. So they thought that everyone should clean up Earth for one day out of every week. It was a BIG hit with the American population, because people would have three-day weekends instead of just two. Mostly everyone just looked at it as a day off, even though it was meant to have a purpose. It's just like how Sabbath Day was meant for church-going, but not too many people went to church. Most people called Sabbath day *Hangover Day* and instead of going to church they would spend their time drinking a lot of bloody marys stepping over newspapers in their underwear. Now, there are no more church-goers and there are no more environmentalists, so every weekend day is Hangover Day.

I don't know why Christians used Sunday as the day of Sabbath and Jews used Saturday (though Saturday is the last day of the week and makes more sense). I think Christians made Sunday the Sabbath because God and the sun are - more or less - the same entity.

Christians made Monday the first day of the week. Monday means Moon Day. Tuesday comes next. It means War Day, named after Tiw, a god of Germanic mythology. Wednesday was also named after a god - Woden, the chief god. Thursday is Thunder Day. Friday is Love Day, named after Fria, Goddess of Love. And Saturday is Saturn Day.

A while back, somebody explained that having an eight-day week would be sacrilegious, but these days *one* person can't make a difference. Hell, a whole barnyard full of people can't make a difference.

☺

As we pull into the Satan Burger parking zone at the bottom of a hill, we see a chair holding a sign that reads. "GRAND OPENING," and a ceiling fan that promotes, "TWO SATAN BURGERS FOR THE PRICE OF ONE."

Satan Burger is at the top of the hill - a jagged steep prick with blackened earth and a step-path seven minutes long. The drive-thru is a lift that pulls your car up the side of the rock face to a pay window. I can see the lift rocking about way up there, and there's a menu on it so you can decide what deep-fried burger you want before you reach the top.

We can't see much from here, so I use my God's eyes to climb up the steps. I see that it is a white building with the red letters *S* and *B* established on the rooftop. It doesn't seem different than any other fast food chain, aside from the fact that Satan himself is the owner/manager and not to mention the strange vegetation that grows on the top of the hill.

The vegetation looks like a forest of black thorn-weeds, tall as trees, wrinkled and crawling like vines, squirreling and generating small scratchy-twitter sounds. The plant leaks a red liquid that people are *supposed* to believe is blood, so it appears like an *evil* place. Maybe they are man-eater trees that came out of the walm, or maybe Satan brought them from hell. We keep away from them, in any case. No telling what they are capable of.

Richard Stein said that Satan was kicked out of Heaven for being a snob. He thought he was the best angel up there, because God loved him the best. And when God decided to love something else (Child Earth) Satan had a hissy fit and called God a *chum-chum*, which was considered an insult back in the days before Man was created.

Sometimes you'll hear someone call a friend a *chum*. Whenever God hears this from Heaven, He starts laughing his ass off at the someone's friend, who just smiles clueless of the insult. One thing God does not like to be called is a chum-chum. Another is an *idiot*. Another is *wrong*. Telling God that He is wrong is probably the stupidest thing you can possibly do, because He is *never* wrong, and He'll make your life wrong and your brain wrong and your face wrong just to make you regret putting the words *God* and *wrong* in the same sentence, unless the sentence is this: *God is never wrong, he knows everything about everything.*

Strangely, however, God finds being called a fuck-o or a fuck-face an amusing performance: after all, these are very fun words to say when you're angry. They launch off your tongue like fists.

☺

I go back to my skin to step out of the Gremlin autocar, preparing my wire muscles for a steep hike, rubbing them with needlelike fingers. I replace some old Gremlin breath with the coldy-crisp air, fresh for the system, wakens me up for the premature morning. It is still silent out, and the streets are still dead, not a living thing in the vicinity. It doesn't bother me right now. The morning light is comforting. It is a shame that most people miss this time of day. Personally, I'd prefer to sleep through twilight than dawn.

☺

Satan Burger is not actually on the top of the hill. It's a little closer than halfway. We get there pretty easily, although irritated by Vodka's moan for German food instead of corporate death burger.

Near the door of the restaurant, a box holds a sign up that says, "Help NEEDED!"

Behind the restaurant, there's a small trail that continues up the steep hill, and near the opening of the trail there's a table with a sign telling us, "Now approaching scorpion fly zone. NO female baboons allowed!"

☺

Upon entering Satan Burger, the only customer we notice besides ourselves is a small troll that only speaks ancient druidic languages. He sits in the corner and minds to himself, drinking a black cup of coffee and reading a collection of surfing anecdotes.

A cigarette machine greets us in the entranceway. It has two signs: "Come this way" and "Two Newports for the price of one!"

The cigarette machine can't speak, because it doesn't own a voice box, but I can tell that it would be complaining if it could. It doesn't have any arms either, so there is no way that it wrote the signs all by itself. Our job is to follow it, maybe decide whether or not the cigarettes are worth buying.

The cigarette machine is our hostess because Satan wants to make it known right off that Satan Burger is a smoking restaurant. It is divided into two sections: smoking and heavy smoking. The machine also sells kaffabud cigarettes and dippy bob rocks, if you're into that sort of thing.

We follow the hostess, hobbling all fat-heavy on its tiny legs, toward the front counter, where a cash register winks and waits for our orders. A crowd of tables and chairs watch us as we travel, staring, shifting, screeching across the tile. The entire restaurant – it's empty of all human employees, run entirely by living furniture.

☺

Satan appears behind the counter.

He is shorter than me, looks middle-aged, with a gray beard and brown-gray hair, a queer smile stretches out his face, wearing a dark suit and red tie, and there's a pin that says *Gay Pride* with a picture of a smiling penis that resembles a cartoon worm going into a butthole.

Mortician sees the pin and hides behind Christian and Vod, whispering, "I told you. I told you he's gay."

Mort is what Richard Stein would have called *homophobic*. It's a phobia usually caused by one of three things:

1) Being raised to believe homosexuals are socially unacceptable.

2) Not coming in contact with any homosexuals during the adolescent period.

3) Being gay and afraid to accept it.

Not too many people are homophobic anymore. Nobody cares enough to hate or fear anyone/anything. The word *faggot* is no longer an insult. And there are no more active second-wave skinheads or nazis or rednecks to go *faggot-bashing*. So faggots are safe from oppression. But they have no interest in going to gay bars and are therefore not actively faggotting, which makes the entire gay and lesbian society a waste of time.

Satan may be the last homosexual on Earth that wears pro-gay pins. Richard Stein said that fighting for gay rights and parading gay pride are two things that homosexuals publicly enjoyed. If these two things didn't exist, there probably wouldn't be as many gays around, because many people find parades and fighting for rights attractive enough to become gay. Stein also said that some people become gay just to be different than everyone else. They don't want to conform to the sexual preferences that authority has bestowed upon them.

In other words: GAY = ANARCHY.

☺

Satan continues his queer grinning for five minutes. We watch him, scared to interrupt.

☺

Then Satan goes into question. "Are you here for food or employment?"

Christian is our speaker. "Maybe both."

I didn't think about the *help needed* sign until now. Christian always talks about getting a job, but he never actually gets one. I would get a job too, but it's almost hopeless with my eyes. We apply for jobs everywhere we can, but never get a response or even an interview. Mort, whose always been a worker, calls Christian and I lazy assholes for never working, but we don't seem to care. Nowadays, the only person you can find in this world is the type that falls into the *lazy asshole* category.

"You're the young man that rented me a room," Satan finally notices Mort, "aren't you?"

"Yes," Mort says. "These are my roommates, Leaf and Christian."

"Christian?" Satan tweaks. "That's an offensive name to me." He's actually joking when he says this, but nobody takes it as a joke.

"Sorry," Christian apologizes, as if he had something to do with naming himself.

"Don't worry about it." Satan waves his hand in a circle. "You're all okay by me. Well, you *are* my landlords. The jobs are all yours if you want them."

"How much do you pay?" Mort asks, still behind Christian.

"I don't pay in money," he answers. "Money isn't going to last much longer anyway. Before the end of the year, the governments are going to say that it isn't worth the effort and discontinue its value. Dollars will become worthless, and given to the bathrooms for toilet paper. You'll see."

"I don't understand," Christian says. "You're talking crazy."

"I don't speak crazy," Satan argues. "Come in the back and I'll explain."

☺

We go through the kitchen to a small office, whose door is angry at us when we open him, waking him up. He hits Mort - last in line - in the back, knobbing him right between two links of spinal column, as if too impatient to wait for him to get completely inside.

"What's wrong with your door?" Mort complains.

"It's stubborn and doesn't like its job," says Satan. "Sometimes it won't open at all."

There are five chairs. We sit in them. All but one of them is alive, the one vodka is sitting in, or maybe it's just asleep. Mine is either nervous or weak, shifting me from side to back to side, with a wrinkled cushy-plastic seat, making whooshing sounds under my butt.

"How come your door is alive?" Christian asks.

"Yes, everyone notices my furniture, everyone *loves* the cute little furniture." A toaster tries to be cute, wagging its cord like a tail. "I'm sick of them!" he screams at the toaster, shoving it off the desk to thump on the floor. "They are so damn annoying."

"Well, what are they?" Christian asks. "How come they're alive?"

Satan lights up a thin homosexual-styled cigar and smokes it like a penis, rolling it between his fingers to ash. "They are my demons. Bet you didn't expect demons to be furniture, did you? Well, there are all sorts of demons. You see, I have the touch of life. Everything I touch becomes a living thing, like that door and those chairs, and everything else that is not living that my fingers come across. Then they become my demons, my servants."

Christian puts his hand in Satan's face. "Let me see," he says, lifting his sleeve to reveal a digital wristwatch. "Make this alive."

Satan touches the wristwatch.

There is a spark of tiny blue light. Then the digital wristwatch becomes a living creature that eats, sleeps, poops, and maybe even reproduces. It cannot speak, but it can beep.

"Weird," Christian says, staring at his new pet. "That's what I call a talent."

"I call it a curse," Satan says, pausing to take a puff on his cigar. Next to his cigars are a couple of packs of cigarettes called *Lung Suicide* and *Cancer Pricks*. Both of them were invented by Satan himself. "Anyway, I need *people* here. These demons aren't working out at all. I've got a television trying to cook hamburgers, a cash register that can't even speak trying to take orders, and a credenza trying to work the drive-thru. The only good they do is clean up the place and hold signs."

"Why don't *you* cook the hamburgers?" Mort asks.

"How the hell can I make hamburgers?" Satan yells. "Every time I touch a hamburger it turns into a demon. Same with fries and vegetables and everything else that isn't alive. Sure, that's how *I* eat my food, but I don't have a choice considering you can't eat food without touching it."

"What about using a fork?" Christian argues.

"Yeah, yeah." Satan gets annoyed. "That's what everyone says, but every time I touch a fork to eat, the fork becomes alive. And when I pick up food with it, the fork eats the food before I get a chance to. It's pretty frustrating. Actually, I don't mind eating live food - it's all I've been eating since the beginning of time. But customers just won't stand for eating a live hamburger, you see. They get grossed out and scared, and it's just not good business to scare away customers with demon food."

"So you need us to manage your store?" Mort asks.

"Yes, completely." Satan starts a *Cancer Prick* cigarette even though he is not done with the cigar. "I'll still be in charge. I just won't touch the food or do any of the work."

"You never told us what we'd get paid," Mort says.

"I'm getting to that . . ." Satan smiles.

☺

Lenny's autotruck pulls into the parking zone outside.

Nan and Gin are in the cab, shivering from the cold and the shock. Gin is dead. He can feel his joints getting all stiff, and thinks his skin is shriveling to rot. Nan takes him out of the autotruck and he stretches his legs. The muscles have no feeling in them, but they still move. He cracks his back and broken neck, hearing the cracking sound but not feeling the relief. Then he cracks his knuckles for the same response.

"Don't." Nan grabs his knuckles. "You're going to get arthritis."

"Sorry," Gin says. He doesn't want to argue. Being dead has brought him down a little, his emotions now at junebug size.

Many people say that you'll get arthritis from cracking your knuckles, but this is a lie. Some people also think that you'll mess up your back from cracking it. This is a lie too. Then there are the people that believe that you'll actually break your neck if you crack it too quickly. These are the same people who say if you cross your eyes too much they'll stick, you get warts from touching frogs, bubble gum takes seven years to digest, and you'll go blind if you masturbate too much. All of these things were made up by parents who didn't want their children to do them.

But most of the parents forgot to tell their children that they were lies once the children were grown up. And the children told their children the same things, thinking they were absolutely true, and the children's children told their children, and so on.

Then, for awhile, no one knew what to believe, because parents didn't know what the right thing to believe was, so the little girls were scared of their stomachs getting all fat with a four-pound wad of gum, and little boys thought they were going to go blind, and everyone says their friend's cousin's uncle's sister-in-law's son's girlfriend's brother is a blind warted cross-eyed mute with arthritis who had to have surgery to get all the gum out of his stomach.

At one point, all the parents got together and made up their minds to go ask "The Professionals" whether these things were true or not. But a few days before The Professionals could be contacted for questioning, all of the parents developed a new interest in staring at their walls and shrugging.

☺

Gin and Nan head to the stairs; Nan holds him as he walks. Normally, Gin wouldn't like to be babied by Nan - she usually thinks he can't do anything without her help - but this time he doesn't mind. She's being nice and caring, which are two things he never gets out of her. Maybe this time he really does need her help.

Lenny stays jerky in his autotruck. Nan yells at him, "You just gonna stay there or what?"

Lenny peeks his nerdy head out of the window. "No, I can't go in. I can't handle the smell of corporate death burger. I'll just listen to some music. I got the new *Cauliflower Ass and Bob* tape yesterday."

"Okay, Lenny." She doesn't seem to mind leaving him.

I called Lenny's head *nerdy*, because that's what Lenny is. He's one of those nerdy punks that dress in classic dork clothes with pocket protectors and thick dork-glasses. Most of the time, a nerdy punk's glasses aren't even real, they're just plain glass or sometimes clear plastic, just to emphasize the nerdy punk style.

In other words: NERD = PUNK.

Nerdy punk is one of the most unusual styles of punk. It is not a style of music though, just a clothing style. Hopefully, there will be a super cool nerdy punk band someday, playing all nerdy punk songs, at a nerdy punk music festival with dozens of other nerdy punk bands. Skinheads will go there too. And nerdy punk will never sellout since trendy people hate everything and everyone that is nerdy.

☺

Satan tells us this:

"I'm sure you've heard about the walm. It is the door that lets people in from other worlds. This may seem like magic to you, but it is not. Magic is easy. The walm is more on the technical side. Technology is hard. What is the one thing you would not sacrifice for anything in the world?"

Our faces give the expression that we took the question as rhetorical. He realizes this and continues.

"Your *soul*. Nobody will ever give up their soul. Really nice Christian people will say they'd give up their *life* for anyone else to live. They say this because they mean it, and really would give up their life to save someone else, no matter how evil or wretched. However, they only say this because after they die, God is going to love them and accept them into Heaven with the greatest of honors. But they would never give up their *souls* for anyone. They sacrifice themselves so that they'll go to Heaven. Would you go to hell or oblivion for someone else? Would anyone do it? Your soul is your everything. Without it, you are nothing.

"Think about this: would a Christian still follow all the Christian rules and standards if he discovered for an absolute fact that God and Heaven do not exist?"

"Maybe," Christian says, backing the people that call themselves his name.

"Well, you'll see pretty soon who will and who won't. Because, as of now, God has turned His back on the world, and nobody else is going to Heaven - no Christian, no human. Everyone either stays here or goes to oblivion. There's no paradise where the world's headed. No hell either."

"What are you getting at?" Mort asks.

"What I'm getting at," Satan says, "is that souls are leaving people's bodies all over the world. They are getting sucked out of the left nostril of every human being. Every night, every day, all day long. Haven't you noticed? The whole world is emotionless. Nobody cares about anything anymore. It's all because they've lost their souls. And it all has to do with the *walm*. You've heard about sillygo, right? Sillygo is created from human souls. Souls are what empower that stupid door so that it will stay open and bring in new people and new animals. In just a month or so, not a single person in the world will have a soul because of that thing. Which puts me out of business. I am a soul collector. My job is to own souls. Without human souls, I'll be out of business. Without my business, I'll no longer be the devil. If I'm not the devil, I'll be human, and then I'll lose my own soul to sillygo.

"That's why I opened Satan Burger. I sell hamburgers that are *so* good that people will trade their souls for them. And, with those souls, I'll *always* keep going, and sillygo will never catch me."

Christian asks, "Yeah, but how are you going to get souls from people if sillygo has taken them already."

"That's the beautiful part," Satan says. "The walm will always provide me with new souls. I'll be in business as long as the walm is in business. And if the walm goes out of business I'll be fine, because I won't have to worry about sillygo stealing my soul after that."

"I don't believe you," Christian says. "If this is true, how come it didn't affect us?"

"You are young. Young people usually have more spirit in them. That's why you'd be perfect working here. I won't pay you in money, but I'll pay you in souls. As long as you work here, you'll still have soul. And soul is the most valuable possession you can ever have. No matter who you are."

ACT TWO
Rising Action

Scene 7
Problems With a Hand

☺

Inside of Satan Burger:

Gin is not taking to being dead. He's not been dead for twenty minutes and already he's going moldy. His skin is all white now, all of the blood cells under his skin have suffocated and died, and his muscles and joints losing flexibility. His mind is getting iron-muzzy and weak, like it wants to rest in peace after death, inside some cozy grave. It doesn't want to live on and on until forever, because forever is a long and boring period to spend in one place. His thoughts go claustrophobic inside the skull, wishing to burst out, leave his corpse and go to Punk Land or some place like it, where bodies do not live. But he's trapped, always-already trapped.

A VCR asks for their order. Of course, a VCR can't speak, so it makes rewinding and fast-forwarding sounds to communicate. Gin and Nan don't understand, so they do not order. Actually, they are getting rather scared.

☺

"Nan is outside," I say.

Everyone gets up to go see her. The chairs are relieved at our departure, a whistling of sighs, especially the chair that held me weakly. Nobody asks how I know Nan's outside, nor do they care. They just assume I know what I'm talking about and go.

The door doesn't give us trouble this time; it's asleep I think. Doors love their sleep.

We go to see Nan and Gin - hands folded together on two chairs that secretly molest their butts.

"How'd you get here?" Mort asks Gin.

"Lenny drove," Nan answers for undead Gin.

"Where is that nerdy then?" Mort asks. "I missed him at the show."

"He's outside," Nan says. "He refused to come inside on the count of his vegan-straight-edge-in-your-face attitude."

"I'm gonna go be vegan with him," Mort says.

He leaves the conversation and then the restaurant. A faint odor follows behind, breathing through the flex-kindly door, which was born in the kitchen's refrigerator.

☺

Satan slups on his queer grin.

Then he aims this grin at Gin and Nan, striking them with happy-laced words, a motion that he has practiced for days: "Welcome to Satan Burger."

☺

Nowhere and oblivion were completely different things/places to Richard Stein. For him, oblivion is when something goes into nothing and nowhere is the place where something can come out of nothing.

Out of nowhere, I cry: "Don't order, Nan."

And there is silence and eyes.

Richard Stein said that some people are allergic to being looked at. I am one of those people. I like being considered a shadow for this reason. If I don't talk people won't look at me, and I won't get an allergy attack - also known as a panic attack.

"What would you like?" Satan asks them.

Christian says, "You'll lose your soul if you eat this food. Don't order."

Slamming fists, mad. "You're killing my business," Satan says to Christian. "Why did I hire you people?"

"She's a friend of ours," Christian says. "I'm not gonna just let you take our friends' souls."

Nan doesn't understand. She shrugs and makes a smacking noise with her lips, tough guy trying to be cute again.

☺

Christian takes her aside and discusses the situation, and I watch a table mounting a peanut. She doesn't like him pushing her about, even if it is important, so she elbows his hand away. He tells her Satan's story and she tells him about Gin's condition, and they both feel the serious weight of the situation weakening their shoulders to the ground. Apparently, Gin is living proof of what has happened to the world. And even without feeling his beatless heart, Christian can tell Gin is dead. He looks like a zombie, or more like a vampire - like Vod. Now they believe Satan's story is *Truth*. Nobody is going to Heaven and nobody is going to Hell. Our boring life is eternal.

Then Christian introduces them to Satan.

☺

Satan shakes Nan's hand. "Hello, Nan."

And he shakes Gin's hand. "Hello, Gin. You are another of my landlords."

However, Satan doesn't realize that in shaking Gin's hand a blue light quietly sparks, turning it into a living creature that eats, breathes, thinks, poops, and sleeps. Neither Gin nor Satan realize what they've done, and I don't feel up to telling them.

☺

Mort comes back alone.

"Lenny's not there," he says.

"What? He just disappeared?" asks Christian.

"I don't know," Mort says. "I saw his truck, but Lenny's not there."

Nan mumbles this: "Where'd that faggot go?"

She does not realize that Satan is a homosexual, and was very offended by that remark. He already hates her. Satan usually hates *all* girls anyway. They always steal men from him.

"He was out in the parking zone?" Satan asks.

Nan looks to him. "Yeah, why?"

"The Silence," Satan says.

Nobody questions him.

"The Silence took your friend."

Nobody says *What's the Silence?*

Satan Says, "It is a creature that came out of the walm. Large as a lake, this creature, but it's not made of water. It is made of sound. And it feeds off of sound, or anything that makes sound, or anything that can hear sound. It will empty this entire world of sound if we let it. It claims this side of town its territory. Anybody that's out on the street is at risk. It will eat anything that it hears and your friend must have been something it heard. He will never come back. Nobody ever escapes from the stomach of Silence."

Satan is wrong about that last statement. I have been to the stomach of Silence, and I have escaped. (Then again, I consider myself *nobody*.)

☺

We decide to eat some sandwiches, which is my favorite style of food. We wanted to eat Satan Burgers, but Satan tells us that it is impossible. If we eat Satan Burgers our souls will fall out of our bodies and the walm will chop them up and turn them into sillygo to make itself go. So sandwiches are fine.

The sandwich is one of the most important foods ever invented. Named after John Montagu, 4th Earl of Sandwich, who also had a pet bulldog named Sandwich. The bulldog had a silver collar that said "Bulldog of Sandwich."

The sandwich was invented all by accident. Someone dropped a food tray at John Montagu's birthday party, which was on a fun-Sunday. The food tray had small pieces of bread, pieces of cheese, and pieces of meat.

Then Sandwich, John Montagu's bulldog, ate all three of them at once. And some woman cried, "What a disgusting bulldog. It ate bread, meat, and cheese all at the same time. Bulldogs don't have any manners at all, do they?" Bulldog just sat there and farted.

And from that day on, Bulldog of Sandwich would not stand for eating anything less than meat and cheese on two pieces of bread.

John Montagu told his bulldog that nobody liked his disgusting eating habits, and that he should eat the meat, cheese, and bread all separately, but Bulldog of Sandwich would not give in to the immature ideals of high society. So he went on eating his food in his own way, and later went on to market this style of food to the public. He called it *the sandwich*.

"How dare you name a disgusting food creation after me?" said the Earl of Sandwich.

"How dare you name me after a disgusting creation like yourself?" said the Bulldog of Sandwich.

Then John Montagu became so angry with his bulldog that he killed him and ate him between two slices of bread just to prove how disgusting a sandwich was. Surprisingly, when John Montagu finished eating his bulldog, he said, "My Sandwich was a genius," but by now, the genius was already digesting in his master's stomach.

☺

When Gin tries to eat, he notices that one of his hands doesn't work right. He looks down to see if it is still there, and it is. But it's moving like a frantic spider, crawling up his side and attacking his other hand.

"WHAT THE HELL HAS HAPPENED TO MY HAND?" Gin screams, crashing backwards to the floor-sickness, sandwich scatters everywhere.

We all look.

The hand is rummage-running all over the floor, slipping in the sandwich mustard and mayonnaise, trying to detach itself from Gin's body. Gin's shock takes control of him and his body flop-jerks crazy. His dreadlocks get covered in sandwich, and his hand eats a piece of tomato and onion.

"What's wrong with him?" Satan yells. "Is he spazzy or something?"

Nan grabs hold of Gin and tightens him in place, trying to stop his hand from eating his sandwich. "It's alive," Nan says.

"What?" Christian screams, examining with wire-eyes.

They think about it for two seconds.

"Satan," Christian yells. "What the hell were you thinking?"

"I didn't do anything," Satan replies. "Just because everything I touch comes alive doesn't mean I have anything to do with his hand. I've touched all sorts of people in all sorts of places, but their parts never come alive like that. I make inanimate things animate, not animate things animate."

Nan starts crying for Gin again. This just isn't his day. First, he gets killed. Then he turns into a zombie. Now his hand is a separate-minded creature that is eating his only sandwich.

"Yeah, but Gin is dead," Christian argues. "He's one giant inanimate object."

"Well," Satan says, "how come his hand turned alive instead of his whole body? Wouldn't my touch just resurrect him?"

"How should I know?" Christian yells. "I don't know anything about dead people. Shouldn't you know? You're the Lord of the Dead."

"I'm not the Lord of the Dead," Satan disputes. "I'm the Lord of Darkness. The Darkness and the Dead are two completely different things. I know more about life than death."

"Well, you know more about death than I do," Christian says. "You've probably met all sorts of dead people in your line of work."

"Yes," Satan says, "but my job is to damn them to hell, not drink tea with them and discuss what their lives are like now that they're dead."

"Whatever," Christian says, and a salt shaker agrees by hopping up and down splashing salt all over the counter.

☺

Nan calms Gin eventually. She tells him that it's not all that bad. Someday the hand will learn how to be a hand again. He'll just have to adjust, and he's got all of eternity to do that, even if his soul gets sucked away.

She says, "Life is funny that way."

Gin names his hand *Breakfast.* It's the first word that poops into his brain. That's the way Gin names everything. He doesn't care if it is a bad name. Names are just names, he says. His dog was named Cancer. His car was named Forward. His goldfish were named Socks, Aluminum, Bookshelf, and Paper Cut. The first choice for everything is always the right one. That's what he says about buying things, that's how he answered test questions in school, that's how he watches television.

His father was like that too. "First choice is best," his father would say. The father was drinking gin when Gin was born. He was drinking vodka when Vodka was born. They also had an older sister, who moved to Colorado and married a man twice her age. Gin's father was drinking whiskey when she was born. If he outlives any of his children, Gin's father plans on drinking a fifth of the appropriate liquor in honor of his lost child, right on the grave, mourning drunk, alone with the corpse. Of course, that will never happen now.

Breakfast is back to normal color again, unlike the rest of Gin's flesh. Eventually, Gin's entire self will be rotten, white and shriveled and crusty. His eyes might roll into the back of his head. All the skin might peel away. Maybe he will become a living skeleton that can't do anything but sit there. Only the hand will be fresh.

☺

Gin ties his hand up for the time being, and puts it behind his back to keep it from his mind. He's still agitated by the whole situation, feeling worse about his hand being alive than the fact that he is dead. Nan gives him her sandwich, even though he doesn't need to eat anymore, and he eats in silence.

Satan's sandwich is alive and screaming as he eats it. If I had emotion enough to cry for the poor thing, I would. It never had a chance. The sandwich's guts - pickles, tomatoes, and onions - squeeze-spray all over the counter. Then it bleeds mustard and mayonnaise until it goes into shock and faints.

☺

Gin feeds Breakfast some of his sandwich. Its mouth is where Gin's lifeline used to be. The mouth is thin and it doesn't contain any teeth yet. Its stomach and lungs have formed beneath the skin of the palm. The digestion track ends at the base of the wrist, where the sandwich will exit once the time comes. The hand doesn't have any eyes, but uses its fingers like antennas which have an extremely keen sense of touch.

Breakfast picks apart the sandwich, using its feelers and mouth. It doesn't like the bread. Hands mostly like meat and onions. Boiled onions in beef gravy is a very popular meal for hands.

☺

After eating is over with, the room goes tired.

The long night has hit everyone really hard. Mortician is asleep on a bench, which is also asleep, his pirate hat rests on his head. Earlier in the night, Satan had touched the pirate hat. Satan doesn't think before he makes things alive, and it's quite normal for him to have *all* objects surrounding him alive. But it's not normal for him to use caution around inanimate objects, so inanimate objects who don't want to be animate must learn to avoid his touch. Now the pirate hat is alive and sleeping on Mort's head.

Satan's hobby is creating new demons. Sometimes he will get some modeling clay and sculpt a large monster with horns and wings and sharp teeth. Its appearance is meant to be *scary*. Once he touches them, they turn into demons and spend most of their time scaring people. This is how humans believed demons looked, but they were mistaken. Only few demons were made in this style. All of them are dead now. The majority of demons are pieces of furniture or doors or tools.

The demons in Satan Burger are all sleeping on their backs, or stirring quietly in the kitchen. The draining feeling of an endless night seeping into a stale morning has gotten into us all. Even the furniture-demons need rest.

Gin, Nan, and Vodka have left for home. They used a teleportation device - a satanic device - to travel back to the warehouse. The device looks similar to a piece of candy corn. When you touch the yellow butt, a door shoots out of the white tip. And you can go anywhere you want through that door, if you program it right. Satan has programmed the door so that all of us can get between the warehouse and the restaurant with no trouble or time wasted.

Vodka found the teleporting door very interesting, but nobody else seemed to care. Doors are doors, no matter how unusual or magical they might seem. Everyone else said, "That's a very convenient door," but nothing else. The door looks even more bizarre than the candy corn remote for it. It's made of energy, orange colors that swirl all around, which is why Vod likes it. He's into bizarre-looking things. He's a bizarre-looking thing himself.

Gin, Nan, and Vodka went to sleep. Their shift is in the morning and they'll have to work all day collecting souls from unsuspecting customers. Mort, Christian, and I have the later shift, so it's not necessary for us to go to sleep right away. My body is getting awfully tired, though, so I let it sleep. But my vision stays awake, soaring into the air above, hovering over Satan and Christian. Neither one of them have tired. Christian doesn't wear down easily, going for days at a time without sleep. He has started on another bottle of gold liqueur, soon to be gritty-mad drunk. This brand is called *Gold Rush*, the second best brand you can buy. Fool's Gold is piss compared to Gold Rush.

Christian and Satan are drinking and smoking with each other's company. Satan is drinking a beer from a living bottle - the bottle's beer is its blood, so Satan is bleeding it to death - but the bottle can't complain. Satan is its master, after all.

Satan gets to talking about where he came from. First, he first mentions his father, Yahweh, who is God.

Yahweh's main job is to create things. It is the job that all gods are paid to do. There is a god inside every living star. Within our sun, there is Yahweh. He is not in our dimension, however. If God was in our dimension, the sun's fire stomach would burn Him up.

Inside of the god dimension, a sun looks like a shopping mall, where the temperature is always perfect, and there are plenty of benches to sit on near fountains and plants. Some people call this shopping mall *Heaven*.

Inside of the shopping mall, God creates all of his creations.

The first thing Mr. Yahweh ever created was a small table. It was not a very good table. The legs were not evenly cut and it wobbles when you touch it. Near the center of the shopping mall, you can still go and see it on display. It's a good example of how nobody is perfect, not even God.

Satan was the first intricate structure Yahweh ever made. Satan was the first angel. An angel is the same as a human, only it's born in the dimension where gods live. They also get special powers. Some angels have the power to fly. Others can see in the dark, or read minds, or run really fast. Satan has the touch of life. Satan was God's favorite.

Gods live very frustrating lives. That's why they are so frustrating to get along with. And they are *bitter* for living such a long-long time with no end, and being responsible for billions upon billions of life forms is a very demanding job. Gods are the fathers of their worlds, but Yahweh seems more like the drunken abusive father that wears a wife-beater T-shirt, who doesn't like his home dirty when he comes back from work.

When Satan came out of the closet, he was sent to hell. Hell was just a giant prison located at the center of the Earth, within the god dimension. Of course, it was the most pain-drudgy prison ever built. All of the evil souls of history lived there, and Satan was the prison guard who monitored the evil. Yahweh labeled him the most evil person in hell, because he was the first homosexual. And God considers homosexuality the most disgusting evil of them all.

Satan is glad Hell doesn't exist anymore. It was a shitty job, and he didn't need it. The walm ate all of the souls from hell before it started eating the ones on Earth, so all the tyrants of history that you've known are in oblivion now. Only your memory of them exists. Satan saved some of the souls, though, because he is a collector of souls. Hitler is one. Kublai Khan is another. Aristotle is another.

☺

Richard Stein said that God is very picky about the souls He lets into heaven. He won't even let you in if you haven't been baptized. And people like Aristotle are the ones that really got screwed, since the art of baptism didn't even exist in their lifetimes. Aristotle was a good man, but he was born too early in history and had to go to hell.

Richard Stein hated God for making up that rule. Actually, he just hated the Christians for it. He never met God. Why should he care about somebody he never met?

Scene 8
The Festival of War

☺

Awake around noon, I tremble my corpse throughout the warehouse, feet sticking to the concrete floor, grits of sand cleaving, devoted to my feet. Going without shoes makes your feet go tough and leathery, but they become susceptible to picking up rocks and bits. A piece of broken glass can never cut you when stepped on, but it will stick to your heel and walk with you for days.

Nobody else is encircling yet. Three of them are at work and the other two are sleeping. My hair is stiff-scrabbled from the hard rest. The head my body owns is heavy, pulling my neck muscles to work. The neck bone is cramped up. A good sharp pain would relax it, massage it. The jab of a knife might do the trick.

I find a knife near the band equipment, one that Mort uses for screwing.

Stabbing my neck's back with the sharp of the knife, I sit on the toilet in the center of the room. As I poop, I put the television on my lap and watch adventure cartoons on the network for cartoons. Johnny Quest is on right now, Thunder Cats is coming up next. As I stab my neck, making the neck tissue loose, and Johnny Quest rides his speedboat in the amazon, rolling in my rolling world . . .

I notice a man through the window.

At first, I don't mind him. He's only passing on the carpet walkway. Then he passes again, and then another again. I continue pinching out the waste-food, trying to pinch faster, hoping that the man outside does not see me sitting here with my pants down and a TV on my lap.

Another man clankers by. He's in a suit of armor, doing some kind of construction work.

I use my God's eyes to investigate.

☺

A large tent picks itself up in my yard. The tent is made of gray

- 78 -

wire lizard tissue - used in underground societies for clothing and other textiles, societies which are widely known as *dark ones*. Black tendons hold the tent sturdy, flags swim from the ropes on small poles, cages and cages of murk below the tent's arena filter a smoldering fatty smell. The workers continue right by my window, annoying us (their neighbors) with a festival, just as we annoyed them with our electronic noise performance last night. Payback.

The landscape is early dark from the smothering rain clouds and a drizzle of pollution. Everyone seems a mess: sludgy clothes, grains of soil and weed milk that dreads their hairs together, and the skin cut by rocks becomes infected with crispy diseases from grooming the caged walm beasts.

I don't see any dark ones, only the medieval tent villagers. The dark ones are a race that came from a diseased world. They lived under the planet's surface with the giant beetles and reptiles that became their food and materials – clothing, beds, bone-weapons. Nobody in Rippington communicates with them except for our neighbors, the medieval ones, who are their friends because they are both very violent cultures. Every so often, the medieval ones and the dark ones will have a battle for entertainment, for the whole world to see, and they call it *The Festival of War*.

The dark ones are probably not out yet: still too bright outside. Dark ones are sensitive to the sun and can only wander during the night moments. They have pale features: white skin, white hair, and white eyes, with a hint of green to their nails and blood vessels. They look a lot like humans, but have cold blood. Some say they evolved from lizards rather than apes. I heard about the dark ones from Christian, who heard about them from our neighbors.

The dark females are known for their unusual sexual behavior. They are the dirtiest, most violent, most revolting, sex-crazed creatures to ever come through the walm. Christian says they are more reptilian than the male species: without any hair growing on their bodies, sharp claw-like fingernails, cold beady eyes, and snake tongues that are up to ten inches wide and eighteen inches long. Their sex drives are intense. They can't be sexually calmed without being gratified at least six times a day. It gets so laborious at times that the males are forced to lock their females away, to keep themselves from injury.

A dark one's sexual performance starts with the female injecting her enormous snake-muscle tongue within her partner's rectum. This arouses the male's penis, which is situated on his chest between the nipples. She can also carve simple designs into his backside to help him bleed. This is foreplay for dark ones. Once the tongue is disengaged, the female squats into the male's erect penis.

As the struggle progresses, the female drives her claws deep into her opponent's flesh, rip-cutting with the magic moment. She will begin licking the blood or eating the pieces of meat she has taken, or she will plunge her tongue into the male's throat and suffocate him. Suffocation is sexually exciting to dark males. And the male will give the female extra pleasure by dishing out fist-blows to the sensitive portions of her skin. The females may look more reptilian than the males, but their skin is gentle and smooth, so the males don't cut the feminine flesh as the females cut into them. They do, however, pound bruises into their milky scales.

After the males first started locking away the more sexually active females, they smiled their big teethy mouths a lot, very happy to be relieved of their sex duties. However, the females found imprisonment very frustrating and resorted to lesbianism.

☺

I've heard of four other new races that are fierce in sexual activity. They include: the aphid clan on the north side, the fire mites, the blue women, and the cockroach people. I've never seen any of these races, but I've heard many stories from Christian.

☺

I finish with the toilet and step outside.

All the medieval ones are at labor on their festival. It looks like it will start tonight, hopefully before I have to work. Some of our other neighbors, the midgets in presidential costume, are watching the creation of this festival. There's a James K. Polk midget, a Benjamin Harrison midget, a Woodrow Wilson midget, a John Quincy Adams midget, and an injured Abraham Lincoln midget. It seems that all of the community, every cultural group in the neighborhood, is excited about the festival, and I'm sure to see them all tonight. There are so many interesting peoples I have never seen before, and I can't wait to meet them all.

Lenny told Nan that *he* was the last anthropologist, but now that he's dead I guess I will take that title for myself. And since I've given up the reading of history books, other than Richard Stein's, I will make experiencing new walm races my hobby. I will try to write them all down, into a book - my history book. The walm might be able to take my soul away and throw me into oblivion, but my life and the memory of all of these races will live on through my writing. There should be at least something of me to live on after I die. Oblivion only wins when you are forgotten.

☺

Once I hear Christian awake, I reenter the warehouse.

Christian, with his flashy pants and buttoning up his white shirt, wrinkled clothes and hair, goes to the steaming toilet for his morning piss.

Christian has a few cuts in his face. They're from sleeping with broken glass. He doesn't know how it happens, but every morning he finds shards of glass under his sheets. Nobody puts them there. There's not much glass in the warehouse at all except for broken beer bottles here and there. He just rolls around in his bed, getting all cut up, bloody sometimes. This time the glass got his face, it must've been sleeping on his pillow.

Normally, the glass only gets his back. He's got extensive scars, like train tracks, like stretch marks on his love handles. My only guess is that the glass hates the cold concrete floor, and at night the shards snuggle into bed with Christian to nuzzle against his warm hips and fat.

Christian notices the festival through the window. "What's going on?" He goes to check it out before I answer.

"Big, big, big," he says.

Many more cultures are out here now. I see a family of the aphid people.

The aphids are standing with refreshments from the refreshment stand, so apparently some festival booths are open. There are four adults and eight children, watching the caged animals growl and sleep. The medieval ones don't mind the spectators, working away at the tents and stages. One warrior says, "Looks like we'll definitely have a crowd tonight." The other warriors practice for their fight in the arena. I call them warriors instead of gladiators - though it is the same type of bout - because gladiators are slaves that fight other slaves for amusement, and these warriors are freemen that fight other freemen for fun.

The aphids are a peculiar ant-like people. Their male/female ratio is one to three, because of their sexual performances. The males have three sexual organs on three places of their bodies. All of the sexual organs look a lot like tennis shoes; one is on his stomach, and two are on each of the hands. When the aphid people mate, three women fuck one man, one woman for each sex organ. They are also joined in marriage in fours. One husband and three wives. Each of the wives have assigned jobs: One is in charge of child care, one is in charge of home maintenance, and one assists the father with putting food on the table. These families usually produce twelve to sixteen children and are prejudice against other aphid families. As a result, incestuous behavior is very common, sometimes encouraged.

The aphid family jolly-walks away from Christian's vision. The husband of the family goes first; and his wife - the second father and also his sister - is in the back to make sure the children don't wander. The children all hold hands, crab-claw hands.

"Let's go check it out," Christian says, stepping out the door.

I follow him barefooted. He already has his shoes on; he didn't take them off last night.

☺

We stroll, watching . . . I waddle with rolling visions of water wheels and windmill turnings being constructed outside of the BIG tent. My shaggy nest of hair, greasy and dry and dready, lonely for shampoo, butterflies in the wet wind.

Medieval ones break apart pieces of wood, shredding them to make the floor for the inside tent. Loud hammering sounds, like metal rain falling around us. We drift closer to the tent village. Most of the spectators are here, watching all the construction, eager for tonight's events.

Christian recognizes a man coming out of a festival tent. It is Cecil Sword Dodd, an older drunk about thirty-five, the only medieval one we know. He doesn't have a family and drinks with anyone willing, even an outsider. Drinking is what Christian has in common with him, which is why they consider each other *drinking buddies*.

Cecil's middle name is *Sword*. All male medieval ones are supposed to have a weapon for their middle name. Common middle names are: Dagger, Arrow, Club, Sickle, Hammer, Trident, and Hatchet. The middle name you have is the weapon you specialize in. Middle names are required and enforced so that nobody gets confused about which medieval one is good at using which weapon. At first, I thought it was strange, but then I got to know the medieval ones. Their lives revolve around weapons and fighting, even when they don't have any enemies to fight.

When Christian met Cecil, Cecil called him over from the train tracks. He offered him a drink and so they drank. Then, when they introduced themselves, Cecil wanted to know Christian's middle name. Cecil said this: "So what's your weapon?"

"Huh?" Christian then said.

"Your middle name."

"James," Christian said.

"That's an odd name for a weapon," Cecil said. "What's it look like?"

"It's not a weapon. It's a biblical figure."

That's when Cecil told Christian how middle names are weapons. And Christian told Cecil what biblical figures were.

Christian then told him his new middle name: "Broken Beer Bottle."

☺

"Cecil," Christian yawps.

We head over to the tent. Cecil looks up from his cake-making. He's the fried cake-maker, and he runs the booth himself. The only customer he's had is an Andrew Jackson midget, who has already purchased a fried cake and is now glazing it with raspberry topping.

"My friend, Christian," Cecil says in a toothless smile, alcohol breath. "Are you coming to the fights tonight?"

"I don't think so," Christian answers. "I have to work."

"You're going to miss a lot. I'm fighting a Carpet Beast."

"What's a Carpet Beast?"

"It's like a small bear, but it has carpet instead of fur, and walks like an ape."

"Sounds tough. I wish I could see it."

"There's going to be fights all day long, including one with a Prowler Beast. You should at least watch the first match. It should start pretty soon."

☺

I stop paying attention to Christian and Cecil and use my God's eyes to go after a naked woman that's passing in the distance.

She is naked, but nobody minds.

She's walking, free from the rest of the world it seems, hidden inside of her mind, smiling like a four-year-old. Thin and perfect. Yes, she is absolute perfection. She's like a machine. Only a machine could be perfectly beautiful, so artistic and unnatural. To me she's the most breath-filching creature I've seen. Nobody else seems to notice her, even though she doesn't have any clothes on.

No sound comes out of her walk.

Only a machine can be flowingly silent.

She must be a blue woman, because she has light blue skin and deep red hair, a fire crotch too, and green-blue eyes that are sharp like turquoise. Her eyes are the largest feature on her face. BIG and innocent.

I bring my vision around close to her face and take a look into those eyes and fall still. One look. I feel weak, small, possessed maybe. Her eyes are so BIG that I get my soul sucked out, drawn into her. She could take my life away in a breath, and I would allow her to, let her inhale me inside of her, just so I could be *inside* of her. And that is all I want to do, with the last of my life - to be inside of her. Forever-forever.

I do not follow her once she's gone.

Christian snaps me out of my God's eyes.

☺

"Where were you?" Christian asks me.

"Over there," pointing thirty feet away.

"What were you doing?"

"I think I saw a blue woman."

"Really?"

"Yeah. It's the first time I've seen one."

Cecil butts into the conversation. "Don't ever go near them blue women. They're trouble."

"How are they trouble?" I ask him, almost offended. The blue woman was *soo perfect*. There could never be anything troublesome about them.

Cecil says, "The blue women live all around this area, but you don't see them too often. They're all lesbians. Don't ever trust a lesbian. They're a race that doesn't have a male species. The women impregnate each other through organs on their faces. Their children are born through the alimentary canal instead of the vagina."

"So what's wrong with them?" Christian asks.

"They're lesbians. That's all," Cecil says. "Lesbians aren't any good. There's no war or fighting without any men. It's a terrible-terrible race."

"So they don't have sex with men?" Christian asks.

"Well . . ." Cecil says, "supposedly, blue women still have intercourse with males of other species, but only for tension release or recreation or something. Males have nothing to do with the reproduction of blue women, so they don't marry men. They're a bunch of sluts and got all kinds of diseases. Don't touch them. They're no good at all. Pure evil, I call them."

Both Christian and Leaf diagree with Cecil. I am definitely still intrigued by blue women. I can tell by Christian's slimy face that he is too.

☺

    As we leave the fried cake stand: mud rocks on my bare feet, more and more people joining the festival crowd, my eyes giving me a small dizzy spell from the drizzling sludge, and Cecil gives us some fried cakes with strawberry sauce.

    Then, walking away with a wooden bowl and wooden spoon, Cecil with his mug of beer asks us this:

    "Where are you headed?"

    We keep walking. The new rain seems to be issuing from the ground and sprinkling on the sky and clouds. Like all of the underground was so filled with water that it had to rain it out, into the atmosphere.

    Christian turns around to Cecil, and answers him this:

    "To oblivion."

☺

    The act of eating cakes persuades us to catch a place for sitting, so we choose the insides of the tent arena. Most of the seats are soaked from the ground rain, a strong wet-forest odor. The crowd is seated with no complaint to the rain or the tent manufacturers or their wet butts, waiting in anticipation for the first of fifty fights that will journey nonstop into late this night.

    We don't bother with searching for any dry seats. The water instantly soaks through my pants to my butt skin, shocking cold, but I let it go. Dark pools will probably be imprinted on my butt all night at work, unless I find my other pair of pants.

    The first fight is between a medieval one and a krellian.

    A krellian is a very tall, very strong, very thin creature/person. It looks like a giant stick man made of rubbery pale skin. They're an uncommon breed that were invented by other men - created to be the strongest and fastest fighters of all time, which means this fight will be a short one. A medieval one cannot defeat a krellian, even when cheating.

    In that world, the men were being overrun by zombies -which were called fortics - and didn't want to be bothered with defending themselves, since there were more important things to be done than worrying about getting killed and eaten. So they made the powerful race of the krellians to protect their cities from obvious destruction.

The krellians live for hundreds of years, usually all by themselves, and never completely out of danger. When they're not killing zombies, they spend their time meditating and practicing religion. Their god is called Crawn. Crawn is the second god of nine in our system. Yahweh, I believe, is the seventh. This particular god has more influence on his followers than most gods in his clique. He gives them powers, even magical powers, to enable them to be muscular and masterful, the greatest race of all for intelligence and efficacy.

Yahweh used to be the opposite of Crawn. He believed in spiritual strength and love. He wanted his people to be powerful in the heart - physical and mental strength meant nothing to Him. But now He has turned his back on our spirits, so I don't want to talk about His good aspects.

Sometimes I wonder if He didn't have a choice.

Maybe He closed the pearly gates so that the walm couldn't vacuum away all of the souls that He collected. Maybe He was afraid that His own soul would be taken away and turned into sillygo. Maybe He cries for the ones he left behind. Maybe He feels guilty.

Or - maybe His soul is already gone.

And that great rotting corpse up in the sky that was once our God, is staring at his great holy wall, shrugging his great holy shoulders.

With his great holy spirit vanished to oblivion.

☺

The fight starts.

Neither of them do anything, staring statues, glacial. The krellian is unusually large, even for a krellian. Intense features. The crowd seems cheer-happy, excited, impressed by the dominating appearance of the krellian versus a very scared opponent, but I get bored. Neither of them move.

A krellian will not strike until his opponent strikes first, that is the moral thing to do if you're krellian, and his opponent is too frightened to attack him.

In boredom, I ask Christian about what he said to Cecil as we were leaving the fried cake stand. "What did you mean? To *oblivion*."

Christian thinks back.

He remembers. "Yeah, that's where we're headed."

"Do you really think so?" I say.

"That's what Satan said, didn't he?"

The medieval one runs to the back of the krellian, but does not attack, still scared. The krellian doesn't even turn around; he's quick enough to turn and defend once his opponent's sword is swung.

"Can you *really* believe Satan?" I ask him.

"There's no reason for him to lie about this," Christian says. "He has nothing to gain."

"Maybe Satan just wants to have us work for free," I say.

"I'd rather take the chance," Christian says.

I nod.

"Satan's not that bad of a guy," Christian says. "He's just a homosexual."

I pause for a minute, finishing up my fried cake.

The fighting medieval one's name is Sanders Sword Sunblanket, or S.S.S., also a friend of Cecil's and is considered one of the better swordsmen here. Much better than Cecil. However, he thinks very highly of himself, BIG ego here, so BIG that he thought he could beat a krellian. Seeing a krellian now, he doesn't think the same way.

"So you think we're going to oblivion?" I ask.

Sanders runs around to the krellian's front. Then he goes behind him again. Then to the front. Circling the stickman - motionless man, does not move, like a mantis, waiting for the man to strike, waiting to make its own strike.

"Of course," Christian says, his eyes not leaving the fight for a second. "Unless the walm is destroyed, it will get us eventually. There's only so many souls we can steal before our own souls are stolen, only so much. We'll prolong the inevitable, and that's okay. But someday, probably soon, we're going to be emotionless, just like our parents."

"You don't seem too worried."

"It doesn't matter," he says. "I'd rather keep my soul, but if it happens, it happens."

"But your soul is the most important part of you. Satan's right about that. Without it, you're absolutely *nothing*, a zombie, a flesh machine. And oblivion is the worst place you can ever go. Everything you ever did will be forgotten. You'll have no future, no present, no past, no consciousness, nothing."

"It's still not that important," Christian says. "Going into nothingness isn't something you should worry about. If anything, it should be a worry-reliever. Your struggles, uneasiness, fears, bad times are all uplifted, erased. It's the only true peace. It is like sleep without dreams, forever."

I argue with Christian because I choose to fight oblivion as Satan does. Oblivion is the only enemy I have and I will not let it win. I think there is still hope for my soul. Maybe the walm will go away in time, or maybe I will be working with Satan forever. Either way, I will never give up, and never go into oblivion.

Sanders thinks about attacking. This thought is such a strong thought that it reaches the krellian's mind, and the krellian *thinks* that Sanders is *really* trying to attack him. So he swings around and clubs the man in his forehead. Sanders completely startled by the stickman moving. And he is more startled by the movement than by his skull being broken indoors, and the blood tickling down his cheek and neck.

"Well, why don't you go there now?" I ask him. "Without a past or present in your future, why live your life at all? Everything you're doing here is going to be for nothing."

"On your way to oblivion," he says, "always take the scenic route."

Christian smiles, watching the medieval one's body as it is hauled away, trailing some roasty hot red, and a chunk of hard white . . .

Scene 9
The Trouble With Music

☺

Rippington is facing an overpopulation crisis today. Word got out through the walm about the festival of war, which most races have heard is the greatest and most violent entertainment in the universe, and hundreds upon hundreds of people are piling into this (my) city every hour. And Satan speculates that all of these beings will take up permanent residence in this (my) world and so will not be returning through the walm.

I'm not positive how overpopulation is going to affect Rippington. There might not be enough food and water to support so many people; everyone is going to suffer. But I'm only afraid for my own suffering, selfish thing that I am, especially because I'm afraid of being inside of a large crowd. I am not normally claustrophobic. Being inside of a closet or a tiny room or a coffin doesn't scare me, but inside of a crowded room or a crowded party puts me into a tornado-like panic. I'm not good with people other than my friends. People that go near me make me uncomfortable; they steal my air before I get a chance to breathe it.

This overpopulation is good for business though. All of Satan Burger is filled with beings on their way to the festival of war, getting some food for the long-long walk across town. And everybody has a soul to sell for a deep-fried grease-filled Satan Burger. I always have to explain to the customers what a Satan Burger is. I tell them, "It's deep-fried in animal fat, which makes it crispy on the outside and chewy on the inside. And remember, they're only two for the price of one."

☺

It is twilight now, but the outside still looks like morning.

I am working the register while Mort and Christian cook. All of us have to where a uniform of red shirts with red hats, and the hats have tiny red horns on the top, to make us seem more satanic.

The line is very dragging and I am the only person managing it. The register is rolling in my rolling vision, making it hard to find the right keys, swirl-whirling off the counter. I hear many complaints in many different languages - complaints that I'm not moving fast enough I'm sure. I go out of my body and into the line to see how I look: I am like a confused old man, hitting only one register key each minute, drugged up in a daze. I find it funny that everyone is so impatient to lose their souls.

Since nobody pays in money, you'd figure there would be no reason for a register – that's what I was thinking yesterday and why I agreed to work the counter. But the register is used as a typewriter that writes down each customer's order, and prints it up for the customer to sign. The signature is an approval for Satan to take the soul away from the customer after the soul leaves the body.

The customers are willing to trade their immortal souls for food. True, it's the best tasting food ever created - so they say - but I wouldn't trade my soul for anything. They do not know, however, know that they are to lose their souls immediately. Most of them think that they will go to hell *after* they die, which they don't think is bad because dying doesn't exist here anymore. But that's not the way it works. Satan Burgers are so good that they make your soul lighter than air, and it floats out of your body and flies around the room.

Right now, Satan is chasing souls around the dining area, scooping them up with butterfly nets, placing them inside of a little tupperware container that says, in BIG black magic marker letters:

H E L L

☺

When a soul leaves a being, the being's consciousness doesn't completely leave with the soul, some of it stays with the corpse. The consciousness is made up of memories, thoughts, and emotions. After the soul leaves, the body keeps a little bit from each of these things. It gets the *soul resin* - the only energy that the majority of people have inside of them now. You can go on living with soul resin, but it won't be any fun. The only real point to living when you're in the soul resin state is to keep on living.

Before, when there were still gates open in heaven, when people were allowed to die, dead corpses would have soul resin still inside of them, left behind. Sure this resin would be useless, because the body doesn't move anymore, but it could still be sensed by certain individuals that were born with the ability to sense creatures from the afterlife dimension.

Now that people can't die, there are all kinds of undead beings drifting about, just like Gin. They are only undead because they still have their life-force. If something like the walm takes away their souls, they will no longer be undead. Their soul will go to oblivion and their zombie body will only have soul resin. And when a zombie has nothing but resin for a soul, it thinks: "The only real point to living is to keep on living. But since my corpse has no life to keep on living, I must go to my grave and fall into a deep, dark sleep."

Sometimes, when you scream really-really loud, you can awaken the sleeping dead. This is the worst possible thing you can do to it. If a woken corpse is notably cranky, it might try to eat your brain to stop you from screaming. If you continue to scream after your brain has been eaten, the corpse will eat more of you until it is absolutely certain that you will not be capable of molesting its slumber anymore. This is how the brain-eating zombie stereotype originated.

☺

Nighttime now, but it still looks like morning outside.

Satan has been playing some music on the stereo system. He calls it *Satan Music*, because he recorded the songs himself. It isn't like anything I've heard before. Seems more like noise than music, but it is much different than the electronic noise that my band plays. Describing it is extremely difficult. Definitely something to be heard rather than heard about.

Basically, it is described as this: put every sound in the universe into one instrument and play a half-melodic tune, with a female vocalist who is being tortured and sexually gratified at the same time; also, throw twelve thousand stones at a single target without rhythm. The music is very intense and very loud, and gives you a feeling quite similar to the flu.

Before I met Satan, I knew of a certain type of heavy metal that was called *Satan Music*. This kind of Satan music was created in the eighties to make bands such as Iron Maiden and Dokken look like wimps. One of the first Satan music bands was called Venom. All the Venom fans would dress in black clothes and dye their hair black and let their faces go pale from lack of sun. This was all an attempt to look scary and vampiric, kind of like Vod.

In other words: VENOM = EVIL.

☺

The music is very intriguing at first, but then it gets annoying after an hour and you just want to get away from it. I keep trying to get Satan to turn the music down, but Satan doesn't ever listen.

> I try sarcasm and say, "Satan, can you turn the music any louder?"
> And he says, "No, that's as loud as it gets."

So I continue with nonstop soul-buying for another hour.

☺

Eventually, business slows and the line thins. Then, all of a sudden, it's all gone. No more orders. Only ten people left in the store, eating their food and losing their souls.

I exit my post and sit into a booth with a hot cup of orange-nut coffee, creamy blend. The music forces my temples to tighten up solid, vibrating my upper spine.

And then an explosion: "SATAN, TURN THE FUCKING MUSIC DOWN!!!"

A yell.

For the first time in years, I yelled. You could barely hear it over the music, but I yelled.

Satan agrees with my nodding head by nodding his head. He turns it down to a nice background score and says, "You're right. Silence is in the parking zone again. It might hear us."

"How do you know?" Christian asks, stepping out of the kitchen with one Newport cigarette on his tongue.

"No more customers," Satan responds, lowering his Satan Music a touch more. "Silence either swallowed them up or scared them into the distance."

☺

"Why do you keep playing that music?" I ask Satan.

I drink down half my coffee and go to refill it. The tangy brown fluid whirls from the cup onto the floor.

"Music attracts customers," Satan says.

"*Good* music attracts customers," I say.

The last of the customers leave, the cigarette machine opens the door for them, to be eaten by the Silence.

"But I *do* play good music," Satan argues, almost offended. "I wrote it."

"It's not good," I say. "You're music scares people. Especially me. The only thing it's good for is making me sick."

"Do you really think so?" Satan says, understanding voice. "This is the kind of music I've always found most appealing."

"Actually," Christian butts in, "I've heard some people say that they came here *because* of the music. They heard it from half a mile away, and they came to see what it was. They seemed really interested in it, until their souls fell out. Personally, I think the music's unusual enough to be interesting. I think it actually does attract people."

"Well, it makes me sick," I say to Christian.

"Really?" Christian sits across from me. "I actually like it."

Satan is happy with his music and turns it louder again. Not *too* loud, I can handle it at this volume for now. As he passes me on his way to the office, he flicks my shirt like a little kid, the red Satan Burger shirt, and the shirt becomes a demon, squiggling on my chest. It doesn't seem to bother me.

I just notice that I've been a part of the past conversation. Normally, I don't speak that much. And I *never* get into arguments or yell or complain like I just did. Also, the shirt that is now alive and squiggling on my torso usually would have put me in suffering, irritatingly squeamish.

Maybe I'm drunk right now, even though I don't remember drinking anything. When I'm drunk, I say things without thinking. Drinking numbs you from your ability to reason. It makes you forget your own character and become a crazy. Maybe I am a crazy now; I'm going through so much chaos these days that reality is hard to grasp.

Or maybe all the sillygo, floating around in my oxygen, is making me go silly.

☺

"Well, Gin's not doing too good," Christian says to me.

"What's wrong?" I ask. "Still upset about his hand?"

"Not just his hand. Early today, when they were working, Satan accidentally touched him a few times, made more of Gin's body parts alive. If this keeps up, Gin's going to have nothing left that he can control besides his brain."

☺

I use my God's Eyes to go see Gin.

He looks the opposite of well, sitting on his bed with Nan, trying to fall asleep, Nan brushing his hair away and holding him, like a concerned lover, something she's never been to him before. Maybe she's getting soft.

Breakfast is attacking Gin's neck, trying to shake him up, but he ignores the hand. Gin's eyes dribble back into his head, with some white on exhibition for the draft to parch. The room is lit by one candle, which is a symbol for Gin. He's the type of person that romanticizes candlelit lifestyles, like the people before the electricity days, nights by the fire in the living room and just a candle for the bedroom. He says that candles make the world a droning softness, a falling whisper.

Gin's new flesh-pets are asleep. They're more upsetting to him than the hand, because they are more numerous. Now he feels his whole being has basically come to an end. It is just a vehicle for other creatures to live. One of them is his left shoulder, who he named Encyclopedia, another is his little finger, who he named Battery, and his right butt cheek, who he named Selenson. Selenson means *Son of the Moon*. Nan created this name for Gin; she says it's never been used before.

Satan also patted Gin on the head, and made eight of his dreads alive. At this point, Gin wasn't in the mood for naming any more body parts, so he calls them Medusa Hairs.

☺

Richard Stein mentioned the Medusa to me. He said that she was a little woman in Houston, who could turn a little man into her slave, making him work his little butt all day long, just for her, just so she could take his money and buy herself things. This happened every time they stared deep into each other's eyes. What the man saw was *love*, what the Medusa saw was *money*. After the man stopped earning enough money, the Medusa divorced him, leaving him broke and empty. Richard Stein said that his first wife was this Medusa, and she had snakes for hair.

Gin's dreads are snakes now too, worming around in the candle flame, in the forehead of a dozen naked beings. I zoom my vision to see what the naked beings are doing inside of the candle's flame.

They are a group of Firemites, beings made of energy, living in fire. They originally came from the surface of the sun, where thousands upon thousands of them live, swirling around in the BIG hot. Without fire, Firemites turn into one-dimensional shadow creatures that eventually die if they don't find fire again, just as we would die without food. This is not a problem for Firemites on their home world, but it is to the ones that are in this candle now. Their sizes change with the size of the fire, a candle will make them tiny, a bonfire will make them man-sized. It may just be a rumor, but the Firemites are supposed to have highly intelligent societies on the sun, that we cannot understand. They don't seem to be very intelligent to me right there in the flame. They seem rather primitive, moronic.

They gaze as a giant orgy of flames, rolling over each other, exchanging energy-like kisses, large fire cocks penetrating fire vaginas. The only thing that matters to firemites seems to be food and sex, which might be why they are considered so intelligent.

Gin and Nan fall into blissful sleep - the best thing in life - with Gin's living body part pets, the dreadlocks wave-snaking inside the air, hissing like Medusa, and the family of Firemites are sweating in their orgy of food and sex, hoping the candle doesn't burn out anytime soon.

☺

When I go back inside my body, I see that Christian has left the room, went to the back of the kitchen, to be with someone more talkative. I totter to the employee section of the restaurant, to where Mortician is working.

Mortician is always the one doing all the work. He's chopping vegetables and tomatoes now, while we sit on our asses. I think he's only like that because it's in his character to do work *all* the time, no matter what it is. He must keep busy so that he won't get bored. And I know that once he stops working, his soul is lost. Soul resin won't have interest enough to do work as obsessively as he does it now.

I hear Christian and Satan talking about the blue women and hurry my God's Eyes inside with them. I can't miss a conversation like this, not when the most beautiful creatures on Earth are involved. I still can't get the face of that BIG-eyed blue woman passing through the festival out of my thoughts. I know Christian is as interested in them as I am. We will both go after them soon enough.

☺

Satan describes the blue women like this:

They look a lot like humans, but they have red hair and what appears to be blue flesh. Their skin is really just white, just like Caucasian skin, but all the fluids underneath the skin are made of blue so the blue women appear to be blue. Actually, they're much different than humans. On the insides, they're more like machines, like the insides of clocks, with gears made of cartilage. They have both male and female sex organs in their mouths, and they reproduce by kissing: two blue women become impregnated by a long tongue-rubbing kiss. The sperm that ejaculates is more like lime juice than regular human sperm; very sour if you taste it.

Another reason why blue women smell like machines is that they don't need to sleep, and instead of eating they run on fuel, a fuel that males produce. Actually, *any* male mammal produces the same fuel, and all types will do them fine, but human-like males are attracted to them and will get inside their vaginas without being forced. Blue women usually molest every male person or beast they can get their wiry fingers on, because they *need* to ingest the cum through their vaginas and into a certain gland that isn't all that different from our stomachs. That's why they still have sexual intercourse with. To men, it is sex; to blue women, it is food.

Sometimes the blue women carry diseases and give it to the males they sleep with, just like some mosquitoes give people malaria when they drink blood. It's very dangerous to be around blue women because of these sexually transmitted diseases, mostly because they are irresistible to men. If one comes in contact with a hungry blue woman, there is no escape; even an old blue woman is irresistible. They must remain irresistible their entire lives, in order to attract males. They grow up to full maturity when they are two years old and die at the age of two hundred, before their bodies grow too withered and smelly to attract men. During their two years of childhood, blue women molest animals, forcing the mammals to ejaculate into their vaginas by handling or sucking their sexual organs.

Blue women are also mute. They only speak to each other telepathically, and they have no vocal chords at all. The only sound that comes out of their throats are soft breaths, and smacking lip vibrations. Other than that, they are as silent as a landscape painting.

"Leaf?"

I hear Mortician calling to my body; my mind is in the next room.

"Leaf, could you take out the trash for me?" he says.

I look over at him, dizzy from the mind-body transaction. I don't say anything.

"That one over there," he says, pointing his knife at an orange garbage bag.

I tie it up and take it out to the thick-greased dumpster behind Satan Burger, out into the fresh-sober morning. Another cigarette machine hostess, not the one at the entrance, opens the backdoor for me. It's the employee cigarette machine, made for employees to buy cigarettes conveniently on their cigarette break, on their way outside. Since they're free, I decide to take a pack. I was never a smoker before - I never cared enough to start smoking - but it's all right to now. The worst smoking could do is kill me, and dying isn't something to be afraid of.

I buy a pack of Carlton's, which were always considered one of the low-tar brands of cigarettes, very sophisticated too I think. I've never tried them before, but I always said that they'd be my personal brand of cigarette if I became a smoker.

If everyone had not lost their soul, there would still be a BIG conflict between smokers and nonsmokers. Neither of the two groups would ever have given up until the entire country, or maybe even the entire world, was split into two parts: a smoking section and a nonsmoking section. Many of the people were neutral, like me, not smoking but not complaining about smokers. I hate the nonsmokers that complain. They're the reason why I take the smokers' side over theirs. Smokers always seem to be more down to Earth, not so uptight, not afraid to die.

The outside is still morning, infinite morning. Richard Stein always called the morning his cool blue lady. It was the only woman he ever truly loved.

I light a Carlton cigarette with an old book of matches I found under some newspaper wanderers, and fill my insides with acid-pleasant harshness. This harshness is what I enjoy from smoking; the nicotine doesn't do much for me.

I look up the hill and see a swarm of scorpion flies, circling, no one is below them, except me, but I'm not worth eating. The scorpion flies find a nice cow and settle down with it.

The scorpion flies are buzzing closer than they should be, all wired in some sort of panic. Like something is wrong. Like disaster is going to happen.

Scene 10
Hog World

☺

After the working day is considered fully cooked, and Mr. Satan is left within his cancer-breathing office counting his newly earned souls, licking chortles and rubbing himself with fruition, Mort, Christian, and Leaf, go out for a night of drinking and celebration. The celebration part is meant to stop boredom and make us *happy*. Without *happy*, the walm might steal our souls before our first paychecks come in.

We go to a pub called *Hog World*, around the side of the Tower Shops - the only business still open at night. It's a dirt-sweaty place, but always filled with new and slosh-interesting people who always know to fun it up crazy.

The owners and most common customers of Hog World are of the Hoggian race, but we all know them as *Hogs*. They are the only race of people that brought their riches with them through the walm. They never go anywhere without their wealth, and were able to fit into Earthling society without difficulty. Hogs are actually the *only* wealthy people left in Rippington now. The original Rippingtonians are all poor or going poor, including those of us at the warehouse. The only income we have, besides life-force, is rent money from John and Satan, and we have to split that up four ways. We're going to Hog World to blow the last of this money, but it is blowing to a worthy cause, so none of us are caring. It is, however, the last time we'll be able to have this sort of fun, which is very ill-depressing. I try not to mull on it.

☺

The walk from warehouse to Hog World is still carpety soft on my bare feet, and I have a constant need to say, "Oh, poor parasites," over and over again, directing it toward the people on the streets, but I mean to direct it toward the rest of the world too. The alcohol has given Leaf some sense of disgust for *all* people, even the thousands of homeless around me. And I think it's fun to be mean to them. They are, mostly, the ones responsible for ending happiness in this world, even their own happiness. So I say, "Oh, poor, poor, poor," all the way to happy Hog World. Hog World doesn't let any parasites inside - they have no money and do nothing but steal oxygen. The Hogs charge ten dollars at the door, which isn't that much considering it's the smug-fanciest pub in town, but during these weeks ten dollars is BIG money, and wasting BIG money isn't that terrible anymore. Money is an endangered species now.

☺

They say, "Fifteen Dollars," when we get to the door.

Face-fuckers, Christian whispers, but I just laugh, not very surprised. And there is a snarled crowd of starving people, watching us as we pay to go inside. A child with penis breasts cries into my thigh.

I just say, "Poor, poor *parasites*," with a cold smile.

Richard Stein always said that the RICH are the scum of the world. He is wrong. In this world, we are all scum.

☺

Inside is another one of these round-a-go crowds that I keep seeing into . . . too many people jolly-dancing in the waves of my vision . . .

God's Eyes:

Above the crowd, a ceiling fan's view, Christian, Mort, and my body walk through to the bar and sit down for some sticky goo-doo - a drink like honey with alcohol mixed in. A shoe spider is on the counter, pulling a small wagon of walnuts for the customers to handle and eat. Shoe spiders are much like hermit crabs, but they live inside of shoes instead of shells.

I take a walnut and put it inside my sticky goo-doo. Walnuts have strong flavor and taste good in thick drinks.

"Let's get fucked in the ass!" Christian says, screeching a party call.

Christian is not as homophobic as Mort, and thinks it's funny to talk like he's a homosexual. But he wouldn't have said anything if Satan had been around; Satan doesn't realize that Christian only says these things when he's drunk.

In other words: GETTING FUCKED IN THE ASS = PARTY.

Christian actually enjoys getting fucked in the ass – that is, if a girl is giving it to him with a strap-on dildo. He feels very homosexual for enjoying the performance and won't tell any of his friends about it. Sometimes a girl will think peculiar thoughts of Christian when he asks her to take him in the behind. Sometimes a girl will become thrill-enflamed by the opportunity to take a man like men take her. Sometimes Christian masturbates with a dildo.

The shoe spider crawls back into his shoe.

☺

"I'm getting laid tonight," Christian burps.

He puts on his girl-maker face - a sly hollow. Then he turns the beams of his forehead *on*, scoping the room for a good score - a woman with six breasts maybe or one with more curves than a human girl would own. I only see two humans in here, females, sitting on the laps of Hogs, very RICH.

Hogs are a flabby sort of people. Not too ugly, but very unexercised. The women have large ears and unusually large breasts that bludgeon their sex opponents. Their eyes are speckled with purple and their clothes, ripped for style, expose the very pale, almost gray, skin underneath. The men are shorter than the women, stocky, BIG teeth in their smiles. They go, "Gar, gar, gar!" when they laugh.

Christian isn't interested in a Hoggian though. He wants the girl with two sets of arms, sitting in the corner over there. She has a very attractive face, but no breasts. Smooth yellowish skin, sliming, which is why Christian wants her. His color is yellow this year. He goes to her without telling us, a man-sly walk to her and she actually seems interested in it. Well, maybe she's just happy that *somebody* is interested in her. She looks very lonely.

Now it's just me and the Mortician. Drinking . . .

☺

I decide to get very drunk, not just *normal* drunk like I usually am. I want to drink like it's the end of the world, which it might be. Where the world ends, hell begins . . . at least in the traditional sense of the word *hell*.

I drink some sticky goo-doo and wash it down with common Earth gin. Mortician neck-dribbles the gin after me, garbling about his philosophy on life.

"That's how every day should be," he says, Japanese accent thicker than usual. "You just work all day and get drunk all night."

"What about weekends?" I ask.

"You get twice as drunk on them."

- 100 -

"Great philosophy," feeling the buzz stab deep inside. He slicks back an oil-stiff drink, hard on his chest. "Goes down like a cactus." He hasn't been speaking in his pirate accent today. I don't wonder why, but I'm glad.

☺

"Speaking of philosophy," he says, making me cringe. "Did you read any Sorpon Black?"
"Sure." I don't get excited. Philosophy is an ugly color, especially when you're drinking.
"What do you think about him?" Mortician asks.
Mort is BIG on philosophy. Always gaming for debates during the drinking times, his way of *socializing*. He does this with religion too, and politics, and food selections. But Mort is more into the arguing part than the deep-thinking part. And Mort is never able to start up debates with enough people these days since nobody believes anything sacred enough to argue over.

As for Sorpon Black, he was an oldtime hippie philosopher, whose deep-thinking came out of his ample supply of repressed sexual energy. Old Sorpon never had sex a day in his life, not even with himself, and he was an extremely attractive guy. But very bitter. The reason why he never had sex was because he was afraid of his own penis. He couldn't handle the way it slunk-stickered in his shorts, so sensitive when rubbed against his thigh. To make matters worse for him, his penis was unusually BIG. It was five and a half inches larger than mine, and my penis isn't considered small – at least for my height.

The sick-scary part for Sorpon was the erection. When erect, there's nothing a man can think about other than his penis, whether he's sitting at work or playing a basketball game or fully-engorged within a woman's vagina. When Sorpon was in elementary school, he would scream blood-shrieks while watching his erection grow and grow and grow to the unbearable maximum. It was like a poisonous salad snake had been dropped in his lap.

This phobia came from a childhood mind-molestation, at the age of six, when his very nice neighbor taught him how to perform oral sex and anal sex by showing him homosexual pornography. But the neighbor never performed these sexual techniques on him. He just liked to mess up the insides of young brains. Experiencing this kind of thing as a child will definitely mess up the insides of your brain. It will either discourage you from being intimate with anybody when you grow up, or it will throw you into the opposite direction: nymphomania for females, andromania for males.

But Sorpon Black's philosophies had nothing to do with his enormous cock. They had to do with the intelligence of sandwiches.

"I don't think anyone *really* believes that sandwiches are the creators of the universe," I tell him. "Sorpon Black was just trying to be entertaining."

"Hardly," Mort says. "It all makes sense because sandwiches are made from all four food groups. And if you compare the four food groups to the four elements, they are relatively the same idea. And if the four elements were layered together like a sandwich, you would create a god. Therefore, sandwiches are gods. Don't you agree?"

"I guess," I shrug. Not actually interested. Like most philosophies, Sorpon's theory is worthless to argue against. And I am not one for arguing.

"You're not a *deep* thinker, are you?" He realizes my lack of enthusiasm.

"I was into *deep* thinking when I was a kid, but then I grew up," I say, insulting his use of the word *deep*.

"Are you saying philosophy is immature?"

"Basically," I tell him. "To most people, philosophies are just common sense." Then I get personally mean – I'm in an odd mood I guess. It's fun to be mean. "People like you don't have common sense, so philosophies seem *new* and interesting to you, but you don't realize that they're not at all new. Only to the immature."

Mortician tries to speak, but I cut him off - the first time I have ever cut anyone off. "Mature people don't need to question the world they live in, because they've already figured it out."

Mort grins at me. "So you think you've figured out *everything* about reality?"

"Not really, but I've figured out that nobody can prove any philosophy theory, so they're useless. Nobody'll ever know the complete *truth*, so there's no reason to worry or argue over petty beliefs. The only groobly thing about Sorpon Black's philosophies is that every single one revolves around sandwiches, and I love sandwiches."

"You're such a philosophy-bashing philosopher," he says.

I am insulted, of course, because he's right. I never expected Mortician to call me a philosopher - he's more perceptive than I thought he was. But I'm happy to be *insulted*. It's a surprise that the emotion is still within me. Maybe arguments are good things after all.

I switch the subject. "What do you think about our situation?"

"What?" he says. "You mean living forever? Sounds boring to me."

"We won't last forever here," I say. Our lives might be longer than those already dead from history, but those from history have souls that are eternal. *They* are the ones who will live forever.

I chug some HOT liquid.

The drinking is killing the poor mood I was in. Taking me from *hating* things to *loving* things, and I smile.

Mortician says, "Yeah, the situation we're in is not good at all, but you have to look on the bright side as I do. Think about how everyone else in the world are all zombie-like. All *gone*. Thousands of soulless bodies wondering the Earth." Brains like pillows. "And we are fine. We have lives and each other. We have responsibilities and fun."

I nod at him, scratching my drink.

"We are the luckiest people in this world. I mean, we still have a chance. I don't want to live like this forever, but it's better than nothing."

"That's what I'm afraid of," I say. "Because I'm positive that we'll be *nothing* before the end of forever."

"Not me," Mortician says. "I'm sure there will be a way out someday. If we hold onto our time and work at Satan Burger, eventually the walm will be gone. Eventually, there will be a new world."

A new world.

I take my God's Eyes to Christian and the four-armed yellow girl he has with him. She seems to be all over his skin, in a slut-ticking frenzied way. The skin leaks a little yellow on him; paint smearing across his neck and face, but it's a sort of grease that seeps through arm-pores. A reaction similar to sweat, but only produced during fornication.

I examine her closely. One pair of arms is human-sized but the other is longer and closer to the hips. The longer arms come thoroughly around Christian's waist section, tugging him into her possession. Her eyes have only one color in them: red. Her lips are thin and curled at the end. Christian digs his taster deep between those rubber lips and he seems *happy*. Well, I would be too if I was with a creature as beautiful as her.

When I was a kid, my parents always told me to *only* marry inside my own race, but I didn't find much fun in that. I always wanted Asian women or African women or the Hispanic ones or any of them that didn't seem to have boring Caucasian skin. I also believe that the melting pot that is America is really going to melt all of us people-ingredients into one product. ONE RACE. That isn't black nor white, but a grayish mud-color. Because people fuck an awful lot and eventually don't care who they are fucking.

Of course, fucking is an endangered performance like everything else now, so Americans will never be gray. But there's a new melting pot in Rippington and there will be a lot of interracial fucking going on. I doubt that this will result in the melting to one color; there's just too many races to mix.

When I was young, I liked to drop a cluster of colors into a paint bucket and watch them swirl around and into each other, color-motley, moving, LOUD. And I kept swirling and swirling and swirling to see what spatter-storm of colors I would come up with, but in the end there was only one color and it was a murky purple-brown-puke that was very boring to look at.

I always thought that the only way to end racial prejudice was to melt us all down to one color, but now I think that God created racial prejudice so that his colorful paint bucket would not turn into a single, boring race.

☺

Mortician is talking about a theory of his, so I go back to my corpse. He's talking about the *new* world that the walm people will make if the walm ever disappears.

"It'll be a shitty place at first," Mort says. "Too many races will produce a BIG ethnic war, and the race with the most people will probably be the first in power. Of course, slavery will definitely come back. The humans are perfect slaves. They won't put up a fight without their souls, no complaints, and they'll last forever now that they can't die. New governments all over the world. Different races will take over different territories. And there will be wars for land and religion as usual. The whole world will be a *new* place and the only memory of human civilization will be on the blank stares of the human zombie faces, working like machines until the end of it all."

"Do you think that we'll be made into slaves too?" I ask.

"Probably . . . but hopefully not."

☺

I leave the conversation and go back to peeping at Christian's situation. The idea Mort has put into my head is very disturbing and I want to ignore it. I don't want to be a soulless person, but it'll be hard to be a slave with a soul, especially if I last forever. But there's always *hope*. And hope is what I am counting on.

Christian is really getting wet with this girl. He's drunk and laughing at/with her, biting on her lip and shoulder. Her stomach is hard with muscle, but she doesn't seem like the muscular type. More fragile. Christian licks her fragile parts.

Creeper-hands caress to her breasts. The breasts aren't BIG at all. They're more like flabby pockets. Almost all races have breasts, no matter how unusual they look. I guess her race is one of the few that don't.

Since there are no breasts for Christian to feel, he goes into her condom-like skirt and heads for the pubic region, and she reaches into his slacks and heads for his.

The two faces flash with alarm . . . then disgust . . .

And the girl's boyfriend - or maybe he's her ex-boyfriend - appears behind Christian. Time for a pummeling. I don't realize what's going on until I see the male species with very large muscles and large breasts - female breasts - and so I seep into the girl's underwear to make sure. I find a penis inside.

The gender characteristics are the other way around in this race. The males are the soft pretty things. And the women are the diesel beasts, hard and tough - men with breasts and vaginas.

Both Christian and the girl-male he's been sexing up begin spitting out each other's flavor. Christian smacks the boy across his face, grinding his teeth and *crazed* . . .

All the people around him are rage-laughing. Music starts up as the power-large woman takes Christian off of her man and throws him into a band of dancing Hogs. And Christian drunk-chuckles at the manly woman, who won't fight Christian anymore. She knows he is a man, and in her race gentlewomen don't hit men, no matter how ugly they are.

☺

Christian is slurped into a breaker of dancing Hogs. The hogs wrench him onto their shoulders and flaunt him around the scope. We are the RICH and deserve to get crazy with joy, because we can afford it. Chris-

tian, in his dirt-rich suit, gaggles at me. Screaming, "Come on, come on."
And I'm pulled in with Mortician and a bunch of other Hoggians. Into the
carousal.

Then the whole pub becomes a fury of movement, with food
drippling from Hog chins, drunken women ripping off their clothes and
showing off sweaty pale bodies, and everything in the room becomes a crowd
of moisture, an orgy without sex. Pure indulgence. The music drive-pierc-
ing the ecstasy. *Laughing screams.* BIG smile across Christian's face. BIG,
BIG smile . . .

A Hoggian woman with wicked eyes pours some liquor down my
corpse's throat, molesting my stomach while I'm out of my body. I go back
to gorge into her, but she's already gone to the next man. So the body tours
into the sweaty food carts that usher the shuffle-prancing mob, with several
other Hogs, scoop-pressuring the pies and meats into my mouth. I'm not
hungry. I do it for *fun.* And I gobble so fast that I don't even enjoy it, but
that's not the point. Then I dunk my face into a bowl of fruit liquor, flog-
ging bubbles. My wetness drizzles inside the liquid.

Next: body twitchings, I throw the cart over and cackle into the
Hogs that were eating there. They laugh with me, hopping on the wasted
larder - a joyous performance.

And the Hog World dance takes me over again, sweeping my con-
science away, *away* . . . Drifting with my rolling life, my round-a-go crowd.
Spin-happy, Mort and Christian take to the top, pouring me onto a balcony
with a round-faced belly woman packaged around me, sinking into my skin
like so much butter, *warm.* I stand whooping with her at my waist, dizzy-
balancing, smiling. She's very pleasurable against my skin, though a half-
ugly race for the most part.

Then, up here above the crowd, I stare out whirlpool. Looking on
the bacchanal-tingle, on the RICH indulging faces. I smirk.

☺

Beyond the happy crowd, I gleam the outside windows, where
hundreds of parasites have gathered, smoldering eyes tearing into me, faces
pressed against the glass. Poor, poor, poor. I put an end to my smile and go
inside my head. At this time, the parasites have sadness and we have happiness.

If all of us were to agree to let them in they would have some of
our happiness, but we would get some of their sadness, and we would all be
at the same level of emotion. However, we would be compromising our

happiness to end their sadness, which is not appealing to us, even though it is the *even* thing to do.

After the moment for pitying the poor slips away, I go back to the *fun*. It was a good, fair idea for me to come up with, but since I'm at the TOP and want to keep my happiness and my luxury, I'm willing to sacrifice the poor ones to the cold.

Richard Stein always said that nobody deserves to live in the cold. But right now, I really don't seem to care.

Scene 11
Another Day In Oblivion

☺

Today, when I wake up with my brain squishing into the back of my skull - Hog World gave me a nasty hangover, with some sour muscles and a bruise - I decide that I'm inside of oblivion instead of reality. I have said oblivion is the worst place in the world to be, but it is okay when you are only pretending. While you are nothing, there's not much to worry about. And doing without worry is the best possible thing I can do for myself.

I say:

"I am in nothing."

This is a very relaxing thing to say. All my nerves trickle right out of me, because *nothing* has no nerves at all. I wrap my whole corpse in a cocoon of blankets, pressing my skin into a small comfort. Only my face feels the fingering draft.

I decide to sleep like this all day, going in and out of actuality. There is nothing more important than being in a dream world when the conscious world is horrible as it is. Christian comes in and out of my closet/room every half hour to see if I'm up for some ugly fun, but I tell him that I'm having all the fun I need for today.

Christian whines and leaves, back to watching old reruns on the pawnshop television. I don't need to explain why they only play reruns on television. There hasn't been a new show for at least three years, which is why I only watch Battlestar Galactica. Christian watches Hart to Hart and The A-Team. Sometimes, while Christian watches The A-team, I wonder if Mr. T is like the rest of the world - boring and emotionless. Christian thinks it isn't possible for Mr. T to get boring, because Mr. T is a national icon, and should've been the messiah instead of Jesus Christ.

I remember that I'm supposed to be in oblivion and not allowed to be consciously aware of the terrible things in the world, such as Mr. T losing his soul. I try to empty my mind. Then I let my eyes put me back into the sleep world again.

Inside of sleep world, I decide I am a butterfly that gets raped by a dragonfly girl in midair. Then a frog slurps us both up and its stomach acids dissolve us as she continues her sexual assault. The dream lasts for about two seconds and then weaves into one where I am five aristocrats eating a sausage.

☺

At work, it isn't so easy to pretend I am in oblivion. I can't work the register if I'm *nothing*, it's just not possible. I decide that only my mind is in oblivion - only because I have decided that - and my corpse is a mindless zombie that can still perform simple zombie tasks like typing and passing out food. Hopefully, the rolling world doesn't make me remember I am Leaf, spilling me into the real world, which is where I don't want to be.

The early shift - Gin, Nan, and Vodka - is still here. Leeching at a BIG rounding table with Satan, drinking storm-warnings and eating beer chips. Apparently they're not interested in going home for the night. Instead, they want to get drunk-happy and be party maniacs all tonight inside of the Satan Burger, while the rest of us work.

But, since I am nothing, I don't care to mind them now. Mort, on the other hand, complains, as usual, about the usual. If he isn't making fun, nobody should be making fun. But I don't blame Mortician for his bitchy attitude; it's in his character to act that way. Without his bitching, he would be as boring as the rest of the world.

Mort hammers at some syrup ants who have invaded his kitchen. Syrup ants are a very pesky type of ant. They are BIG like fingers and have large butts filled with syrup. In the world they came from, people would squeeze the syrup from their butts and put a collection into bottles. On the label of these bottles would be the words: "Syrup Ant Syrup," with a BIG cartoon syrup ant smiling away as his syrup-butt poops on a stack of pancakes. However, on their planet, pancakes are made from sawdust, because flour doesn't exist there, not to mention that wood is one of their four basic food groups instead of breads and cereal.

As he hits them, their butts explode and a pool of syrup occurs, getting his counter goo-sticky. Tiny drops of the sweet juice slop onto his wrist skin, pasting the hairs together. And nothing frustrates Mort more than having pasty wrist hairs.

Mortician decides there isn't time to bother with the ants and sends a demon stapler and a demon meat cleaver after them. These objects have never eaten syrup ants before, but they are willing to try anything with syrup in its butt. At first, the demons chomp at the air, spinning in circles, unsure how to work their invisible legs. Once they learn the how to move, however, they gobble up the pests no problem. Exploding the ants in their metal jaws, leaves the counter a gooey mess. Mort continues his working and bitching.

☺

I come out of oblivion and hear this:
"WHAT THE HELL DID YOU TOUCH HIS PENIS FOR?"

☺

I see Nan in an argument with Satan. In my rolling vision: three stretched figures like radio wax, melting into each other with their screams at each other. There are three distinct voices: Satan's is calm, Gin's is a choking cry, and Nan's is a hysteric shriek, like a mother whose seen her child ruined.

"I didn't touch it," Satan replies, shaking his head childishly.

Nan unzips and drops Gin's pants to reveal a dancing worm, "Then how the hell did it come alive?" she says. The worm wiggles excitedly. Its mouth has developed from Gin's pisshole and Gin's bladder is now its stomach sack, two small eyes on the sides of its head, quite like a snake's.

"I'm sorry," Satan says. "I couldn't help myself. You know, it's not easy being the only gay person left. I have urges that are hard to resist."

"Well, you better resist," Nan argues. "Gin is mine. And he's not like you. Only I can touch him in that way. Why can't you stop touching him? You're turning him into a freak. Why can't you leave him alone?"

"I didn't think he'd mind," Satan says.

Nan seems more upset by the situation than Gin, shouting and mewling like it's *her* penis and not Gin's. Actually, that's basically the truth. Gin and all his parts are Nan's personal property, somewhat like a slave's parts would be. When Gin is looking shabby or unclean, Nan will order him to shower and put on fresh clothing. Until now, I never realized that she had *complete* control over him. I always thought Gin was a free-spirited guy who refused to be held down. But things are clearing. I don't know if Gin has become this way recently, just after his death, or if he's always been like this and I just never realized it. Maybe he's losing soul, losing his will to resist her commands. If I was in his shoes, I would give up hope altogether. Maybe I'd even embrace oblivion - the *real* oblivion.

"What the hell am I supposed to do with a living penis?" Nan says, shaking Gin's penis around. "It's not going to work right. I need a real penis, not a snake attached to Gin's body."

Satan doesn't seem to care. He says, "I don't care."

"You better care!" Nan yells. "You keep touching and touching and touching but you don't take responsibility for the things you make alive. You better figure out a way to put him back to normal."

Satan shrivels his lips. "There's a person who can lift a demon spirit out of an object. But I haven't spoken to him in years."

☺

Satan goes on to talk about his twin brother. He is supposed to look exactly like Satan, but his complexion is pale and he's not a homosexual. And just like Satan, his touch is magical. But instead of a touch that makes things alive, his touch makes things dead.

He has the touch of death.

And the man's name is *Death*.

Satan and Death were both created to perform specific jobs in the world. Death's job is to touch people when they are supposed to die, making up some ridiculous cause for each death. Sometimes he touches people to give them a heart attack, sometimes a car accident, sometimes a bullet in the head; it all depends on what seems reasonable to Death at the time. Sometimes Death screws up and gives a little girl a heart attack, or once he had a young mountain climber who was falling to his death die of natural causes. One of the world supervisors (those angels in blue suits, red ties) got on top of Death's case for that one, and suspended him for three months. During the three months that Death wasn't working, nobody died.

Satan's job is to collect and separate the souls from the people that Death touches. He puts them into two groups: good and evil. The good souls are the ones that the rest of the universe can use, so they're sent to heaven to be processed. The evil souls are either recycled and used for soul-fueled machines like the walm, or Satan keeps them in hell.

Satan and Death haven't spoken to each other in years. They never really got along. Death thinks that homosexuality is unacceptable. So unacceptable that he created a disease called AIDS to make men think twice before having sex with other men. Death was almost suspended again; once his supervisor found out that he was being discriminatory on the job. But there were people that needed to be killed, so Death only got a decrease in pay. And to make things right, Death had to make the AIDS virus just as common in straight sexual relations as it was in gays.

"Death has no prejudice," was once a very popular catch phrase, but it was obviously written by a man who had never shared company with Mr. Death.

The catch phrase was meant to scare people away from dying. It didn't work. People were still becoming dead.

☺

"So your brother can make him normal?" Nan asks Satan.

"I don't know. I don't speak to him anymore," Satan replies.

☺

Christian decides to make a fort underneath one of the tables. He can't work ten minutes without taking a twenty minute break. The engineers that made Christian did not take durability into consideration. They just molded and bolted him up in the cheapest way possible and shipped him here. So you can't really hold Christian accountable for his laziness.

Christian's fort is designed to prevent industrious people from verbally assaulting him while he relaxes inside of it. The design doesn't work, though, and unfortunately, he's too lazy to try and fix it.

Which is why this discussion takes place:

Satan complains to him, "Get back to work. I don't pay you to sleep and make table forts."

Christian says, "Screw off. You don't pay me at all."

Satan says, "You won't get any souls if you don't work for them."

"I don't care. What do I need souls for?"

"Don't be an idiot."

"Go to hell."

"I'm going to fire you."

"I'm going to kick you out of the warehouse."

"I'm serious."

"*I'm* serious."

"No, I'm more serious."

"I'm 150 percent serious."

"I'm infinity percent serious."

"I'm going to punch you in the stomach."

"I'm going to punch me in the stomach too."

The argument continues but nobody wins.

I take my break from work - and oblivion - outside and decide to smoke another Carlton, pissing out by the dumpster which coughs at me in disgust. For some reason I feel *good*. My eyes rolling, breathing in the cold air and then some of Carlton's temperament. Nicey thinkings run wild inside my blood. *Sharp* emotions. I look up to the clouds - an attractive day, even with life so glummy and sick.

Then I see a storm on the horizon. Headed this way. Blue lightning bolts with curvy rounds, like noodles, and instead of raining water, I see it will rain madness.

The storm will go for eighteen days, not stopping until everything is wet and insane. A blubbery storm. I can smell its odor from here. My eyes open and then close a few times.

☺

In the background, the walm licks its fleshy lips with anticipation, hungry for the force that makes men move.

Scene 12
Pleasure Features

☺

The window still says that dawn is coming. It's getting very old. It's been saying that for three days now, nonstop, without saying anything else, like "What's for breakfast?" or "Look at all the people in the street."

The window says, "The dawn is coming! The dawn is coming!" But nobody is listening anymore.

I'm still on break, ignoring the windows, pretending to be in oblivion instead of in Satan Burger. Thinking a blank wall, drinking some black caffeine, echoing a tap with my heel.

Ogling a table:

The table flat and square, colorless. It doesn't breathe very much. Demons can go long periods of time without oxygen, like dolphins, but dolphins are much smarter than this table, so they shouldn't be compared - especially since dolphins are very prejudiced against tables.

The table gets me thinking about a world that Christian has heard about, where almost everything is cubic.

☺

This cubic world is made out of wood, carved from a branch of a universe tree.

There's a forest of these trees that lives in the center of the universe. The sole purpose is to grow wood for planet-building. Each tree stretches into the tall of space, dark spider-crawling trees rooted inside planets that are three times larger than Earth's sun. The trees only need starlight to grow.

Nobody lives in the forest except for the forest creatures and the forest ranger, who guardians the trees from brigands and comets. He inhabits a hut-like creature that lives inside of a dead star, drinking moonshine made from a moon. Besides protecting the forest, he chops branches down for the wood merchant, who comes around every Erdaday.

The wood merchant sells the wood to the world-makers, who carve planets from it and sell the planets to gods. The gods put them into orbits and make the planets alive if they want to. The world-makers don't always make their worlds out of wood, because wood isn't very durable and needs to be replaced every three thousand centuries. But it is the quickest and easiest way to make a planet. If I was a world-maker I would *only* build my planets with wood. That way, gods would need new worlds every three thousand centuries, and I wouldn't have to worry about going out of business.

One time, a world-maker who liked to create wood worlds decided that he would make a bunch of square planets instead of round ones, trying to be more creative than his competitors. He found only one god interested in owning square planets, and the god filled an entire system with them, not a single one being round.

On one of the planets, the god created people out of cubic shapes to live there. These people ate square food and drank square water in square glasses. And there were square mountains that would get square rain that would drain into square lakes where square fish would swim around and eat square waterbugs then poop them out in square little turds.

And when the square version of Christopher Columbus tried to prove the world was round, he fell off the edge of the planet into the sun.

☺

"Let's go outside," Christian says, trying to make the best of our lunch hour.

I agree, even though I should already be done with my break.

Time to end the boredom that work has brought, before our souls go away completely. Satan says that boredom has nothing to do with losing soul, but I don't believe him. I don't think the walm will steal a soul from an interesting person filled with life. It prefers easy prey, like my boring parents.

Outside, padding down steps, the Silence seems to have left a warm presence behind, and there is another lifeless calm. The street is empty, but it will soon fill up with new people. Overpopulation is really starting to show in the city - especially around the warehouse - since yesterday's festival. None of the peoples that attended the festival ever left, so now we have a city full of homeless oblers, aphids, kruuty pods, gobbobops, strik pickies, krellians, hontolos, muckies, turtle nesters . . .

"Where should we go?" I ask him, as the sky melts like candles and drip-drips onto the empty parking lot's swirly-thing.

"I've got a place."

Christian smiles and I follow him, up for anything.

We go silently, trying to avoid Silence. The streets remain lifeless-calm the whole way to there. It must have been a BIG feeding today, taking dozens of new ones out of the population and into its belly.

Christian seems to be slinking as we go, only half-excited at the exciting thing he wants to show me. I'm noticing that Christian's soul is losing him today. Maybe he's just hungover like me. He isn't the same as he was yesterday, rowdy at Hog World, but even at Hog World he wasn't as soul-filled as he was the day before. I can't tell if the others are losing soul. But it shows with Christian. He was always vigilant and aflame, even hungover, without giving one minute to depression, but now he's a drone-slinking downer.

And even though I am positive my best friend is dropping his soul, I don't seem to really care. Am *I* losing soul too? Or am I just losing concern for other people?

☺

We arrive to The City of Scrap Metal - Christian's destination. Darker inside than the morning street that we are on. An infesting darkness.

A sign on the gate tells us, "Yard of the Autocars."

☺

A trillion tons of speckled metal meat stacked in piles of piles, into skyscraper buildings. Half eaten by the rust parasites, all in the sweating dirt yard, where the children live, where automobiles are left to die, left to suffocate.

All the poor autocars . . .

Living like the dead, every day in a painful festering heap. They can feel every second of time tearing at them, breaking them down to ruins. There's no gas or oil or passengers for the cars to eat. They are left to cannibalism. They eat the other autocar corpses: cars that are too damaged, cars with broken arms and legs, devoured by the stronger trucks. And the people come everyday to pick at them, stealing pieces of their brains and insides, taking the last of the good parts and leaving them with rotten metal oddities and the rat-infested seats.

But the poor autocars try to tell themselves that the parts will help other cars, even though their selves will remain in the autocar yard, suffering and dying.

And all the little autocars cry out: "Why can't they just crush us?" And the elder autocars answer: "Don't worry, eventually they will." Richard Stein said that he cried every time he passed an autocar yard. Now I understand why. It's a graveyard for the not-quite-dead. And all of the metallic body parts whirl me dizzy-sick and disgusted.

☺

"Why'd you bring me here?" I ask Christian, sick and hunched, drooling in the center of the lanes of Autocar City's main street.

But he doesn't have to answer. I see her. It's the same blue woman I saw at the festival, the one with BIG eyes and deep red hair. Still naked but not dirty. As beautiful as a machine.

She's coming to get her food. Two others join the advance. One is short and very thin, with short hair and large breasts, and the other has straight hair and Asian eyes, breasts perky but small.

The blue women seem to have the power to lure us to them, melding our minds to theirs, communicating with emotions rather than words. I find that the short-haired one is the oldest, almost a hundred years. The others are just children. One is seven and the other, who is my girl, is only four. Despite their ages, they all look their twentysomething prime. The youngest one comes running to us, childishly.

"I get the first one," Christian says, meaning *my* BIG-eyed blue woman.

"Fuck you," I tell Christian, very strongly, with all my steel-jagged emotions. That's all I need to say to back him away from her.

I know that the girl is only a four-year-old. It sickens me if I compare her to a human four-year-old. But I can't let it bother me. They're from a different world, where sex is as common and no-big-deal as going to the bathroom. And, strangely, her immaturity makes the attraction stronger. She is innocence. Full of life.

When she arrives to me, all she does is leer into my eyes. Sucking all of my power into her possession. If she asked me to go into oblivion right now, I would do it for her. I would put on chains and be her food slave, a cow in a dairy farm. Sex slave to a four-year-old.

She puts out her hand and embraces mine. A slight smile on her face, childish, biting the corner of her lip in a mechanical way. Her fire eyebrows curl, and I'm sucked into her BIG pools again. Swimming in shiny blue-emotions.

And now I know I'll actually get to taste a little while of this perfect creature.

As Christian tries to figure out how to get them back to our warehouse, I notice two small words printed on the blue woman's stomach.

They say, "Pleasure Features," with five arrows pointing at her pleasure parts: her mouth, butthole, both breasts, and her vagina.

Scene 13
Frog Crimes

☺

We decided to have lots and lots of greasy sex with the blue women instead of going back to droming work, Mortician probably shitting his pirate pants right now - all of his anger drooling out the back, down his legs. He won't forgive us.

I said *lots and lots* of sex, but I didn't personally get lots and lots. I only got a little. The blue woman was so hungry that she shoved my shank inside her and made me cum in less than two minutes. And one spurt was enough to fill the four-year-old up. The best two minutes of my grim life probably, but a disappointment afterwards.

Christian, on the other hand, is lasting, getting sexed inside and out and all around his room, grunt-thrashing against the walls, trying to please the two beasts he has with him. But it's more like them trying to please themselves. BIG hunger. BIG crash-noises and screams. The blue women can't really scream, but their mouths can make a whistling sound. And they make him feel cheap.

I decide to peak in on them.

☺

God's Eyes:

My vision doesn't come across right once it goes inside. Too much drum-movement, and a strobing light that Christian bought at a pawnshop four years ago goes pity-pity-pity-pity. A broken zoo of water creatures attacking a cloud person, shifting around each other for a comfortable screw. And the screwing works like batter-pulp, water sifting through hairs, going *Mmmmmmmm* . . .

It all frustrates me. I go back to my corpse, to my blue woman, who seems very bored and agitated. She just stares at my self, says nothing, just stares. Eye-gazing and I am too shy to handle looking back at her, drinking on a cup of brandy.

Peripheraly, I offer her some of my liquor. "Do you want a drink?"

Then I realize she's only four. "Oh, nevermind. You're underage."
I feel like such a pedophiliac.

☺

   When the two blue women are done with Christian, they brush off some wetness from their smooth blue skin, curling sight, and then they depart. Leaving two things behind: One is my young blue woman, still staring at me without blink; the other is the performance of shutting the door behind them, which exposes us to a large gang of tree frogs, who are in the act of fleeing from something, like criminals.
   "Why didn't *she* leave?" Christian asks, gesturing to the blue woman. Croaking frogs.
   I shrug and he squats down on a milk crate next to me. Half-shaking from his fierce workout, he befriends a freshly lit cigar.
   He says, "They're like cockroaches."
   "Who?" I ask. "The frogs?"
   "No, the blue women. They're disgusting."
   Alarmed, I drink some brandy. "What . . ."
   "Cecil was right. They're dirty, disease-ridden whores. Disgusting."
   "I don't know what you're talking about," I tell him, upset but not showing any emotion. "I like my blue woman."
   "She's not leaving." He looks at her - sitting there, staring at me. "What are you going to do with her?"
   "I don't know, keep her in my room," I say.
   "That's disgusting."
   "Why do you hate them so much?" I drink. "They are so innocent."
   "That's why I hate them. They are *innocent*. Innocence is disgusting."
   "That's kind of a harsh statement," I say. "What do you hate about it?"
   "I just hate it. I hate kids, I hate retards, I hate idiots. Simple minds are boring as hell and I hate being around them. Innocence is just a nice word for *ignorant*, and I hate the ignorant."
   "Stupid people can't help being stupid," I tell him and take a sip.
   "I don't care. Stupidity is *evil*."
   "Evil? Calling innocence *evil* is what's evil."
   "Children used to be considered pure evil once - *born* evil - be-

- **120** -

cause of their ignorance. Their parents would have to beat the evil out of them on a daily basis, so that they would not be evil in adulthood. That's why children are so cruel to other children and to animals and so on, because man is born from evil. That's also why the only adults that are prejudiced and mean are the ignorant ones, who are too stupid to grow out of their childhood attitude."

Christian puffs on his cigar. The blue woman watching the wheels churn in my brain.

"I don't get it," I tell him. "People used to *beat* ignorance out of their children? Those people sound like the ignorant and evil ones to me."

"If I had kids I'd beat the evil out of them."

"Well, you better not make kids then."

Richard Stein always said that children came from *good*. Before you are born, you are with God, which is Happiness. So during the early years of life, children are filled with good spirit and are happy and comfortable. The older you get, the further away from God you are, and you become *bitter*. That's why so many old people are crabby. They've lost their memory of the good spirit.

☺

"You know why I think the walm is here?" Christian puffs and gurgles.

I shrug, watching the blue woman smile at me.

"I think that the walm people are prisoners from other worlds, that have been sent here because all their prisons are full. All the governments in the rest of the universe decided to make one planet the BIG prison planet, so they chose Earth. It makes sense in a way."

"I guess it makes sense," I tell him, but I don't like it when other people think their ideas are clever. I believe that my own ideas are clever, so I don't like me either.

☺

The frogs hopping indoors agree that we are on a prison planet. They themselves are frog criminals that were convicted of doing frog crimes. But the frogs are trying to escape imprisonment. They're getting out of Rippington, out of Earth.

Richard Stein said that frogs were invented for a special purpose. They are the containers for dreams and fantasies and ideas. He said that

- 121 -

there is no such thing as creativity/originality and that everything that can possibly be thought up has already been thought up; before time began, every different story existed in every different way. And every idea is stored in a huge vault near the center of the universe. So every time you create a song or draw a picture or write a poem, you're not the true inventor of it, you're just stealing it from the vault and calling it your own.

Frogs are the beings that disperse ideas to people. In some worlds, rocks have this job. In others, caterpillars do it. Sometimes even a strap-on dildo has the responsibility. But in this world, frogs are the dispersers. So there's no such thing as *originality*. Sometimes an idea will seem original to a world, because that world has not experienced that idea yet, so it's called *new*. But it's not. Of course, the word *originality* contains the word *origin*, and origin means something that has already been done . . . my diction must be getting confusing. What I should say is that nothing will be *fresh* ever again. All creativity is just musty and stale.

But frogs must disperse fantasy because fantasizing is extremely important to the soul. It's a mental block from reality, which is needed at times, like my go-away place. It is my stress-reliever. Without fantasy, reality would be hard to stomach.

The frogs see the storm moving in from the distance. It's approaching very slowly, which means it will be leaving very slowly. The frogs are trying to flee, hopefully off the planet. Of course, if they get off the planet there will be no more imagination left in anyone's brains. So hopefully they don't get away.

Besides the storm, the frogs are fleeing imprisonment for having committed frog crimes. Frogs break the law when they don't hand out fantasies. But it's not their fault. The frogs stopped handing them out to the humans of the world, because nobody cared to have them. Soulless people have no need to meddle with imagination. So the frogs gave up on all of our world, except for Rippington. Some people still have souls here. That is why the town is overrun with frogs.

I finish my brandy and go to shut the door, kicking all the frogs outside. I'm not at all gentle with them and smear them against the concrete. I wonder if frogs are judgmental when they give out ideas. I wonder if my dreams are going to suffer tonight for hurting them. I wonder if I would be a very imaginative person if I became very nice to frogs.

I shut the door and turn to the blue woman. She's still ogling me.

A curious look. I hope I can feed her before I go to sleep.

Scene 14
Listen Day

☺

Bladder: puffed to full, teeming with truncheons and pressure pain, the creature's weight motivating it tighter tighter . . .

I awake early today, underneath the blue-skinned woman, whose sweating-smooth face is pressed into my flabby chest. Soothing skin against my body, eyelashes fluttering on my nipples and tickling . . .

I do not want to wake her, so pacific, but my bladder can't hold in the pain for much longer. Her hair combines with the fire sheets, motions to billow-waves, a sea of flames crashing against my coast-like ribs . . . I'm still not moving. Still contemplating how I can get out from under her without waking her . . .

I'm still not moving.

☺

God's Eyes:

I go to Christian. He's pacing in a dust suit, chalk white against black. His pacing goes back and forth from the thin of the warehouse to the metal-work sculpture section. Faster-faster . . . Then he slips into the teleporting portal and transfers himself to Satan Burger.

My vision follows:

There's a sign on the Satan Burger window that tells me, "Satan Burger Closed For The Holiday. Reopens Tomorrow at 8:00 a.m."

All the demons are resting. When no work needs to be done, the demons go back to standing still, acting like normal furniture. They let the warm sun dry their skins, and let the dust collect on their backs. Dust-bathing is very smoothing to furniture.

Satan is also dust-bathing. Cherry-red face pressed asleep against the table. Dreaming dreams of stories older than Earth I imagine, when he was God's favorite invention, God's first born son, born several minutes before his twin brother. His dreams make him cry, like my dreams used to make me cry. When I dreamt of the past - the time before my parents

- 124 -

turned their back on me, just as Satan's father did him - crying was frequent. It's hard to stop remembering.

I don't cry these days when I think back to my childhood, to the happy times before my mind caught a disease. I guess I just don't care enough to cry. I lost the part of my soul that found caring necessary. Even when I'm sad, I cannot show the tears. I can only show a silent expression.

"Where is everyone?" Christian wakes Satan to ask. "Why is Satan Burger closed?"

Satan awakes. He shakes the bad dreams from his skull and flops them onto the demon table like jelly. "It's Listen Day, nobody works on Listen Day. My twin brother is having a get-together to celebrate, and he invited your friends. Hopefully, he'll be able to make Gin's body parts dead again."

"Why didn't they ask me to go?" Christian complains.

Satan places his head back on the cold of the table surface. He says, "Nan is still here. You can go with her." And then he closes his eyes so that dust can pile onto the lids.

☺

Today is Listen Day, a holiday that the gods and everyone from the god worlds celebrate. Even Satan, who doesn't believe in celebrating any holiday, celebrates Listen Day.

Everything was invented by someone or something, even time, space, love, sight, physicals, mentals, sound - and whatever you can think of. Most of these were all created by the Creators, which came from outside the universe's understanding. They're the gods of the gods, you could say, and they made time and space and the universe and the gods. Almost everything. Nobody knows who made them.

Sound wasn't invented until recently, though; about a few billion years ago. It was invented by a god named STNT (pronounced Stint). He chose to stop existing so he doesn't exist anymore. Some say he's in hiding, others say he went to join the Creators. But according to history, he just stopped existing completely. He wanted to be *nothing*, and now he is.

At the end of Stint's life, he invented sound. His last gift to the universe. Though his inventions were all revolutionary, humans have yet to understand the importance of the things he created. They're all ideas that exist in the god world; we can't even begin to comprehend them. "Complex things are easy to invent," Stint said after he created sound, "it's making something basic that is difficult."

Sound was then known as the forty-eighth sense, and to the planet beings like humans, it became the fifth sense. Stint created only the plans for hearing. He left the universe before he got the chance to hear anything.

The manufacturing of sound took months. Millions of workers offered their services for free. Needing to make sounds for every object, they made creations called *vocal chords* to communicate sound, and objects called *ears* were made to hear them. They made loud sounds for BIG objects crashing, and shrilling sounds for small objects rubbing together. Every sound all had to be different. Every sound needed to be special/unique, like how every being is special/unique.

On the last day, sound was thrown across the universe. Every entity that existed had the capability to hear. But nobody was allowed to listen until the start of the next day, waiting with earplugs through the remaining hours. It was decided that the next day would be a celebration, dedicated to *sound*. It would be called Listen Day.

On the start of morning, everyone was allowed to use their new sense. The beginning of a world with sound. They spent the entire day listening to their new hearing worlds, listening to everything and everything, whatever they came across. It was a feast of audio noises. The first BIG celebration in millions of years.

From then on, Listen Day was considered an annual holiday and nobody was to work on that day, every year - though years go by differently depending on where you live in the universe. There were celebrations where everyone would make noise in the gathering areas. A festival phenomenon arose. Eventually, music was invented, and the whole celebration became a music festival, where a non-stop concert replaced the noise-making. And beings would feast their ears to several music compositions, and they would sing.

All over the universe, these festivals are cooking up right now. But my God's Eyes don't go far enough for me to see them.

☺

Christian finds Nan masturbating in the bathroom. She's holding a picture of Jesus Christ. Jesus is hanging dead from his cross. Blood prickles from his nails, from the crown of thorns.

"GET THE FUCK OUT!" Nan screams, throwing the picture at Christian.

Throwing the picture was an act of violence. It was an attempt to explain to Christian her level of anger. It wasn't meant to cause him pain.

But if Nan was using some kind of dildo or any object pretending to be a dildo, she would have thrown that at Christian to cause him both pain and disgust. Getting a smelly dildo thrown at you is extremely insulting too.

Christian steps out of the bathroom with the picture of Jesus Christ. He doesn't seem to be bothered by Nan's performance.

He says, almost laughing, "Nan still masturbates to pictures of Jesus."

Satan hears this, since Listen Day is all about listening. "She's attracted to Jesus?"

Christian nods.

"Why?" Satan asks. "Jesus is BIG and fat. Why does she masturbate to him?"

"Jesus is obese?" Christian smirks slightly. "She's obsessed with raping the messiah, got a sick little head on her shoulders. She only knows the paintings of him though. Nobody knew he was fat."

Satan says, "You know he's here, right?"

"What do you mean?"

"Jesus. He lives here in Satan Burger."

"I never saw him."

"His room says *Men's Bathroom*. Haven't you been in there?"

"Actually, I did see a fat guy in there before. I thought he was a customer."

"He was kicked out of heaven just like I was, so I let him move in here. Our dad doesn't like it when we rebel against him. It's a common thing for kids to do, but God doesn't accept rebellion from his angel children. After awhile, he banishes you to a place where you can only interact with humans and demons. It's called damnation when your God banishes you, but it's not all that bad - I guess."

"I thought you and Jesus were enemies," Christian ponders.

"We were, not anymore. Now our father is the BIG enemy. We team up together so that we can take him out of power, to make heaven a more democratic place. Of course, we're only kidding ourselves. Angels can't destroy gods."

"So you and Jesus are friends?"

"Let's not go overboard now."

☺

Nan gets out of the bathroom and starts out the door.

"I'm coming with you," Christian tells her, ensuing.

"Fine," she says. Incensed.

They go blue, bottomward to Lenny's autotruck, no Silence but it's quiet, and Christian remembers her masturbation sequence. He laughs . . .

"Talk shit and you're dead!" Nan says.

But Christian laughs again. He doesn't need to mention anything to be teasing. And he mostly laughs at the idea of Jesus being a large fat man instead of the *perfect* man that Nan fantasizes about.

I go back to my body:

The bladder is in worse shape than before. I see a large yellow pulsating creature as I go inside my body with God's Eyes. Neglecting to urinate any longer will give me future urinary problems, like kidney stones or golf-ball-sized testicle disorder, so this blue woman needs to roll off me, or I need to wake her off, or push her off.

I hear somethings crawling in the walls. Rats?

It's okay, rats in the walls aren't uncommon for warehouses. Right now, nothing in the world matters except getting rid of my bladder pains, even if the rats are really squirrel-sized spiders. And a spider is the only creature left that scares me, besides the scorpion fly. The pain pounds hellfists at the surface flesh.

I try to move, but it only makes the pain worse.

The somethings in the walls continue to make crawling sounds.

Eyes to Death's house:

Gin, Mortician, and Vodka are sitting in a sitting room there, drinking dog tea, with Gin's living dreadlocks serpenting, jellyfish. They're waiting to meet Satan's twin brother, but they haven't seen him yet. Supposedly, he's doing business somewhere.

Mrs. Death is there with them, petting her daughter, who has three years. Her other daughter, who has eleven years, is in another room, listening to things that have interesting sounds. Mrs. Death says Death will be back soon, and Gin says that Nan will be encompassing shortly. The word *encompassing* is a good adjective for Nan

Mrs. Death says to them, "He is out with our son, Jerry Jr., getting some music for listening today."

She eats from a pretzel-cheese mix, crunchy-crumbs crumble and fill her dressy lap with snacking food.

Mortician says, "Is that Mr. Death's first name? Jerry?"

She looks up. Her pudgy lips, cherry red lipstick (a child's brand), smacking at the cheesy pretzel mix. "Oh, no. He was named after me. I'm the Jeri that Jerry Jr. was named after. My husband's first name is Chuck.

She pauses to choke down a mouthful of martini.

"Our other daughter, in the listening room, was named after him. But we call her Charley. Do you like that name for a girl? I always thought Charley was a cute name, but she doesn't find it aristocratic enough. She wants to change it to Adelaide."

"I like the name Charley," Gin says. Breakfast spasms to the discomforting cold.

"Good. I like it too." She smiles pleasantly.

Jerry Jr. has six years. He is Death's only son, and he is Death's love and pride, his will to live. Everything that Death has accomplished means nothing in comparison. The universe means nothing, life means nothing, everything means nothing except for his son . . . and the rest of his family.

But Death has never been able to touch them, because of his Death touch. He could never caress his wife in passion, could never hold her, never sleep with her. Just a little brush of his fingertip would put her down . . .

They still created three children, but it was done in the least passionate way possible, without even touching, without even having sex. He didn't want to risk killing his wife, even after she suggested handcuffing his hands behind the bedpost, where they would be safe and clear from touching her.

Worst of all, Death will never be able to pat his son on the back when he gets an A in geometry, or when his football team goes to the state championship.

Because his touch brings death.

Back at the corpse:

The infested spider-sounds refuse to stop.

The blue woman still in her position on my bladder, pains do not desist.

I move, quick without hesitation without worrying about her, or the pain in my bladder.

A sharp blunt pain, but not as bad as I anticipated. It's just like me to exaggerate something so inconsequential.

The blue woman doesn't even wake up. A slight vibration-fizzle whimpers from her throat, which is supposed to be snoring, and she plops down where I was groaning. Her ocean breasts squishing into the mattress brings me a smile.

Then I rush out of my bedroom-closet to the toilet, which is still situated in the middle of the room instead of in a bathroom. And I leak away a pain-filled balloon.

I am surrounded by people that I have never seen before. All walm comers, all *new*. None of them stare at my penis, but it's still disturbing to have it flashed out to them. My pissing is more important to me now than my embarrassment. I let the urine leak completely away, but there is still a slight pain in my bladder from the stretching.

For one reason or another, the new homeless people in my home aren't much of a bother. There's about three or four medium-sized families that all look human and decent enough. The overpopulation in the streets was too much for them, I'm guessing, and forced them to take refuge inside of the warehouse. It was going to happen sooner or later.

On the way back to my azure woman/thing, my mouth speaks to the new people - and let me mention that my mouth says this and not *me* - as if my mouth is their governor:

"I will allow you all to live here for free on two conditions. One, you can't ever go in any of the bedrooms. Two, you have to stop any other outsiders from moving in here and crowding us. Be the protectors of this place and it can be your place."

Then I say, "Smile, it's Listen Day."

And go back into my cozy closet-room, where the most beautiful creature ever created is sleeping.

☺

I curl up next to her and go into my God's Eyes:

Nan and Christian are just arriving at Death's door. They are saying their hello-greetings to Mrs. Death and placing themselves next to Gin and Mort - Vodka is there too, but he hasn't said anything for two days. Mrs. Death seems quite scared of Nan; she's never had a skinhead girl inside of her home before.

"So what are you doing for Listen Day?" Mrs. Death says to Mort and Gin, ignoring her new guests - Skinhead Girl and Skinhead Girl's friend - smiling in her very energetic style.

"We're going to have a concert at our warehouse," Mort says in his very fake British accent, a slight modification of his pirate accent. Of course, he was going to have the concert anyway. Listen Day just seems like a good excuse to have a concert, even though Mort has never heard of Listen Day before and is trying to impress Mrs. Death with a lie.

Now that I think about it, Mortician seems to be attracted to Mrs. Death. She isn't a bad looking woman for her age. She has cute white skin, chubby lips, farmer-blonde hair, and an old-fashioned style of clothes. Her body is the same as any healthy thirty-eight-year-old, but I can see why Mort would be attracted to her. Especially since Mort is obsessed with pirates, and Mrs. Death is the type of woman that pirates would love to conquer and rape.

☺

Mrs. Death starts lunch.

Mr. Death still hasn't arrived, and Mrs. Death is worried. He's way past due, four hours past due actually, and it's unsociable to not serve lunch at lunchtime. She's left with no choice.

Since it is a Listen Day meal, the lunch consists of foods that make sounds. For an appetizer, she serves them the squishy sounds of stuffed mushrooms, which is Charley's favorite food. She likes fungusy-tasting things, I guess. She also serves an orchestrated salad, with crisp vegetables, crunchy croutons, and gooey dressing. They listen to their food carefully as they eat. It's a tradition, on Listen Day.

☺

I go back to my body, shivering excitedly because of the thought of the girl I'm sleeping next to. My palm squeezes a blue cheek, then rubs its smoothness. She doesn't wake up. Blue women are deep sleepers. All they need for survival is sex, and all they need for enjoyment is sleep. Their lives are complete perfection because of this. I wish humanity's culture was more like theirs. Then again, blue women are machines, and humans are the opposite of machines (whatever that is). They have too many emotions and imperfections.

The scratching-crawling sounds continue. They're concentrated in a single spot, in the corner of the bed's wall. The blue woman doesn't wake to the sound even though it's right next to her ear. Deep-deep sleeping . . .

The scratching/crawling turns into scraping into tearing into pounding/ripping. It's trying to get through the wall into my closet-room, to my bed, to my blue woman. Then there's a crack. In the corner, the wall's cracking right through, it's going to come into my room. Blackness takes over. I can see it coming out. A rat maybe, or a thousand-bug army. Coming from their world into mine.

The crack splatters and the blackness gets BIGGER. But nothing moves inside of it . . .

☺

Mr. Death enters as a zombie, the same way I was always said the grim reaper would walk. But this isn't a robed skeleton; it's a man in a normal suit, an average American man. Cold from the cloudy day, but sweating, nervous. A horrifying expression on his face.

Mrs. Death smiles and says, "Hello, precious." But the rest of us, all of my friends and the two daughters, frown and say nothing.

The bringer-of-death is actually a *normal* person, well-dressed, well-groomed, well-classed, average. I didn't expect this. He's just like any other father – well, besides Nan's father, the alcoholic.

They watch the man discreetly as he begins crying into the table, wetting the table's cloth, making small whimper sounds.

Mrs. Death smiles without concern - a natural reaction to everything. Or maybe she has lost soul too.

The man doesn't speak. He just cries.

Cries.

☺

My body:

Something appears from the hole near my bed. It's a small man, the size of a human child's action figure, who looks like a cockroach. Cockroach man. Staring at me with its pickax, which it used to break my wall apart. Tiny, spider-like eyes.

The cockroach people look just like humans, but have many cockroach characteristics. They're the size of cockroaches, they eat shit like cockroaches, and they live in the walls like cockroaches. Millions upon millions of them live on top of each other because their tribes are so BIG. A single mother produces at least one hundred offspring with each pregnancy, and reproduction is their main activity. Each cockroach person lives from one to two hundred years and usually produces two thousand children.

Every father abandons his mate after intercourse, and every mother abandons her children after birth. The schools take care of them during childhood, which lasts about twenty years. The cockroach people have the intelligence of any normal human, but they don't use their intelligence for intelligent things. They prefer pestering larger creatures, eating shit, and fucking out more and more and more pests to clog up the walls.

Their lives are long, but unfulfilled. Their whole point of living is to act like bugs. But in the cockroach people's dimension, the mammals are as small as bugs, and the bugs are huge like mammals, so there's probably no point in bettering themselves.

"A storm is coming," the bug man tells me. "It's going to be a bad one."

I nod to him and the little man smiles.

He climbs my bed, and up my blue woman's fire hair to her shoulder, around her neck to her chest. Then sits down, nuzzling his back into a plump mound, a massive ocean breast, her clock-like machinery pulsating into him, vibrates his back and buttocks. And he blurts, "Comfortable."

I hesitate to speak with the small man, rolling through my dizzy vision.

He says, "I'm sorry about the wall, but we needed a fire exit."

"You live in the wall?"

He doesn't answer me.

He says, "There will be lots of lightning, lots of wind and fire, lots of people going insane. Lots of people dying."

"What do you mean?" I ask.

"Child Earth wants to have some fun with us."

☺

The blue woman awakes to the little man on her breast, calm to his presence. Calm. She picks him up, looking down at him, studying.

"Innocent and curious . . ." I say to myself.

The blue woman tosses the cockroach man against the wall. He screams and breaks his neck and back and insides, and the little body plops to the floor, limp and dead.

Her blue face rests against my arm. Her mouth is wide open. The liquid flowing out of it is icy and ill-flavored.

☺

God's Eyes:

Mr. Death stops crying. He looks up at his audience, at his wife and kids' unfeeling smiles. Vodka is still silent and also shows no feeling. Nan and Gin seem concerned for him, but probably just because he's Gin's only hope. The room is dim. The room is always dim when you're at a table facing Death.

Death speaks:

"I killed him . . . my own son." He looks up at Gin, curling his lips. His words begin slur-sobbing as black tears fall from his eyes. "He was about to get hit by a car and I pushed him out of the way . . . I was trying to save his life . . . I didn't mean to . . . but my touch killed him."

He starts crying again. The wife gets sympathetic now - out of habit - but not as much as she should. She doesn't break a tear.

Gin says, "But I was killed, and I'm not dead. How did your son die?"

Death responds, "You are not dead because I did not touch you. I was fired by God, my father, and was ordered to never touch anybody ever again. My touch is what kills the body and sends the spirit to its destination. Without my touch, people that die become zombies, like you. When my touch killed my son, his soul was released from his body and sent into the walm, to be turned into energy. He is erased from us."

In oblivion.

"About my hand . . ." Gin interrupts him as if he was talking about weather, holding up rotten Breakfast, who squirms in rhythm with his medusa hairs. "My hand was touched by your twin brother. Can your touch take the life from it?"

"I cannot help you," Death whimpers. Then he stands up and reveals his hands. They are gone. Not cut off, just gone. There isn't any blood or signs of chopping. They're just stumps, like he was born without them.

Death says, "I will never touch anyone ever again."

One of his daughters chuckles at him.

☺

The wrist between Breakfast and Gin rots away as Gin holds it up to Mr. Death. Then there is no wrist left at all, and the bone breaks from Breakfast's weight. It falls into Gin's Listen Day dinner plate and begins to do a happy dance.

The two girls laugh first, then Mrs. Death and all of Gin's friends, and even the miserable Grim Reaper, starts chuckling. Soon the room is filled with insane giggling, all for the dancing demon hand.

Gin doesn't respond. His eyes look like they're tranced.

Then Gin hard-blinks and shakes his head, looking around at his hand's audience and their jubilation. And after a few more hard-blinks, he joins in. But instead of a laugh coming out of his mouth, it is a long red cry.

Scene 15
Boot Lips

☺

I am watching the baby blue woman watch television with awe-filled eyes, and many walm people are watching from behind me. Probably never seen a television show before. All of them are enthralled within six-year-old news reruns. I'm surprised they still have shows on, surprised they didn't shut it all down completely, the whole damned entertainment market. Surely they will soon, and it won't bother me much. I haven't seen Battlestar Galactica in days and don't seem to care. I've already seen them all, but that never stopped me before.

The blue woman is on the floor instead of on a milk crate, comfortable with the cold hardness on her butt flesh, or maybe she didn't want waffle prints on her skin. I haven't given her a name yet. I don't think I'm going to get around to it either. Blue women don't need names. They don't seem to own enough individuality to have them.

Richard Stein said that names are inconsequential within a race of *perfect* people. If they all look reasonably alike, if they wear the same clothes, and have the same style, speak the same, maybe they even think the same. If individuality is wiped out then names should be nonexistent, or maybe numbers should replace them - I should call the blue woman *Number Nine*. But Richard Stein wasn't talking about blue women. He was talking about the nazis. If the nazis would've taken over during WWII, overpowering the world with their Hitler-loving ideals, they would've made everyone identical. They would've killed their enemy, which was individuality, which would've made for a horrible world, maybe even worse than the one I'm living in now. Because without individuality, everyone would be as boring as a blank piece of paper.

In other words: NAZI = FRAMED PIECE OF BLANK PAPER.

But the anti-nazi people had too much soul to let the nazi utopia happen. Souls were very bright back then and individuality won the day.

☺

The others arrive in time, just before the boredom's arrival. I sense cold crisps and meat flakes on their minds as they enter from the queer world. The cold crispy emotions they emanate were created from thinking too much while within the untamed outside, mad-agitating streets, which has happened to myself times before. But I'm not sure where the flaky meat emotions came from. It probably had to do with being around Death for so long, or maybe they're getting disgusted with Gin's appearance. I'm not for sure, it seems like a very uncomfortable emotion to have.

They tell me about their encounter with Death, taking off their outside clothes and getting drinks from a flapboard box they've brought with them, and I try to sound surprised by their story, even though I've seen the whole thing in the third person.

I say, "You poop-dicks ate without me? What am I going to do for food? I'm not going out by myself with my crappy vision." I say this because I want to go do something. Eating seems like the logical activity for me. And I think my whining is funny.

"Take your blue woman with you," Mort says snobbishly. He doesn't enjoy the blue woman's presence either. Maybe he's jealous.

"We'll go with you, Leaf," Nan says for Nan and Gin - Gin completely overrun by the flaky meat emotions. "I'm kinda getting sick of this place. These *people* are getting to me." She looks straight at the walm people in the corner, unashamed of her rude, ugly smirk.

"I'll go too," Christian sputters, quiet.

Mort gets all rut-pissy. "Who is going to help me set up the stage and the equipment? I'm not doing it all by myself like the last show."

Christian sighs. "Vodka will stay and help you."

"No, he won't," Vodka says.

"You're all a bunch of twats," Mortician says.

☺

We leave after an hour of drinking small scotch bottles and watching Scooby Dooby Doo – who the blue woman finds extremely fascinating. She seemed to understand how the news show was brought about, because they were real people. But she doesn't seem to have a clue how animation came about. She doesn't know about drawings or moving drawings, and she probably thinks they're *real* creatures from some strange cartoon world on the other side of the universe. *Captivation* leaks out of her gluey, wet eyes.

Of course, she probably likes Scooby Dooby Doo because she's only four.

I thought I would've been able to leave the blue woman in the warehouse watching the cartoons, but she wouldn't let me leave without her. Sleek-gloss in her eyes when I tried to lock her in my room, a look that almost made me cry. She sometimes seems emotionless, *cold*, but has an ability to push emotions into me. Love and regret are two of them. Obviously, she has control over the way I feel. Maybe I like it that way.

I didn't want her coming with us. I was afraid she would run away or get lost or hurt.

Mortician is already on top of the concert preparations. He wheels around in my vision as a twisting robot worker. Spitting. And he doesn't respond when we tell him goodbye and head back into the cruel streets of Rippington.

The first thing I notice as I get through the door is the gray blob of sky overhead, storm clouds moving in, vein-puffed and breathing. I walk and enjoy the cool air and the different colored street people. The crowd they make is *everywhere*. Thick with ugly. But I can enjoy it from the distance.

I just smile and say, "Nice day for a walk."

Surprisingly, the tower shops are still open. We go there. But they've changed the place quite a bit since the beginning of the week. The upper levels now say, "OFF LIMITS," due to the accidental assassination of the female baboon that was living up there, which means that the high area is vulnerable to scorpion fly attacks. And which means that the burrito stand that was up there no longer exists. The emotion monitor on the neck of my mind tells me that I *do* feel some sadness from this happening and I pretend that it feels good. "Sadness is better than *nothing*," I whisper, and try to believe it.

Nan takes me to *Sid's Apple Barn*, a place that looks like a toilet stall and is located up inside the brain-tangle section of the tower shops. It's kind of a hangout for her almost-friends Liz and Toma and Sid, who owns the Apple Barn. Sid is a good guy, happy all the time; he's one of the few people I look up to. A strong-headed man, violent like the color purple. He goes by the nickname, *Boot Lips*, and if you ask him why that's his nickname he will make up a new reason just for you. His favorite one to say is this: "My skinhead friends always wrestle me when I'm drunk and they like to kick me in the face when I'm on the ground, right in the mouth with their combat boots. The morning after, my lips would get all swollen and purple. So my friends'd call me Boot Lips and think it was funny."

I'm not sure about a place called *Sid's Apple Barn*, but I'm no longer dead set on eating good food. Anything will suffice.

☺

We see Nan, Leaf, and the unnamed blue woman go up to the counter, leaving Gin and Christian to find a table over in the Food Court Seating Area, which used to be called the *Emergency* Food Court Seating Area. Nobody ever ate or sat there unless the female baboon wasn't on the rooftop. So with the female baboon permanently gone, the Emergency Food Court Seating Area is just called the Food Court Seating Area. But it's very badly arranged with autocar seats and wood planks on piles of broken television sets or other useless appliances found in the streets.

The only good thing about the tower shops now is that there are still security guards that make sure that the walm people don't crowd the place or turn it into their home. Which makes it a refreshing place to go. And they let some of the skinheads hang out, because they're native Rippingtonians and have the driver's licenses to prove they are.

Right now, there aren't many skinheads around, just a small group of them, and one of that group's members is Sid's Girlfriend, Aggie, who never liked Nan because she screwed Sid once in ninth grade - long before she met Gin or any of us, and even before she became part of the skinhead crowd. Nan isn't considered a skinhead anymore, at least not by other skinheads. But she still shaves her head and dresses and acts like one.

We go to Sid so Nan's old friendship with him can rekindle. Nobody seems to notice that I'm here to order food. I just swirl the counter in my vision for fun, with the blue woman rubbing my elbow and smelling the dirtiness on my skin.

Aggie, coated with dark red paint and piercings like facial hair, leans against Sid's counter. She curl-bobs her eyes at Nan, then coughs and pretends to be a nice person. She feels threatened by Nan, as always, because Aggie was Sid's second choice - Nan being the first - way back in the day. Aggie feels even more threatened by my blue woman; Sid can't help but stare in her direction between sentences. I don't blame him. A naked woman with rare beauty and turquoise skin is hard to resist.

Nan and Sid and even Aggie spray some words back and forth, mostly about Gin, but my mind wanders and I don't get to listen to them. I look at Sid's menu and see that it's full of apple-based foods with alcohol mixed in. It sounds strange to me that an ex-gutterpunk would open an apple barn, but Sid thinks he needs the money. His parents own an apple grove outside of town and he drives there to get bushels of red-yellow apples for his pies and ciders and casseroles all the time. "It's the only work I could get," he claims. And it's a good business since overpopulation is making food places scarce. In a couple of months, I bet *all* restaurants and grocery stores will be gone, extinct, and everyone will have to kill themselves and become zombies like Gin so that they won't need to eat anymore. Or maybe they'll all get in line at Satan Burger and sell their soul to oblivion. If, that is, Satan Burger doesn't go out of business before then, from losing its suppliers.

☺

I order the apple-vodka cobbler - not sure how Sid got his hands on the vodka - and some fritters. I pay with some change I found in my second pair of pants, eighty cents away from becoming broke. Then we go to the table that Gin and Christian picked out. It's a stripped pool table with no legs and chairs from the old high school, but there aren't enough chairs for the blue woman who sits on my feet. Sid and Aggie come too, with Aggie's two girlfriends who don't speak at all and seem to have no soul left, or maybe they're just goths who find it trendy to act that way.

Nan and Sid continue talking. Then Sid begins talking about what's happened to the world around us. He still has lots of soul, it seems; he's not hunched over or anything. It's funny how he wants to talk about the human situation here. Most people try to ignore it or don't have enough lifeforce to mind to it.

"It's crazy," he says. "I love it. It's *chaos*."

"Anarchy," Aggie says.

Boot Lips doesn't understand that he is at risk of losing his soul, nor does he know about heaven getting shut off for good. He never believed in heaven anyway. Boot Lips is another person who wants to go to Punk Land when he dies, but I don't think Punk Land really exists. Maybe my faith isn't strong enough. He doesn't realize that the world is bread festering with mold, nor does he realize that Gin is dead and still walking around, and hisself could soon be like Gin too.

Gin is still stiff with flaky meat emotions. Scared maybe. And Breakfast is hidden away in his patched pack, scraping to get out, hungry.

"The world is just as I always wanted it," says Boot Lips.

"Apocalyptic?" Nan utters.

"I like living in craziness and being unstable." Boot Lips begins picking at a wart. "Nothing makes sense anymore and I want us to hold on to that. The world has always been a boring place of order, at least in America, with chaos only in some ghetto areas. But even the ghetto chaos was boring. They were all about who's who; ghetto gangsters were childish and superficial. They weren't much different from rich white preppies from the suburb areas who hated anyone different, hated anything that wasn't part of the *trends*. Even punks were superficial back then, confused about what the definition of *trendy* was. Now there's no trends to follow. Nobody to look up to or down to, besides yourself. And nothing gets boring here. *Nothing*."

Right now, I want to tell Boot Lips about how our situation is more serious than he realizes, and how the walm will take his soul, and how he's damned to this world forever. But I don't tell him. He looks too happy and too excited about the world. I don't want to bring him down.

☺

Boot Lips tells us about his band *Slaughter Shoes*. Nan invites him to play at our Listen Day Concert tonight, even though Nan has no business booking bands at our shows. She has a new swimmy personality around Sid and starts to realize that she would rather be with him than Gin. Normally Gin would've cared about Nan's change of heart. But now he's consumed by writhe-suffering today.

A few seconds later, Nan takes Gin aside, around the back of a water store, to tell him how she feels. I want to follow them, but my God's Eyes decide to go inside of Boot Lips' brain instead. I discover that he doesn't have any more interest in Nan. He wants to stay with Aggie.

The only thing I hear Nan tell Gin is: "I don't want a man with an wormy penis."

I'm sure Nan and Gin will stay friends. They've been close for quite a long time and Boot Lips doesn't want Nan. But, surprisingly, Gin's emotions don't seem to get any lower after Nan's breakup statement; he's already hit the craggy undersurface. The sight of his hand dancing in his food was the breaking point. It doesn't really matter what happens to him now, with or without soul.

☺

I eat my food slowly because Nan wants to hang around here until the show starts. Aggie and Sid take off to get ready, pull Sid's band together and maybe practice a little. Nan and Gin act like nothing's happened between them, like they're still together, but that's because Gin is in agony and Nan pities him enough to try and make him feel better. As a *friend*.

"It's over," Gin says to us.

I suddenly get an odd feeling. Like the world is about to end, even though it can't. Like something cataclysmic is about to happen, in Rippington, or maybe just in my life. Terrible.

Richard Stein once said that there will be a day when the world will crossover from its tiresome yet basically happy state to a place of PANDEMONIUM.

I think that day is here.

Scene 16
The Rabid Storm

☺

The storm comes first.

It goops in as the sun blobs out. Orange fuzz dissolves into the skeletal-patterned skip-clouds, frigid with gray and hints of blue. Spider limbs talon-reach for the soap mountains on their avenue. Uneven faces secrete slowly out of it - the cloud is going to leak more people-creatures instead of rainwater, spat-splashing onto the great mob of overpopulation below.

It rents through light, oozes sideways, chokes it into darkness.

And dusk becomes night.

☺

The mob:

Crowds of people sleeping in the streets, the carpet walkways, smushed into buildings like snail shells. All different races, sizes, shapes, colors, clothing, trying to ignore claustrophobia. Every empty piece of ground taken up by a living being. Rippington is Earth's toy box, overflowing with piles and piles of action figures. They are motionless and hushed. Some coughs and shaking. Waiting for starvation to kill them and make them like Gin.

The roadway people become aroused when they see sheets of lightning dazzle-striping from the clouds. Flashes reflect against their BIG glazed eyes, haunting their children. Coils of wind corrupt their naked parts with invisible fingers. Some people enjoy the storm, for now - the water clouds aren't collapsing yet - because there's no amusement in Suffocation Land besides what's up in the air.

☺

The warehouse is ready for another concert. It's burning warm with gum-crammed groups of people and thick sweaty air. Mostly filled with walm people trying to get off the stormy streets, and some of the usual crowd of punks and skinheads, trying to get rid of their boredom. The rest of the usual punk crowd - the larger portion - must have lost too much soul to make it here.

There won't be another show after this one.

Only two bands are playing tonight: *The Oi!s* and Sid's band, *Slaughter Shoes*. My band was supposed to play too, but Christian refused. He said he wasn't in the mood, and neither was Vodka. And Vodka has BIG round pads on his breasts. I don't care for playing either; playing with my blue woman is more fun. I'm in my room with her right now, caressing her perfect ocean skin. Her sensations not as quick as a human's but that's because she is like a machine.

Slaughter Shoes starts playing - a melodic hardcore sound with a saxophone player. Boot Lips, the singer, hop-bangs to his songs, more soul-filled than anyone else here; it's like the walm hasn't touched him at all. He's even more up-up than he was back at his apple barn. I'm sure his soul will outlive everyone's in town. Good luck to him.

He really adored the steel sculptures that live inside the warehouse and ordered them to be placed in the center of the crowd, surrounding the toilet where Vodka is sitting. The sinister/gruesome aspect of the sculptures is what he liked. They are black and rusty and crude, also very sharp. One looks to be a palm tree of knives and another is like a tangle of meat hooks and a headless woman with spiked skin and sword nipples. She smiled at Boot Lips with her prickly vagina and he immediately fell in love.

The name of this unrefined sculpture is *Fria*.

Vodka sits alone on the toilet, staring at Fria's butt and the butts of every other sculptures around him, boxed in like he's in the bathroom stall of a sweat-dizzy night club, but the stall doors are sharp and spiny and stabbing inwards. He complains to the sculptures for crowding him, but they won't give him anymore room. His stare is blank and evil, but his response is *silence*. And nobody outside of his little boxed space realizes that he's in there.

The blue woman begins to touch me now, to excite me, trying to get my penis erect so that she can eat. She's *always* touchy-feely when she is hungry, and very alert instead of inside her dream world.

Mooshing her plump breasts into my stomach, digging into the skin with flinty nipples. BIG eyes looking into me - she knows I like that, it jingles our souls together. I'm not certain that blue women have souls. They're more like machines or like animals, and I've been told that neither of the two possess souls.

I slink into her neck, washing the azure plastic, feeling her smooth-fleshy. She doesn't have human neck bones. The neck is more like the human calf - lots of meat with one hard bone . . . but her bone is soft and thin, flexible. I can also feel a slight tube, probably for mouth reproduction. It creak-chirps when she slavers on my chest.

☺

It begins raining.

I hear it tinkle-clanking against a metal shelter from my sex bed as the blue woman rubs me. I eye to the outside, leaving my corpse with the four-year-old creature engorged.

The rain clouds weeping needle-goobers, thick and colored like pig snot. But I know the rain drops are not made of water. They're particles of madness instead.

"The storm will bring insanity," said the scorpion flies.

"The Earth wants to have some fun with us," said the little cockroach man, still dead and now crunchy in the corner of my room, listening.

The insanity leaks onto the unsheltered street people, sloshing onto their naked faces, seeping into their minds. Their mental states become schizophrenic at first. Slow and scared . . . paranoia. They begin shivering. They are unable to move.

The insanity rains onto the warehouse as well, dripping only the madness-scent through a few cracks, but the smell alone is enough to drive lunacy through your skull.

The aroma fills everyone's breath, even mine . . . and peculiarly, it also affects the blue woman, who doesn't breathe.

☺

This is where the fun begins . . .

ACT THREE
The Supreme Ordeal

Scene 17
Maggots In The Brain

☺

The madness comes second.

It starts when Christian goes outside for a cigar. He lights up under the dry clanking metal, looking up at the grotesque patterns in the clouds. They remind him of my descriptions of my acid ocean eyes, wondering if my vision looks similar to this. But my vision doesn't make me see evil-sickly patterns like these, only swirl-whirls.

The warehouse doesn't mind the maddening rain too much. Neither does it give a fuss over the crowd inside its belly. We asked if it would be okay to have another concert, but the warehouse just stared at his carpet walkway and shrugged.

Christian is very calm. He's been very calm for a long time now. Very unlike him. He doesn't seem totally emotionless, but surprisingly laid-back, strutting around in his zoot suit like a real classy gangster. The loss of his emotion has actually helped make him more appealing to people, especially women.

He looks into the BIG crowd of street people and their malformed-minds, all of them beady-watching him back. He knows something is wrong with them, the way they are staring. But he tries to ignore. Cool smoking.

☺

Richard Stein would have said they all have *maggots in the brain*, which he used to say about his wife. His wife was quite the insane one back when she was alive. She was afraid of almost anything, especially moving things. She didn't feel comfortable in cars or walking near cars, or taking the subway or trains, or airplanes, or even riding bikes. She couldn't leave the house on some occasions, paralyzed on her sitting chair.

Richard Stein was attracted to her because of this insanity, which is why he married her. There is something passionate about crazy women that can't be described, he said, you know you are absurd for getting into these relationships but there's nothing you can do. And he was happy with her for several years, even though he never got to know her completely, never figured out what made her tick so awkwardly and without rhythm.

Once age turned her ugly, Richard Stein initiated hate towards her. The crazy personality no longer cute. And the older she became, the more maggots crawled inside of her skull. Eventually, she drove her crazy emotions into Richard Stein's skull as well. And he spent a lot of his time hiding under blankets in the attic like a piece of furniture.

☺

Christian glances away from the crowd of sniveling insane ones. Looks up into the sky, with droplets hitting his cigar.

☺

The rain's influence starts to alter the warehouse crowd. Finally there are enough droplets indoors, enough punks to breathe in the lunacy. And the crowd of emotionally weak people begin a dance. Crooked-slowly at first, then fast and slamming, smashing into each other, moshing. The ultimate of all round-a-go crowds. Boot Lips, a screaming machine, starts punching the skinheads that get too close to him, kicking over tables and stands. The band plays chop-chop. Consumed by the insane energy, they sing song after song without a break.

Then the entire crowd is throw-slamming themselves against themselves; even the walm people that live in the corner of the warehouse join in. Battering into the walls and each other, pounding and skull-blasting . . .

Wild maniacs around the crude sculptures.

☺

The insanity hits the blue woman. She sucks and rubs faster on my stomach, trying to swallow me. She puts her vagina into my face and a small tongue emerges. It laps at my nose and an eye. The itch-meat slides into my mouth and squirts a sweet flavor into me, a strong aphrodisiac - produced under the blue woman's vaginal tongue like a salivary gland.

She slides the little tongue down my neck and body, leaving a trail of sauce. Then it takes a couple licks off my shank skin and slides me into her feeding hole. Immediately pounding, bouncing on me, rubbing my chest hair with her blue claws. Eyes in deep contact with mine. Whirlpool.

☺

God's Eyes to the outside:

Christian puts out his cigar as he notices the street people dancing as madly as the ones inside the warehouse, like the thrashing hardcore is powerful enough to hit anyone that hears it.

Then a small group of them charge the warehouse screaming carnal violence. Christian falls back, stumbles inside, kicks the door shut . . . He locks the door in two places and throws his weight on it.

The insane ones attack the door, booting, ramming . . .

Christian yells out for help, but the words drown under the singing.

☺

The mosh pit gets out of control. People use chairs and guitars to beat each other. Beer bottles smash over heads, glass covers the floor, a skinhead uses a broken beer bottle to stab everyone as he dances, the wounded keep dancing, showering blood onto the stage . . .

Mort tries to stop them from ruining his equipment, but a large walrus-shaped man hits him with a speaker box, knocking him into painful sleep. Some blood tangles down his neck.

☺

The blue woman uses her mouth-tongue on my face now. She leans forward so that her breasts can massage my skin.

She bites into the fat of my shoulder, moving it in circles with her screwing, drooling out the cold liquid of the yellow-violent pleasure.

☺

People brush against the scornful artwork. They cut themselves on acute edges and knives. Fria's blade-like nipples slice into the dancers, two or three at a time, and their tips become red.

Nan and even Gin join the slamming. They're near the sculptures and hold onto each other, Nan laughing insanely at the pain of broken glass digging into her feet. Gin's dreads do a snake-dance. They attack skinhead faces, whipping with excitement. Breakfast holds onto Gin's pocket, regretting that he was separated from his wrist/womb for the first time.

☺

Christian braces the door with the little of his strength, as the insane ones shriek-slam the outsides, ripping apart the windows and yard decorations. Some make it on the roof, stomping on the shelter, trying to tear it down. Others send rocks through the windows toward the dancing crowd, bludgeons on their meat.

☺

The blue woman leans back, still glaring into me, and my rolling vision at her. She uses her leg powers to fuck faster. She spasms her back like caterpillars, smack-bouncing her breasts . . . ocean waves ripple through the soft fleshies. She drives my body with mean thrusts, fucking my skull into the concrete, hard, nonstop, a spark of pain flashing in every drum . . .

She makes her hands into claws and strikes my chest, digging them with purple nails, enticing my blood to come play.

When I scream, the pain becomes bliss-intense. Furious animals tearing into me for food - I notice myself enjoying the idea. I'm weak and whining under her dominion.

And she's only four.

☺

A skinhead is thrown into Fria's nipples. The nipples pierce through both of his lungs and kill him instantly. After this first death, the mosh pit becomes a giant murder-dance game.

People are toss-hammered, mangled into the knife sculptures, thrashing to the music. And stomachs are opened on the palm tree and the windmill and the cactus and the monster and Fria.

Vodka's pale skin is drenched with blood and chunks of hamburger fat. He begins masturbating, greasing up his shank with shredding men's red fluid.

The slicing massacre continues until most of the crowd is covered with slash marks. But nobody dies, because death doesn't exist anymore. So the crowd continues to slam each other, cut each other, with no blood left, with missing limbs and facial features, and everybody slips in the blood pool beneath them and sometimes gets back up again.

Gin stumble-slides into the cactus sculpture, and gets his leg stapled between two limbs, with a dozen long needles through his ankle, trapping him beneath the stampede. All he sees is a repeat of combat boots stepping on his body, but his body can only feel mental pain.

☺

The blue woman slices reckless, trying to claw all the way through my body. Blood whipping off of me with the pulsation, soaking the sheets brown.

My screams continue. She starts punching me with her left arm as she continues to cut me with her right claw. Fists nail my face and mouth, maybe so I'll stop whine-yelling.

I put my arms around her neck and squeeze, choking some pain back in her direction, but she seems to like it. And it gets her more excited, throwing more punches, with both hands this time. Beating my shank inside of her, beating blue knuckles onto my face . . .

☺

The front door breaks away and Christian is tossed into the blood dance that cyclones him away from the street people, who begin crazy on the punks as they dance by. Battering orgy. Boot Lips continues screaming with gore leaking from his forehead into his eyes.

The street people enter the dance. Their skulls smash into the deadly artwork as they try to get to Sid to stop him from singing so harshly. Some begin ripping the place apart. Skinheads slice into them with knives and hammer them with chains belts.

☺

The blue woman stops beating me when I climax - squirting blue woman food into the eating hole. She seems to climax too, vibrating her thigh muscles and lower lips. But it's not a real orgasm. It's just the blue woman's mouth-like vagina slurping up my juices to process them into her system. I go dry and her vibrating stops. She falls onto my mutilated body, stinging the wounds as she rubs herself . . .

I can sense her smiling with satisfaction, licking the blood from my face with her chilly tongue. Then she falls asleep with her face on my raw-beaten skin.

☺

The street mob makes it to the band, to Boot Lips, and destroys all the equipment.

The music ends.

I hear the combat-scramble continue - yelling, smashing, pounding - throughout the rest of the night. Falling into my head, staring at the whirling ceiling. I am a shredded towel underneath a sleeping dog.

The blood trickles quietly.

Scene 18
The Death Of A City

☺

Rippington died last night.

It just looked at all the people in its belly and figured that its life wasn't worth carrying around anymore, since the citizens were ungovernable and incapable of becoming civilized ever again. It found no reason for itself to go on.

So it rolled over in its bed and died.

☺

This morning, its rotting corpse can be sniffed in the air, all over the streets and inside buildings. Madness-rain is pepper in the grey sky. There aren't anymore businesses or any money being circulated. No one has any food or water left to survive on, and nobody cares. No one even has sense enough to leave town to search for food; they're all just waiting to die and become zombiefied.

Rippington is no longer here for us. No more city for us, we're just living inside its remains, mutating into nothing but remains ourselves.

And little boy Earth watches us die and giggles.

☺

I awake to the rain tapping on the ceiling and the blue woman lapping at my damages, sucking on my shank with her eating hole - not hungry enough to eat, just vagina-licking it, like a funpop - propped on top of me again.

When she sees me awake, she gives her tongue a rest and glares at me. Her BIG eyes - engulf-swallowing me like normal, but something is not all-normal about this look. There seems to be something new added. It almost seems like . . . *love*.

Just as I see this look, I feel it coming on . . . a love-passion moment, which she hasn't felt for me even though we've had sex many times,

- 153 -

thinking that it was impossible for her, impossible for blue women to love because they are machines.

And just as any two regular human beings tossed into such a situation, we bend our necks forward and wrap ourselves into each other, lips into osculation, *kissing*.

I soon feel human again.

☺

I thought the act of kissing became extinct long ago, even before the walm, people just stopped caring enough to kiss before fucking. Love is a dead performance. Only the hardcore fuck job is required.

But here love is, right between us, flaming up and stabbing us.

And it is almost beautiful, in a pedophiliacal sort of way.

☺

Richard Stein said that love pops up when you least expect it.

He also said that alcohol can play a BIG part in the birth of love, even though love is only love because of drunkenness.

The killing of a buzz can kill this emotion very quickly.

☺

After a few minutes of passion, a slug of mucus-goo - a squirming worm-ball - crawls up her throat and into my mouth, sliding down my throat too quickly for me to react.

It chokes me with its intense, porkfat scent, this large regurgitated stomach booger, which goes down my throat and into my stomach bag like a bowling ball.

Then I cough her kiss away from me. Push her back like she just took a shit in my mouth and hack up the bad taste.

I dip my face over the bedside to puke up the snot ball, but nothing comes out. It resists. I turn to the blue woman to see her face, wondering what she did to me. Was it some accident that she'd be sorry and disgusted for?

But she just smiles and grabs my stomach for a caress.

Her touch burns cold.

☺

I forgive my blue woman once the taste leaves my mouth. I *must*. She is something I cannot stay mad at. Besides, without her my world would be blunt-somber, perhaps *nothing*.

☺

I stagger from my room, slight hunger. Into the meaty wreckage, swirl-whirling me into dizziness, tornadoing red.
An arm hangs from Fria like an offering, and her companion's disfigurements received body chunks as well.

The storm and madness are still fill-screaming the streets outside. People are babbling crazy and beating and killing each other. Some rain-pounds fall through the roofless section of the warehouse, almost a *Hell* carnival outside.

My feet stick to the floor, and my eyes dizzy-roll as usual, as they walk to the toilet, pass a few sleep-dying corpses in the corner. Not too many homeless ones in the warehouse today, just a few. The rest must've been sickened away. I guess there's not much point in them staying; half of the roof is missing along with the entire front wall; not much shelter for anyone here. If there was another place to go, I would've left too.

I piss in a corner, too weak to move the sculpture gore. It burns, and I like it . . .

When I turn around, the blue woman is there; she has been behind me for the whole piss. An inch away, watching me go to the bathroom. She's not sleeping like she usually does at this time, like *all* blue women do for entertainment, like I figured she was doing now.

She has the same happy look on her face that she had when I awoke, issuing *love* emotions from her blue skin that sink acidly into mine. I grab her around the back and pull her closer. As I caress her buttock-mounds, she caresses my stomach.

☺

Vodka groans from his toilet seat, trying to push his way out of the sculpture-fortress. He crawls out with palms flaky with dried blood-film. The blood isn't his. It came from the wounds of skinheads/crazies. Coughs take turns burst-popping from his lungs.

He sits and lights an old cigarette, sitting next to the corpse of John

- the weird old guy that lived in back of the warehouse. John isn't completely dead, as everycorpse else in the room, just sleeping without a heartbeat. Vodka uses the perverted man's back as an ashtray, spitting *shhh*-dust all over him. Vodka always loved his smoking. But he doesn't seem to be enjoying the smoke now, even when defacing a half-dead man's back.

"Where's the portal?" Vodka asks me. The tone is unfamiliar. A *normal* tone - not a fake German accent.

I look around the room for the portal, but it's gone.

☺

When my mind goes back to my girl, I feel a sharp pain of perception. It creeps up on me and swims through her skin into my mind.

Looking into the blue woman's eyes, I figure her all out. I see all of the plans she has for me and know that I'm not just sex-food for her. I feel that emotional-telepathy the blue women have. And my mind snaps with a greenish-red color, the color of unbelief, mistrust.

Her eyes glitter into me, guided by icy fingers to my stomach.

☺

Her telepathy-emotions tell me: You are *pregnant*.

She had shot her cum ball into my gut - tongue-kissing gave her an orgasm - and now a baby blue woman is squirming in me.

She smiles, proud of herself.

☺

I start thinking. Seriously. Men can be the *only* creatures to spit cum into someone else. I come to the conclusion that blue women are actually *men* with breasts and vaginas.

So . . . I must be *gay*.

☺

With the rage of homophobia - a phobia that's very strong in me because I was never exposed to homosexuality during my younger years, and it is yellowish-gray in color. Blaming the blue woman for turning me into a pregnant homosexual - as if I didn't have enough problems - my fists decide to break her face.

- 156 -

She doesn't swell or bleed from the punches. She doesn't seem shocked at me either. But she does fall down into a comfortable sleep, curled up in a red film. Some of my knuckles go fat. They darken around the edges and say, "Why'd you do that for? You don't know how to hit anybody."

☺

"Why'd you do that for?" Vodka asks from another side of the warehouse.

I grip my swelling parts. "She turned me into a pregnant faggot."

"A pedophile, too," he adds.

☺

Sighing, looking down at her/his sleeping body. And even though I hate homosexuality, I still find her/him amazingly attractive. Which means I'm in the middle of a sexual identity crisis.

"Fucking bitch," I tell her/him for putting me in this situation. "I'm getting an abortion."

☺

Of course, I'm kidding myself. She/he has me now. I'm the wife of a four-year-old blue woman and there's no getting out of it, because she's an absolute beauty - even if she *is* male - and I'm slave-weak to her.

"Go back to being a street whore," I tell her.

Then I carry her into my room, into my bed.

☺

Suddenly I realize something else:

My God's Eyes have ran away from me.

I can't see in the third person anymore.

I panic, sick.

A whirl of gin-dust heat pours over me. The only sight left is the crippled one, drug-damaged. It makes me frenzied and ill.

The power left me the second I tried to look into Satan Burger.

It has to be the storm that cut out my vision, cut out my vision like it cuts out electricity. Or maybe it was God. Maybe God stopped feeling sorry for me and wants me to use my normal sight. Or maybe something happened at Satan Burger that I'm not allowed to see.

☺

"There must be something wrong," I croak at Vodka. "At Satan Burger, I mean. The portal wouldn't be down like this."

"It's just because of the storm," he answers, cigarette calm.

"The Crazies probably got in and ripped apart Satan Burger, like they did to the warehouse."

"Nothing's wrong. You're being paranoid," he says.

"I'd be lucky if paranoia is the *only* thing I'm being." I hear my words freaking, silly-going. "*Everything's* wrong. Let's go to Satan Burger."

"I don't want to go to Satan Burger," he whines. At least he can still whine.

"You don't have a choice. It's the end of the world."

"We're not going anywhere, not with the streets clogged up like they are."

"We might as well try," I argue. "Unless you want to become one of these living corpses on the ground."

He says, "That doesn't sound like a bad idea."

Scene 19
Streets Raging

☺

I convert Vodka to get himself up and going, trip-boring into the car. The old lightning Gremlin starting up a *whir*, with a good collection of gas still in its gut.

A puddle-mud row is the closest thing to use for a street; we spark-scrape over curbs to get there. People and debris and handmade shelters - cheap patchwork or plastic tents, boxes, piled up scraps - clutter all other areas; even the carpeting on the sidewalks are not accessible. The rain seems to be black-yellow in color, I stare up at it in the sky. Mud water splashes under the wheels, greasing up the windshield.

The street is furious. The rain is sinister and the ill-fighting people are all coated with blankets or trash and plastics over their tops, trying to stop the cold and the plague-rain. The rain's consistency candywrap the street people, melting them it seems, leaking over their eyes and faces to make them blank or inflamed or uncontrollably nervous.

We find an empty spot in the street and take the opportunity to merge. We plunge into the ocean of people, surrounded by Crazies zombie-walking in circles, all trapped inside of their minds - their own little terrors.

☺

The driving is slow.

Vodka travels with caution. I'm not sure if he's afraid of the Crazies or just too bored/lazy to use force. The street people soon crowd us into small sections of off-street. Then it gets too thick to make through at all. The Gremlin comes to a snarling halt and I shiver-cough.

A boy without hands crosses and Vod decides to drift from consciousness. He flows outside of reality into his go-away place.

I tell Vodka, "Just run through them. Force 'em out of the way."

☺

The Gremlin finds its fashion through without hurting anyone, not terribly at least, just toughguy shovings. A woman spits on the car for touching her. The spit might be blood or vomit. Vodka frowns at her. She glances at me as she spits again, a dead stare, almost a doll-face looking at me. Her eyes don't seem to be inside of the sockets anymore - I see two yellow eyeholes screaming at me. Her face wrinkles in and around and *dissolves*. A good many Crazies give me the same horror-melting look, all soggy with yellow gleams. Paranoia washes over me. The sick rain seeps into my skull. Some of the devils punch and kick the car. Bleed-slashing claws attack and splatter against the metal. The autocar drips blood.

Vodka doesn't seem to care. He continues to drive as if the traffic is normal.

A small tribe of microwave ants crawl on my arms - not certain whether they're real or just a rolling vision. It's getting unbearable to be alive without my God's Eyes. Can't escape the uneasiness. Maybe I'll get them back after the storm. Hopefully, praying . . .

I'll be praying for a *real* death otherwise.

☺

"This is going to take forever," I tell Vodka.

"I told you," he says.

Vodka's voice is too foreign to me; he sounds like another person completely. I can't tell whether he's still himself or somebody new. Maybe this is the real Vodka, Gin's brother, the way he was before he started pretending. Maybe his soul is so far out of him that he doesn't care to pretend. He says, "Oh, well," more than occasionally.

☺

"I'm going through them," he says. "I'm sick of waiting."

At least he is sick of something.

"Finally," I say.

"What do you mean, *finally*?"

"You've been driving like a scared old lady."

"I didn't want to hurt anyone."

"Who cares about hurting them? Go ahead and *kill* them, nobody dies anymore."

- 160 -

☺

The car hits its power chords, Vodka's foot full on the gas. The engine fart-rumbles and we go faster, beating our way through the Crazies that scatter in an ant-frenzy.

Only one person goes under the wheels, lifting the car upward on my side, and I feel a little *pain* for that person, but it soon passes. It's more important to get to Satan Burger right now. Much more important than worrying about millions of crazy street people that can't be killed. If people could die, the population problem would be easily solved.

Speed builds. We're still moving slow but at least we feel like we're *driving* now instead of slim-rolling. The crowd seems cautious of us up ahead. They bowl out of the way easily enough, gleam-yellow eyes on all of them as we go. The population seems smaller too. And for litter in the gutter, we have human corpses too soulless to ever get up again.

I don't notice - because of my rolling vision - what race of people we have gotten into until I see them coming out of the sewers and shadow-corners.

The dark ones.

All pale features, mostly naked, more reptilian than I heard - tough skin, lizard-sharp faces, snake eyes - we see a male stamper to our car. Evil white eyes. I can tell it's a male because he has long pale hair and is veiny with muscles.

☺

My eyes skip a beat.

And then I see that we've been thrown into a reel-violent situation, flee-flying out of the scene. Vodka jammed the gas, maybe out of fear, as the dark male approached us. We just crushed his ribs underneath the Gremlin wheels.

☺

And the lightning Gremlin breaks some legs underneath the wheels, curling through Crazies, and a few dark ones are chasing after us - two females and one male. Looking back: a thrash-tatter of movement ripping through the crowd. Our vehicle is the wind. It splits open the air and through the street people . . .

- 161 -

The crowd is thicker up ahead. The Gremlin accelerates, hoping .
. . Vodka gnashes his teeth, squeezes his eyes, locks his joints. I watch the
dark ones fall further and further behind us . . .

The car beats into the ruff ahead, popping. Some of it over the
hood and knocking some of the Gremlin's life out of it. But we don't stop .
. . and then we do stop. The Crazies' faces shriek at our lack of motion . . .

And the dark ones catch up to us. The females, with their hook-
blade claws, rip into street people who are too close to the car. They frighten
into balls and some of them run away, clearing a path for us to fly-flee again.

☺

But the dark ones come too quickly, one female gets onto the roof,
straddling the Gremlin. Another female pop-breaks my window and tears
into my shoulder, worming its claw-fingers deep-deep into me.

I don't seem to feel any of the pain.

Then her face appears to me, as her other arm grabs my neck. She
pauses, stare-growling. Fang-like teeth and snake-like eyes. And I just stare
at her . . . she's actually a beautiful creature - maybe it's because I'm drunk-
crazy from the rain, but she is extremely attractive to me right now. Her
slender white body, chiseled breasts. Her eyes are black pools, trancing me.
She tears at my shoulder, howling at me like I'm her food.

She reaches her head inside, my body shock-shaking at the pain I
do not feel, opening her mouth to expose sharp snake teeth to my neck. She
lures my body closer. My head penetrates the window, my skin is opened by
the glass shards, cutting folds of meat from me. Vodka screams in a faraway
place . . .

My head emerges into the outside whirl . . . ruffling around me . .
. her face wrinkles lewdly. A naked feeling seeps into me, like the passion of
being born; this must be the passion of death as well. Orally defeated by a
beautiful snake woman. And the dark female screeches, leans closer to chew
my neck apart. But stops biting . . .

She gushes out her BIG goo-tongue, pressing against my chest,
long-long and thick but like a human's, and tough. It gorges into my shirt,
probing, tasting the blood that streams there. It's large enough to drench-
hug most of my torso, and it caresses my neck and face, a pepper-melon
flavor that drools into my nose and taste. My hand begins to polish one of
her breasts. They're rubbery but *nice* - a nipple harder than a human's could
get. She is powerful and strong, not a soft little girl like my blue woman.

She grips harder into me, clawing upward under my skin. I don't feel the pain; her nails soothe instead of worry. She bites my chin to the bone. Then the tongue slides over the wound, tasting, healing it. She loosens her grip and slithers her giant tongue into my mouth. She pulls my jaw far out of lock and forces it down my throat, painfully shoving it in and out. Fucking it.

☺

I awake a few minutes later, detached from the dark female.

Vodka is covered in red and whine-driving uncontrollably over curbs and street people - they come in flashes as we go through, skiing in a forest. They had cut him, the dark male and female, from his neck to his stomach, jugular open and sheeting him. His eyes are fading in and out, but he won't die. A large hole is in his stomach, and his insides mumble-screech and bubble. My body seems fine, though bloody and molested. I look around at what's going on with chaos-eyes.

Vod's voice makes a gurgle-blood noise. "Get it off the roof!" he shrieks.

There's still one hanging onto us. She's trying to cut into the car's top, holding on tight and getting in a scratch or two at Vodka's face. His whimpers turn to shrieks at each of her attacks.

The dark female's yowls scorch into me, just above my ear, in a torture-fury, and I scream, "How the hell am I supposed to get it off the roof?"

But Vodka doesn't answer. He's zoning zombie-minded and curling at the eyes, driving *harder*. We destroy anyone/anything in our way, breaking through crowd and rubble, unstoppable. The dark female cuts into him again, screaming at him, and again, but he doesn't feel it or seem to care. His meat is dead, and all of his blood is resting on his lap.

Then there is Silence.

☺

The Gremlin piles straight into the Silence, and everything clears.

No more crowd ahead, just quiet and deserted . . . The dark female's howls continue for a few more seconds, then fade away, eaten. Even the engine sounds go away, we feel deaf. The car razors into a wall, near the autocar graveyard - where I found the blue woman. I don't scream before we hit, I let it come, I don't even bracing myself.

Vodka just didn't seem to care enough to hit the brakes.

☺

I awake alone, Vodkaless. In the rain-molested autocar.

The Silence is gone too, traceless as it came, and another crowd of street people has filled the area, gushing in as the Silence cleared the way. The pain starts in, from my forehead - broken over the dashboard. Skin flaps from my shoulder, where the dark woman's nails screwed like shanks.

I feel sick.

I have to get to Satan Burger.

☺

The crowd is too BIG. There's more people here than there is space. Head-dizzy and *grrrrr*ing, I can't even open the car door. I climb out of the collapsed window, to the roof. Vodka's living corpse is up here. He's sitting there wet and soggy, like the street people, rocking-rocking, red-stained clothes.

"I thought you were dead," I tell him.

"I wish it were possible," he tells me.

☺

The street people wave-ripple in the storm. Miles, miles of ocean-crowd, rolling with patchy colors, dissolving in the distance. They really seem like an ocean now. The car's roof is our raft.

"We need to swim for it," I tell Vodka.

I can't hear his reply in the metal-clanking rain.

☺

I lug-haul Vod off the raft. We go into the water – sweaty smells from the water-people. He's lunked over, drug-headed it seems, not swimming very well. I have to pull him so that he won't drown.

The ocean people press tightly together, then roll-expand a little so we can move a few feet, then they crash together again. Everyone is struggling to move but nobody's getting anywhere. We get shoved back toward the raft, then forward across a building wall. A piece of the water claws another gash into me. Blood drips through my fingers when I hold my face.

My breathing is weak. I'm trying to stay above the water, trying to get some breath going. I find Vodka's hand slipping from mine . . . he's getting away. The water behind me is moving back toward the raft. My body is going forward. I stare Vodka in the eyes, examining his stone expression. Then I let go.

The force wasn't even that great. I could've kept us together easy. But I let him go.

Looking into his face, I didn't see Vodka in there at all. I saw an empty container. There was no soul behind his eye-windows, just a calm *brrrr* noise. So I let him go, and the crowd swallowed him up, another one of *them*. It doesn't take long before he gets to the distance, and I can't tell which one of them he is anymore.

Vodka didn't seem to mind.

Scene 20
The Man Who Loves Everything

☺

I flow a few miles, emptying into rivers, taken by the people-current toward Satan Burger, ignoring the faces on the water surface. When I get there, the lot is brimming; persons climbing the steps to get out of the people-ocean, some falling off. They're screaming insanities at each other.

Then a *swish* of thinking bleeds into my emotions, a grind-spinning view of the area above me, on the hilltop.

And what I see is: Satan Burger is gone.

☺

I swim to the steps for a closer look, but there are too many people, too many rage-frustrations inside of me. The sickness gets stronger. I get claustrophobic.

I start climbing.

☺

Halfway, I meet a familiar face. It's soggy in the rain and I'm surprised I recognize him with my acidy eyes.

"Satan," I call.

He notices me and squeezes in closer.

"What happened?" I scream over the insane ones before he reaches me.

The insane ones hand out jabs and tickles.

Satan Burger was destroyed," he yells, getting closer . . . His face is sooty and blood-cut, his nice clothes are rip-sliced apart too. As ironic as it sounds, he looks like he's been to hell and back. I can't even see his gay-pride button.

He shouts, "An earthquake hit, tore the whole building in half, into pieces."

I shout, "But there aren't any earthquakes in New Canada."

"It doesn't matter," he yells. "Child Earth did this, the little shit.

- 166 -

He was pissed off that I was stealing the souls of his new toys and sent an earthquake after me. I should've never touched the fucker."

"What do you mean, *touched*?"

Still screaming: "I'm responsible for putting breath in this planet's lungs. I touched it. I have the touch of life, remember. I made it alive. I made almost every planet in this damned universe alive, with my *gay* fucking hands."

The sense of the whole situation hits me, and I say it to myself: "Earth is a demon?"

☺

"I'm getting out of here," Satan yells. "I suggest you come with me."

"Go where?" A headache spikes me. "Where is there to go?"

"Through the walm," he says.

"That's crazy. You could end up anywhere. Even in a place without oxygen and die."

"I'm willing to take the risk if you are." Satan grins darkly.

"Where is everyone else?" I ask.

"Who cares." Satan drops himself into the water crowd. "Come on, let's go before another earthquake hits."

"Where are they?" I scream-ask again, but Satan gets carried away by the people current. He lets the crowd take him. The distance between us is suddenly very BIG.

From the edge of the parking lot, he yells, "I'll see you in *hell*," which is the common thing for him to say when departing. Sadly, it makes him laugh.

Then his body is gulped away from my sight.

☺

I find another way up the steps, on a side path, and I'm able to get up pretty quick, but on the wrong side of the hill. This side is open, and I have to stop to breathe in some *space* . . . Then I realize I need some time to sit. I find a rock underneath a demon-tree, who shelters me from some of the irritating rain.

"He's right, Leaf," says a nearby voice.

I don't turn around right away, still breathing in the space, trying to relax this dizzy head of mine by squeezing my eyes closed . . .

"Who are you?" I finally ask.

I hear him sitting next to me. Dead leaves crackle.

He says, "I am Jesus Christ."

☺

When I open my eyes, I see a roll-pudgy man with a beard wearing a janitor's outfit. A tag on his shirt tells me, "This is Jesus."

I can't say anything, or maybe I can't think of anything to say. I've never met the messiah before and I've never met anyone who ever has. I don't seem to care.

He continues, "Satan was right. The walm is your only out."

My mouth doesn't say anything

He says, "You have to save your immortal soul."

Then I shake my head. "I don't know if it's worth saving anymore."

"Don't say that!" Jesus says, waggling sense into me. "That's the walm stealing your lifeforce that made those words. You have to fight it."

I realize Jesus is right. Sort of.

☺

Richard Stein always wanted to meet Jesus Christ. Of course, he never got to. Maybe he did *after* his death, but I'm not sure how the afterlife situation works. I don't know if you get to talk to Jesus right away or if you have to wait a hundred years. I think I'm one of the only living people to ever meet Jesus Christ after his crucifixion. I should probably feel special or something. But I don't.

Richard Stein was very Jesus-curious during his early thirties. This Jesus-curiosity caused him to accept Jesus into his life. But Richard Stein didn't like God. He didn't like the way God capitalized the word "He," in regards to Himself. God seemed too-too superior to Richard Stein, and Richard Stein called superior people like Him *Hot Shots*. This is the way I figured it: "God is the ultimate authority figure, and people like Richard Stein don't like authority figures."

Jesus was a lot like Richard Stein, though. Jesus was a human, he could be killed, stopped. He was the savior, but still needed saving. He could walk on water, but could still drown. He caused the better organization of society, but also caused wars over faith in him. To Richard Stein, Jesus was both a saint and a devil, and that's what he liked about him.

Richard Stein always wanted to meet Jesus so that he could see what he looked like, what clothing styles he liked, what foods tasted best to him, what regrets he's ever had - all the small things that would make Jesus more human. He especially wanted to know if Jesus *hated* anything. He wondered if Jesus hated Satan - or if he pitied him, or was frightened by him. He wondered if Jesus hated evil and sin.

Once Richard Stein said, "I already know that Jesus hates sin, I just want to hear him say that he *hates* something."

☺

If Richard Stein was in my position, he'd have a whole bundle-pack of questions lined up for the savior. He would have loved the idea of Jesus being a BIG fat guy, ugly instead of the beautiful image people paint. But of all the questions he would've had, I can only think up one for him.

I ask, "Why are you wearing a janitor's uniform?"

At first, I figured he wore it because he was the janitor at Satan Burger, but Satan said his demons did all the cleaning, so I just had to ask him.

He responds, "I am the janitor of mankind, not the *shepherd* as the BIG bible says. I clean up the dirty parts of society, the dirty sides of men's souls. It is the job I was born to do, and I don't get paid anything to do it."

"God won't pay you anything?"

"Well, God isn't the person who would pay me if I got paid. He hires accountants from an agency to handle all of his income. But his chief accountant doesn't think there is a reason for me to be the janitor of mankind, so he does not pay me. It is volunteer work."

I say, "It sounds too hard to be volunteer work."

"Hard work doesn't bother me. To tell you the truth, I *love* to work."

"What?" I'm shocked to hear *love* and *work* in the same sentence. Jesus is beginning to seem crazy.

"Work keeps my life in order. Keeps an even amount of hard times and good times in my life. When I work, I learn to appreciate the free time I have, I don't waste it on trivial things like music and television."

"You don't like music or television?"

"Are you joking? I *love* those things."

"I don't like commercials," I tell him, wand-spindle voice. "That's what makes television a waste of time."

"Commercials are better than nothing," Jesus says. "If there were no commercials, what would fill the spaces where the commercials are supposed to be? The announcer would say 'we'll be back after these messages.' There would be three minutes of black space. There would be nothing. Wouldn't you prefer commercials over that?"

I guess he's right, He *is* Jesus, but I think television networks would just make television shows longer if there weren't any commercials instead of add in black space. Jesus knows best though. "I guess you're right, but commercials represent corporations and money. And money is the ultimate evil."

"No, I don't believe so. Money is extraordinarily *good*. Money gives people a reason to work. Without work we'd still be sleeping in caves."

"Oh." I seem annoyed by his replies.

There has to be something that Jesus Christ doesn't like. I've already asked him about the three evils of the world. Richard Stein always said that nothing is more evil than work, money, and commercials.

"Is there *anything* that you don't like Jesus?" I ask.

"I love *everything*," he responds.

"You can find good in every single person, every single object?"

"Of course."

Thinking of Richard Stein, I say, "But there is *one* thing you hate. You hate *evil*."

Jesus just shakes his head.

☺

"People don't understand evil," Jesus says, pinching a piece of sand. "Nobody realizes how absolutely necessary evil is."

He pauses, staring at the street people in the rain. The water drops are getting slender, and shrill-winding waves start in.

He continues, "Satan wasn't the person that started it either. Of course, the bible says he did. But *God* was the one responsible for evil, and everyone in heaven knows this. He made Man with an evil side, but told him not to use it. God expected Man to succumb to his dark side eventually, *wanted* Man to, because without evil there is no God.

"After evil was invented, there had to be an opposite to it. That is where good came from. So you see why I have to *love* it? Good comes out of evil. Without bad in the world, there cannot be good, because there is nothing to compare good with. That is one reason why I am not in heaven. Heaven is a terrible, boring place. It is too *perfect*. It is *paradise*. Sure it seems nice, but there is no evil there, no conflict, there is no such thing as satisfaction. And people forget how beautiful satisfaction can be."

He gives examples. "Nobody works in paradise, so there is no such thing as coming home after a hard day of work, and just sitting on your ass, doing absolutely *nothing* and getting absolute pleasure from it. Even *love* is boring in heaven, because there is constant love all around you there, and no hate at all. So love is nothing special. And you never go through the hardships of falling in love, which is what gives the winning of love a feeling of victory. And all the food is perfect in heaven, so you can't compare it to bad food. And there is no excitement in heaven, because conflict and danger makes excitement. There is also nothing there to fear. Everything is comfortable in heaven, so even comfort isn't satisfying. You last about two months in paradise before you get completely bored. And if boredom doesn't find you, you'll become one of the *heaven zombies*."

The word *heaven zombies* makes me turn my head to the crowd of insane ones. I ask myself, "Are *they* the same as angels are?"

☺

Jesus says, "There *is* one thing that I do hate. I hate it with passion. I *loath* it . . ."

He hates perfection.

☺

"What are you going to do?" I ask Jesus, ready to leave. "Are you going to go through the walm like Satan did."

"Never."

"Why? You'll lose your soul if you stay."

"I have already lost my soul, so it is no use going."

"What? You seem perfectly fine."

"That's because I am Jesus. Jesus is supposed to be filled with love. It is just routine for me to act this way, emotion has nothing to do with it. And also because of routine, I will never leave my people. I am their last protector. Even if I still had soul, and still cared about things, I probably would've stayed."

But then it would've been out of love, not routine.

☺

Jesus says, "I need you to do something for me, Leaf."

- 171 -

I nod.

"I need you to survive."

I nod again.

"I have been writing a BIG history book." Jesus pulls out an old-skinned pack. Patting it - a hard drumming. "This is the book of Man, all the events since man's birth are in it. And it has been handed down and down and down, until it reached me. Man will never die if he is kept in memory. Memory saves people from oblivion. So I need you to get through the walm with this history book, and save it. Then you need to continue writing in it. Write about you and your friends, the society that you start within whichever world you end up in. Breed and build your numbers, see if you can create a human civilization again. Before you die, hand it over to the next generation. And hand it down and down and down. Until there is only one human being left alive."

"What about the humans we leave here? What is going to happen to them?"

"They have no emotions," Jesus says. "They are not human beings anymore."

He places the history book in my lap. Then a hand on my shoulder. "And the very last human alive must bury this history book on a high peak, and the words written on the tombstone must say this." He draws the words in the dirt:

HERE LIES THE HUMAN RACE.

Scene 21
Flying Fish

☺

I climb the hill to the ruins of Satan Burger and see a flock of flying fish scavenging for scraps of food. The fish aren't the winged, footed fish-birds that I once saw in the midget president territory. These are normal-looking fish that seem to have confused the air with the water, swimming through the oxygen with their flappers, and getting rained on quite a bit. Maybe the fish confused the air with water because they are insane.

I walk up, up, watching the fish dive down to the Satan Burger rubble to piles of burger-wastes, dead customers, bloody demon corpses. I see Mortician up there. He's climbing on top of the rubble. He's probably looking for water, or maybe for his pirate hat, but I don't say anything to him.

At the flat edge, Christian is relax-sitting on a piece of sign. Smoking a cigarette with comfortable breaths - a pile of cigarette boxes near him taken from the broken cigarette-dispenser demon. I go to him.

The only thing I can hear is the train-roaring wind and Nan's cries coming through it. I see her once I get to Christian. She's on top of Gin's body, wrapped around him, punching him for not working right.

"What's wrong?" I ask Christian.

"Not much," he says, shrugging. "Not much."

"What happened to Gin?"

He looks over at the corpse on the ground. "He's gone."

Finishing his cigarette, Christian stands up and looks at Nan. "While Nan was unconscious, after the earthquake took down Satan Burger and knocked her asleep. Gin ate a Satan Burger, right there. He put his nostrils inside of Nan's mouth while he ate it, and his soul wandered out through his nose holes, just like Satan said, and it was absorbed inside of her. He was gone before Nan woke up. Gone to . . . oblivion."

I watch Nan pushing at him, screaming, swirling. Gin's body parts are still moving, still alive. Breakfast runs around Gin's face. It smacks him, but the face is soulless tissue."

"Satan was wrong," I say. "There *are* people that will give up their immortal soul and go to oblivion to save another person's life, even if that person doesn't love him."

She loves him now.

☺

"What're we going to do?" Mortician asks. He jumps down from the rubble toward Christian. "Satan's gone and he was the only one who could help us."

"We're basically fucked," Christian says, lighting another cigarette, this one a menthol.

"What do you think, Nan?" Mortician yell-asks her. "What do you wanna do?"

It takes her many cries, getting them all out. A gash bleeds down her forehead.

Mort asks her again.

More talking between Mort and Christian. Then she interrupts with her answer: "I want to *die*! All what I want to do is die. That's the only thing I was guaranteed in life, how come I can't anymore? If only there was an afterlife, any sort of small afterlife, I wish Gin and I could go there. I wish we died last week, when death was working right." But they pay no attention.

"Give up, Mortician," Christian says. "You know we're fucked."

Mort says, "I know we're fucked, but our souls are running out. We might as well do something before we're boring zombies like everyone else. Let's do something *fun*."

☺

"We aren't fucked yet," I finally tell them, wondering if they would've thought about it themselves. "If we go through the walm, we can find another world. One where we won't lose our souls."

"Dumb *ass*," Christian says. "Whichever world we end up in will still have a walm in it, and it will still eat our souls. You can't get to a walmless world by going through the walm."

"But then we'd be new people," I argue. "New people don't lose their souls to the walm here, so I'm positive we'd be fine."

Christian shakes his head in an *I don't know* fashion.

"Let's do it," Mort says. "Even if we lose our souls, at least it is something we can do."

- 174 -

"But how are we going to find the walm?" Christian asks. "We've never been there. It'll take us forever to find it in this city, especially with all these crazy people around."

"I think there is someone who knows where it is," I say.

"Yeah? Who's that?" asks Christian.

"Stag and Lenny."

"They're gone," Christian says. "The Silence took them. Nobody comes back from the Silence."

I shake-spin my head. "I'm willing to go. I've been inside of it twice already. I've been inside of its stomach bag, and I have returned. For some reason it will not digest me. I'm probably too disgusting. One of them still has to be alive somewhere inside of it. I'll find the Silence and get them out."

"I'll come too," Mortician says. "It sounds like fun."

I say, "No, you don't need to go. I should do this alone."

☺

I go to Nan on my way down the hill.

"Nan," I say. "Stay here, okay? We're going to go through the walm once I get back. I'm going to get us out of this place."

She's calm. Well, she's not as hysterical as she was before. "I'm not leaving Gin," she says.

It's a hysterical idea.

"You *have* to come," I say.

I sit down next to her and the corpse. All of Gin's living body parts are cut off and hugging Nan's lap. There is Breakfast, Battery, Encyclopedia, Selenson, Tofu, Beer Mug, and the Medusa Hairs. I wonder if part of Gin's soul is inside of his living parts. Did some of it survive? Nan seems to connect to them. She holds the body parts like she would Gin. Her behavior doesn't frighten herself.

"Nan, please," I say. "We'll escape and be *free*."

"I want to die," she says.

"You can't do that here," I say. "Come with us and live a life. Eventually, you'll die and your soul will go somewhere. If you stay here, you'll never die. And your soul will leave you. You will live for eternity without a soul."

"I don't want my soul anymore. Once my soul is gone I won't be sad anymore. I won't ever have to deal with my emotions ever again."

"What about the good emotions? Like love and joy and pleasure and excitement. Don't you want them?"

"They aren't all that great. I'll give them up if it means getting rid of sadness." Nan pets Breakfast, crab-crying. She's a little girl again. All of her toughguy features are gone. "I've had too many depressing moments in my life. I can't ever escape sadness and *hate*. Never. If I go with you through the walm, it will follow me. It has always followed me, going to another world is not even far enough to escape it. I want to stay. I want the walm to rip that sadness right out of me and grind it up inside of that machine. I want sadness to be *destroyed*. So I'm not going with you. This is my only escape. My only *revenge*."

"This is hard for me to say, Nan," I put my hand against her polite-fleshed shoulder. "But the future of mankind depends on you."

"Don't say that," she growls. She knows what I'm about to say.

"You're the only woman left. Without you, mankind will go extinct."

"Let it," she says.

"Don't be selfish."

"Humanity doesn't deserve saving. And there's no way I'm going to fuck any of you three."

"You don't have to fuck any of us. Someone will jerk off in a cup if you want. We'll figure it out somehow. Don't worry about it being me, if that's what you're thinking. There's no way I'd force my shitty genes on anyone."

"It's not going to work, Leaf. I don't want to take part in making a society of inbreeds."

"It worked with Adam and Eve," I say. "Plus, it was Jesus's idea. You, of all people, have to listen to him."

"I don't like Jesus anymore. He's a fat guy. I liked him before because I thought he was the guy in all the paintings. That Jesus is sexy. And even if *that* Jesus told me to become Eve, I would refuse."

"I see."

"I just want to die," she says.

"Good," I say. "Come with us and die there."

☺

She sits in silence for awhile, thinking, pouting.

Then she says, "Whatever."

But "Whatever" might mean "I'm sorry, Leaf. I'll go with you and see what happens. Maybe I'll change my mind in the future, but we'll have to see. I just wish I could *die*."

"I know, Nan," I say to myself. "I wish we all could die."

She's staring at the ground and holding me with one of her arms. I don't remember when she put her arm there, or for what reason. I grasp her hand, and squeeze, pretending she is physically familiar to me.

Under the rain's patting, I hear her say, "I'm already pregnant."

I'm not surprised. But for some reason, she gives the same response when I tell her, "I am too."

Scene 22
Horse Mansion

☺

Back to Silence.

It wasn't difficult to find it boom-sweeping through the streets like the shadow of a thundercloud, sucking up the insane ones into its gut - which was called Humphrey's Pub back when it was behind the gas station but that doesn't exist anymore. The pub had to be torn down and replaced with a larger building, since the Silence has been eating so many street people and needed a stomach structure BIG enough to fit them all in. The building that has replaced the pub is the largest building that has ever existed in the universe. It's called a *Sutter*.

Sutters are machine-mountains. They're sky-bathing power plants that are used on planets whose god has been killed by Time. The Sutter is the mechanism that takes over the god's duties; it's the autopilot, you might say. It's not as good as a god, but it works. But a Sutter isn't capable of performing *all* of the god's duties. Nothing can *completely* take the place of a god because gods are very complex life forms and are easily offended by men who compare them to machines.

But all-in-all, the Sutter can handle the basic god tasks that are important to human beings: creating life, changing Mr. Sun's batteries every hundred years, dispensing good and evil evenly throughout the world, and bringing souls from death to heaven. Sutters do not have the technology to access heaven, though, so they were designed to summon the souls inside of them into the wing called *Heaven Two*. The wing is large enough to possess about eight hundred generations of souls before a new one needs to be built.

Heaven Two is not as enjoyable as the original Heaven, but it's better than oblivion.

☺

A Sutter is powered by the same energy that powers the walm: lifeforce. Lifeforce is the universal fuel. It's used in the god dimension much more than electricity or gas. But Sutters don't use humans as their power source. They use the souls of horses. Horses have small organs inside of their brains that have regenerative abilities. These organs - known as *Tompets* - will rejuvenate any lost soul particles in the horse, making it impossible for horses to lose their souls until they die.

The organ was discovered accidentally by a man named Philip Tompet, who was trying to prove his theory, "Horses are superior to humans," which was published in a book called, *Horses Are Superior To Humans*. He wasn't trying to stress the importance of horses, but rather to demean the idea that mankind is the best meat-form that has ever been pooped into being. Four more books were published under his name that corresponded to his original theory; they were, *Dolphins Are Superior To Humans*, *Polliwogs Are Superior To Humans*, and *Somebody's Nose Is Superior To Humans*.

After Mr. Tompet presented the Tompet Organ to his world, many people started to agree with him. And after the publication of his fifth book, *Venereal Disease Is Superior To Humans*, he was killed by the rest of his race, who said to him, "You took that last one just a little too far."

So each Sutter is chocked full of millions upon millions of horses, and there are four immortal humans - more like machines - who take care of all of the horses and make sure the Sutter is nice and clean. Still, it's the closest thing they have to a god, so they treat it with respect. If you ask them where they live, they'll tell you, "In the Horse Mansion," because it's a more descriptive name.

☺

Richard Stein never got to read *Horses Are Superior To Humans*, but I'm sure he would've enjoyed it. He always said that horses are the greatest creatures invented, because they are BIG and strong, yet still beautiful. He said humans can never have beauty when they are BIG and strong, and neither can any other animal, even lions and bears. Unless you're an artist, that is, because artists usually find all creatures beautiful, especially the ugly or peculiar-looking ones.

He was a BIG man himself. Not extremely defined with muscles, but pretty massive. He found himself disgusting, an ugly beast with pants. He cringed in the mirror every day, just like me. And he found all of his BIG-strong friends disgusting as well, even though they found themselves beautiful, and so did their women.

Richard Stein always envied all of the thin-small people in the world. And all of the thin-small people in the world envied him back, just for not being thin-small.

☺

    This Horse Mansion doesn't work anymore. It was swallowed up by the Silence just yesterday, when it took its morning stroll through the walm and back, leaving a world without their god machine, which means that that world will probably die soon. It has already digested all of the horses inside of it and rendered it a BIG useless building. If it did still work, it would be a perfect solution to our problem. We could've gone to Heaven Two instead of oblivion.

    Now that I think of it, God could've put a Sutter on Earth after Heaven filled up, but I guess he just didn't care enough to do it.

    Of course, even if there was a Sutter, we would've had to kill ourselves before the walm took our souls, and that would've been a pretty hard thing for us to do. It would've been a good backup plan anyway. Especially if there's something that will try to stop us from going through the walm, like a prowler beast or a gatekeeper, which is a good possibility.

☺

    I was expecting the Sutter to be crowd-stuffed, but I find the opposite when I go in. It's totally empty. I go inside, my steps echoing, echoing . . . I guess all the crazies were too loud and got themselves digested already.

    I just used the word *praying*, but I meant *hoping*, because praying is a pointless act in this world.

☺

    Walking hyper-stretched. Vision sick, lunking through horse-scented spaces. Some people here - walm people. Just a small *some*. A couple quiet blue women feeding from a wormy teenager. A few scraggly ones and a dark male are here. All of them are in their miserable insides {?}, sitting.

    Keeping my mouth shut, I walk on . . . If I'm wrong about the Silence and it digests me, all of my friends - who happen to be the last *real* humans left - will become walm fuel. I can't let that happen. They're counting on me to be a hero. A *hero*. A human fuck-up is mankind's only hope. It scares me. Obscene colors leap into my head. I murder the thought.

After an hour of striding through hallways and finding only twenty-two sad-sad beings, I go to *Heaven Two* to satisfy my curiosity. If Stag and Lenny aren't in this area I'll at least be able to say that I've been to heaven.

Inside, I can think of only one descriptive word for heaven: *carpet*. I'm not sure if I can describe what I mean, but I feel all *carpety* inside of here. I feel comfortably drugged and released from all stress. The whole panic of the world has slipped right off of my shoulders.

Of course, this isn't the real heaven. It's just an imitation of paradise. And the only thing great about it is its comfortable atmosphere. I'm sure that the comfort gets boring after some time. At the moment, though, I am tempted to stay.

☺

I don't find Stag or Lenny, but one of them finds me.

I hear his voice calling me from a dark section of Heaven Two, where the words *Punk Land* have been hand written on a carpet wall. It was Stag's little joke.

"Where are you?" I say, not perceiving *anyone* in Punk Land.

"Right here," Lenny says.

Then I notice that he's right in front of me, but transparent. A fading image. He's half-digested and now only half-exists, sitting in a queer position and trying to hold on to his remains.

"Where's Stag?" I ask, not whispering.

"Gone like the rest of them." His voice isn't a whisper either, but it's not as loud as mine. "You got eaten too, eh?"

"Yeah, but I'm not staying here. I'm indigestible."

Lenny doesn't believe me. He says, "Cock wash."

"I just came for you. We're getting out of this world."

"I'm not going anywhere," Lenny says.

"It doesn't matter then," I gripe.

☺

I tell him the story of Satan Burger and how we're going to restart the human race. He doesn't seem to know where he is. He has cotton stains on his mouth and doesn't speak. Speaking to me has already caused him to be digested a little more.

He tells me where the walm is. "Near the center of Punk Land, where they filmed *Death Corpse*." That movie I was in, as a zombie in the back of the zombie crowd. There was a close-up of my back when I and a few other corpses were killing a major character that was dressed up like a butt-rocker. Mortician and Lenny were in that movie too, but I didn't know them very well in those days.

"Is it dangerous?"

Lenny shrugs. "There'll be something waiting for you there. It's the Movac and it knows *everything*. Everything about everything. From how the universe began to how the universe will end, to what you are thinking to what you're going to think."

"What is it doing there?"

"Answering questions."

☺

"Do me a favor, Leaf." Lenny scratches his chest and fades a little more.

"Sorry, I'm in a hurry." I get up to leave.

"Please."

"What is it?"

"Kill the Movac for me."

"Why do that?"

"It doesn't deserve to live. Nothing should know *everything*."

Scene 23
Carnal Run

☺

I leave Silence as slip-easy as before, and feel a tremendous smile overtake my face; I'm the *only* person who can escape such a creature after being swallowed. I am special. Just how I am the only person owning God's Eyes, though they have been repossessed. I walk out calm-slinky and go back to Satan Burger, through the street that Silence emptied for me.

The walk is not dangerous anymore, I think, with more Silence-emptied streets, but danger can come from within you. Right now my head-visions seem like danger - my eyes are going hell-whirl. It's enough for me to commit self-murder, but I won't give in to the suicide voices in my head. I have mankind to save. And besides that, I'm sensing a hard-on coming. A BIG bulge in my pants. Richard Stein always said that hard-ons are bound to happen when you least expect them, but nobody ever thought that the hero of mankind would be having trouble with a hard-on during the moment of his ultimate test.

I am guessing my shank is craving the blue woman - maybe the blue woman is craving it too - but it's not getting any blue pleasures any-more, because I will never see that creature ever again. She tricked me into pregnancy, without even loving me, but she was *so* beautiful . . . I'm defi-nitely going to miss the sex. But I'll have another blue woman soon enough. Once I give birth to it, I'll *have* to feed it in the same manner I fed my old blue woman. Sure it seems like incest to molest my own child, but blue women belong to another culture.

☺

My hard-on is still going strong when I get to Satan Burger, trying to hide it from my friends when I see them (I use the history book of man-kind as a shield). Mort, Nan, and Gin's body parts don't seem to notice *my* hard-on. They probably don't care enough to let themselves notice.

"We need to get going now," I tell them. Then I realize one mem-ber of our group is missing. "Where's Christian?"

Mort sway-looks around. "Must've wandered off."

"Where?" I stomp toward him.

He shrugs.

"Stay here. I'll find him."

☺

I jamble-hike to the other side of the hill, searching, searching . . . but my vision is too harsh and unclear, so I call to him. Three yells, but he doesn't give an answer. If he's joined the crowd of insane ones, I'll never be able to find him. I won't even bother, not even for my best friend.

Richard Stein's best friend was a guy nicknamed *Hobby*, who produced twenty-six children from thirteen different women, none of which he was married to. It had something to do with his brain, but Hobby loved to impregnate women, more than one woman at a time, and every pregnancy happened to manufacture identical twins. His friends, like Richard Stein, thought he was funny, but thirteen pairs of children thought he was a jerk.

They ended their friendship the day Hobby was arrested for giving twins to a sixteen-year-old. Richard normally would have thought it was a funny thing for Hobby to do, but Richard's little sister was where he drew the line.

☺

I find Christian across the street. He managed to climb to the roof of the bakery building on the left foot of the Satan Burger hill.

"What are you doing?" I yell to him. "You lost your fucking mind?"

Christian stands there messiah-like, his arms spread. "It's beautiful, isn't it?" he calls.

"What?"

"This place is groobly-goo. The whole world. The streets full of creatures and colors. I feel like Mr. T."

The rain has gotten to him, or maybe it's the silly-go.

"You're going crazy, Christian," I say. "Stop it."

He laughs. "I know. It's great."

"Try to fight it. We need to leave."

I see him swaying and twisting in my ocean eyes, drowning. The rain has drizzled him soggy and he can't stand up on his own anymore.

"We need to get to Punk Land," I scream to him. "That's where the walm is."

"Sounds like fun," wobble-words from his mouth.

Christian looks at a point high above me.

"Scorpion flies," he says.

"What?"

"Scorpion flies."

I see the swarm tornadoing above me. Buzz-whirling for an at-tack. The scorpion flies have gone crazy as well, and are actually coming to ground-level to kill. A BIG panic hits my face. A smaller one hits Christian's.

"Get out of here!" I scream to him. "Meet us in Punk Land. We'll be waiting for you."

Christian nods, jumping onto the whirl crowd below, and I run back to Satan Burger, slipping every footfall and moving in circles with my rolling world.

☺

"Let's go!" I yell to Mort and Nan, who are already up and ready to run. Staring dead into the millions of beady-minded insects in the sky.

I glance up at the sky on our way down the Satan Burger steps, wheel-screeching black ones in the orange wind.

"Where is it?" Mort screams.

"Punk Land."

We jump full into the crowd of insane ones and barge our way through. Breakfast and all of Gin's other body parts begin fall-hanging from Nan. She loses one of the Medusa Hairs and keeps moving through, pulling off her shirt and wrapping the demons inside of it. Her skin now exposed to the dirty world, cuts and bruises from the sex with Gin and her bra is ripped in places where Gin's teeth had been. A pink nipple smiles in the soaking air.

My hard-on will not go away, especially with Nan rubbing her open breast against my arm, trying to keep with me. Also, all of the insane ones seem to have gotten into a rumble-orgy of licking and rub-scouring. Pressing against my shank as I barge my way through, feeling very displaced by the performance . . .

A masturbating woman with green-speckled hair licks the sweat from my neck, trying to keep me with her, trying to pull me down. She must realize my condition and wants to release the pressure, as a favor to me. And I want to go into her. But I must shove on. I try to pull her forward, to come with me toward the walm, but she releases her grip and continues pleasuring herself.

- 185 -

I keep going, pushing through the rolling insane ones, trying to keep my shank from running into any other hungry women. I wonder if the rain is what gave me this unstoppable hard-on. Maybe my penis has maggots in its brain.

☺

The scorpion flies attack.

I hear the people scream from behind us, dropping paralyzed. Running begins.

The whole insane crowd, just now getting a glimpse of reality, filling their nerves with fright over lust, terror. Then trampling starts. Screams and thrashings through the puddles of pulpy yellow.

My legs and eyes don't communicate properly, but I'm moving. Jumping over the already-paralyzed. Fighting the slow ones in my way. I still feel Nan's arm and breast wrapped against me, running with my speed. I'm not sure if Mortician is behind us, or if he's been taken down, but I keep going, crushing MAN's history book against my erection.

Some people take to a manhole, to the dark ones' territory, which might be the safest place to go. But I don't follow them. We might get trapped down there, unable to reach the walm, or maybe the dark ones will hold us there and let their dark females molest us beyond death. I push into my erection again and groan. I still have the dark female's love wounds from when I was with Vodka, and the open sores are still numb-felt. Even the flaps of skin hanging from my shoulder feel like cloth, or something not attached to my nerves. Maybe the rain is some kind of special acid juice and melted my nerves.

The crowd is thinning, too many fallen prey to the scorpion flies. It doesn't seem like the scorpion flies are eating all of their victims. Normally, a swarm of a hundred would sting one human-sized creature and it would be enough food for the whole family. But the scorpion flies are crazy now. They're trying to take down every member of the group, as if the crowd is one prey instead of a group of prey.

Nan cries out and goes limp, falling from my grasp. Turning, huffing, I stomp on the scorpion fly eating her stomach, grinding its insides out, pushing all the wind out of her. I gawk around. Gin's body parts are squirming in Nan's shirt. There aren't too many scorpion flies attacking nearby, just a couple. I can't see Mortician. He's gone. He must be one of the frozen bodies in the distance, where some scorpion flies start feeding. I'm not going back for him.

I am alone.

I stare down at Nan's thin, vulnerable body. She looks as if she's asleep, but her eyes are open and blinking a little. Her legs have fallen open and there's a wet pond between them. Her exposed breast is now sweat-dungy, glistening and oily. The history book pressed against my shank is only making things worse.

She can't do anything if I pull down her tight shorts right now, and give it to her right in the middle of all this chaos. I never liked to think about Nan sexually, but the rain must have gotten to me. We *need* to get going. If I do this here a scorpion fly might get me. Then we'll both be devoured, without dying. And even if a scorpion fly doesn't attack me, she'll kill me once she comes to. Literally *kill* me.

I feel so perverted, but I can't stop feeling it. I wish the tables were turned and Nan was the horny one, molesting me while I was paralyzed, with the insane screamers stampering around us.

I bend down to pick her up, podding my arms around her hips. I lift a little with my weak muscles and take her shoulders off the ground, but then my penis stabs her in the side with a shock, and I drop her. Her head claps against the street. My erection doesn't leave her side, though, it presses further instead. I must be insane, truly insane. I feel my way up her stomach to the unexposed breast and pull the bra down. Smoothing my palm into it. I can't stop myself now. My penis has taken full control over my body. Screaming-commotion all around this performance, people being eaten alive, beating each other to escape, and my other hand decides to go between Nan's legs, feeling the outsides.

Then, before my hand goes any further, I stop. The hard-on is gone, the penis has shriveled . . . I pull both of my hands away from her skin, lean in to her ear and whisper, "I'm sorry, Nan. I'm going crazy." Then I plunge my head into her bloody stomach, but I don't cry. My mind doesn't care enough to feel the disgust I should be feeling now.

☺

"Leaf!" I hear from the distance.
Mort limps toward us, smiling at his act of survival.

☺

"What happened?" I ask Mortician when he arrives to us.
"I almost got it back there," he says. "I tripped on some bastard

and fucked up my leg. I'm surprised those things didn't get me. Especially with my slow ass."

Mort pauses. He looks down at Nan.

"Did they get her?" he asks.

"Yeah."

"She's fucked."

"I couldn't pick her up."

"We're going to have to leave her."

For a second, I feel relieved, because I won't have to face her after she wakes up from paralysis. But I know that would be very wrong.

"We can't just leave her. She's our friend, and she's the last human female left."

"Well, my leg is crippled and you're weak, plus you have your fucked eyes. How are we supposed to get her out of here?"

"We'll have to both carry her," I tell him. "I know she hates me, but I can't leave her here."

"Fine," Mort says. "But if you get stung, I'm leaving you both here."

☺

As we leave, I see a human clown with its arms missing. They look like they've only recently been severed. The clown is wandering incoherently toward the scorpion flies. Blood drip-drips onto his side. He doesn't seem to notice that his arms are missing, and it's almost funny. Richard Stein said that clowns are goofy people that know how to be funny. I think he's right, because even though this clown is in a terrible state - losing his arms in a violent sort of way and all - I still cant help but laugh.

Richard Stein also said that there are only two sorts of people that would laugh at someone so pitiful as a clown with its arms cut off. Those people are the *mean* sort of people and the sort that have maggots in the brain. I wonder which sort I am.

But Richard Stein said that there are very few people in the world that *don't* laugh at the pitiful and the misfortunate, which means that most human beings are generally *mean* and/or have maggots in the brain. But mean people and maggot-brained people can be pitiful themselves, so there was a lot of confusion among humans before their souls were lost.

Scene 24
Ocean Man

☺

The drizzle-rain dies as we arrive at Punk Land - not the punk version of heaven, but the place where punks acted punk before the walm took it over.

We're not strong enough to pick Nan up off the ground and her knees are raw-bloody from scraping against the asphalt. She has yet to become un-limp, but I'm not impatient for what she will do to me when her strength returns. I cringe at the thought.

I left Gin's demon body parts where they were. Besides Breakfast, that is, who refused to be left behind. He followed for almost a hundred feet, crawling on fingers, before I noticed him. Then I stuffed him down Nan's shorts, hoping she wouldn't mind. She'll probably kill me for that too. Waking from paralysis to find out she's been pervert-handled by both myself and her dead boyfriend's demon hand will probably be damaging to her mental health in some way. I hope I can make it up to her in the future, after we start a colony in a different dimension.

The scorpion flies are behind us, feeding probably, but we can't be too sure we're safe from them. And there are other creatures to worry about as well. Like the dark ones and the prowler beasts and the krellians. And the Movac, who knows everything, who is awaiting us at the walm.

Richard Stein said that it would be a terrible thing to know everything about everything. I bet he would've agreed with Lenny's statement that *nothing* should know *everything*, and whoever does know everything should be killed. Richard Stein also said that all human beings are born with the *wish* to know all there is to know, even if it is such a terrible thing.

☺

The park, which used to be punk-filled, is now flooded with a miniature ocean - one that must've been brought from a miniature world. At first I see it as a giant puddle, through gyration eyes, but once I scoop a handful of the water I can see closer-closer. Turns out there are tiny whales and sharks and sailboats inside. So small that a sandwich bug can eat them in a gulp. I drop the chunk of ocean back into place, probably drowning the sailboats that I had. The ocean seems to go for half a mile, all the way through Punk Land.

Richard Stein said that the ocean, not old age, is where all the world's wisdom comes from. He believed that oceans produce an aura that seeps into the souls of anyone around it, so people that live in or around the ocean are generally the most enlightened people alive. Mr. Richard Stein never knew this for fact, though, because he didn't know any wise people that lived near the ocean. He just assumed he knew what he was talking about after he visited the Atlantic one summer. He said, "The vast emotion was overpowering and my thoughts were never so clear." But he never went inside of the water, since Richard Stein couldn't swim. One of his legs didn't work correctly.

Water-wisdom is what he called it. He said that it's much more powerful than old age wisdom or educated wisdom or the common wisdom you're born with. In fact, he mentioned that if there was someone who knew everything about everything, that person would've gotten his/her knowledge from water-wisdom. If this were true then more schools should've been built on beaches or near lakes, because *wisdom* is more important than school-learning - which is *intelligence*. The thing about intelligence is that it revolves around memory. Those with good memories will learn more. Those that forget easily will not be intelligent. And those with photographic memories will be considered geniuses. I don't like to hear that someone with such good memory can be called such a name, a genius is one who has *both* intelligence and wisdom.

The man who knows everything is an exception, however, because he was probably born with the knowledge to know everything - at least in my opinion. So memory would not be an important commodity for him, since there is nothing he can *learn* that he will need to *remember*.

By the way, I have been addressing the man who knows everything as a *he*, but I perfectly well know that it could be a *she* - the woman who knows everything. I will have to start calling it the *Movac*, so that I do not ruin its gender.

☺

Richard Stein figured that he could find total enlightenment by heading out to sea in a little sailboat. In fact, he said that he would either find enlightenment or die trying. With his spouse gone and without giving the world any children, there was nothing he really had to lose. Except for his life, but by then he was so old-hugging that he would've died soon anyway. He was probably going out to sea to kill himself. That's the way he wanted to die.

On the side of his little boat, he printed the words *Ocean Man*, which was the title of his ship. He took two months supply of food and three months supply of whiskey and a few books; one was Hemmingway's *The Old Man and the Sea* and another was Kafka's *The Castle*. Then Ocean Man shoved off from the port in Gloucester, Massachusetts, where he lived for two years during adolescence. His girlfriend back then was called *Nina*, and she was the first woman that he ever loved. The one he never forgot.

Richard Stein said that you'll always love your *first* love, no matter how many partners you may go through. The *first* is always special. His second love, which became his first wife, did not compare to the memory of Nina. Neither did his second wife, who was his eighth love, and who died in an institution populated by crazies. Besides Nina, Richard Stein loved his *Cool Blue Lady* the most; she was the only woman who stood with him throughout his entire life.

The Cool Blue Lady hovered over Richard Stein solemnly as he washed against the sea, kissing him with her breath. Yes, the Night was his *love*, deeply. He embraced her with passion, allowing Ocean Man to drift him into the betweens of her firm dark legs. Richard Stein called this voyage the *supreme ordeal* of his life - the climax of fire, his grand finale. It was the first and only time he truly felt *alive* and he was glad he lived so long to reach it. He was glad he never put the gun to his head as he always figured he would.

Mortician and I find a dry island underneath a tree and set Nan down. On the swap-side of the tree is a miniature city by the ocean that has a port leading out to the sea. Dozens of fishing boats are coming and going. I wonder if this port is similar to the one in Gloucester, where Ocean Man set sail. I wonder if there is a character similar to Richard Stein over there, setting out to find clarity during the twilight of his life, trying to get in his grand finale before he dies.

"What are we going to do?" Mortician asks.

"I don't know," I say. "Wait awhile, for Christian."

"Do you think he will make it?"

"He better."

I pressure-thumb Nan's eye open to see how she's doing. Still unconscious. Her nipple has been covered over with a coat of mud. I'm guessing that Mortician is responsible for earthing Nan's breast, because he was probably disgusted by it. Mort finds Nan dyke-hideous because she's too thin, bald-headed, and without many curves. Skinhead girls are dirty to him.

I hit myself in the skull, thinking about how I almost raped Nan back there. Then I hit myself again.

Some walm people pass by, through the tiny ocean, slug-legged people with no eyes. I often wonder how significant the human race is/was compared to the other peoples of the universe, wondering if we were superior or equal or less. So far, I haven't seen any race that is technologically more advanced than humans. I have seen some that were emotionally more advanced, or physically more advanced, or own better lives than us, but none are particularly evolved scientifically.

Can it be that humans are ahead of their time? Can everyone else out there be as primitive as the walm races? Are we something *special*? Maybe we were put to an end because we evolved past the danger zone - which is the zone where even gods are vulnerable to man's destructive power. Maybe we invented a device that could blow up the sun, heaven, where Yahweh lives. Maybe He cut us off because He was afraid we would destroy Him.

☺

"I've got an idea," Mortician says.

I glisten to the rolling water and stutter-mumble a word.

Mort asks, "Why do we have to leave?"

"Because of the walm. Forget already?"

"I didn't forget," he says. "But what if we get rid of the walm? We wouldn't have to go anywhere. I think we should just destroy it, just fuck it up with an ax or light it on fire, damage it enough so that it won't work anymore. If the walm is gone we can stay without losing our souls."

"You're forgetting about the Movac," I tell him. "The walm is guarded by something that knows *everything*. How are we going to beat something that knows everything? It's impossible."

"Nothing's impossible."

"The Movac knows *everything*, understand? It would know exactly how to stop us. Even if we had a gun, it would know where to go to dodge the bullet. Lenny told me to kill the Movac also, but he's an idiot. It's impossible."

"We might as well try," he says. "What's the worst that can happen? Get killed? So what, we can't *fully* die anymore."

"Don't be stupid. I'm not living here as a corpse, waiting for the walm to steal my soul. I wouldn't want to stay even if we *did* destroy the walm. There's no future."

"But there's probably hundreds of people around the world that still have some soul left. We'd be saving them."

"You don't know that," I tell him. "We could be the only ones. I'm not going to risk restarting the human race so that we can save a few half-zombie people. Besides, we don't stand a chance against the Movac."

Of course, there is *one* way we can defeat the Movac, although it's a long shot. The only way you can beat a man who knows everything is if he *wants* you to beat him. If the Movac *knows* someone is trying to kill him, he has two options. One, he can take the necessary steps to stop that someone - not to mention the Movac already knows he will succeed, because he knows the future, which can almost be considered cheating. And, two, the Movac can accept death and do nothing - but the Movac would already know this before needing to decide.

By the way, *decisions* are just as irrelevant to the Movac as memories. You don't need to make choices when you already know which ones you will choose.

Then again, the Movac may *want* us to kill him, because the one who knows everything must be waiting for death, out of boredom. Everything must be so *boring* to him. Then *again*, the Movac has *always* lived knowing everything about everything, so he's probably so accustomed to knowing everything that he wouldn't have it any other way. *Humans* may want to better themselves and better themselves and better themselves without being the best - because the best, since they're the best, can't better themselves - but the Movac's point of existing has nothing to do with bettering itself, so these rules don't apply. The Movac's point of existence must be something I can't understand, something beyond my personal knowledge. Something *godly* . . .

I'd prefer to leave the walm in soul-sucking order anyway, instead of destroying it. Even if the Movac would allow us to kill it, I wouldn't hurt the walm. Because I'm hoping that it will go out of control, become unstop-pable. And it will suck the souls out of everything nearby. It will finish off the human race, then go to the walm people, then go to the Movac or whatever other super-beings are here, then go to Child Earth and suck the bratty little soul out of it, and then it will start taking the energy out of heaven. It will suck God's soul away, chopping it up into the walm, into oblivion. And I'll be laughing safely on the other side of the universe, be-cause that's what He gets for turning His back on us. A taste of His own medicine, you can say.

Of course, this is very unlikely. I'm sure that God is the one con-trolling the walm and has the ability to turn it off. I don't even know if the walm can reach that far. Of course, God might want the walm to take Child Earth's soul away, which is good enough for me. If I was God, I would've straightened out this bratty planet a long time ago. I think Child Earth *deserves* oblivion. On the other hand, I'm just an action figure. I don't have any say in the happenings of the universe, and I'd be laughed at if I thought otherwise. I'm just a form of amusement.

I wonder how amusing Richard Stein was to Child Earth, when he shoved off an old man into the sea without any sailing experience, and with-out any company besides his Cool Blue Lady during the second half of each day. I wonder how Child Earth felt about old men in their twilight mo-ments altogether. I wonder if he gives them their grand finale without kill-ing them off first, if he thinks it would be funnier to not satisfy a pitiful old man. Or was the distribution of such grand finales God's job?

Scene 25
Brain City

☺

An hour or two passes and still no Christian.

He went crazy, so who knows what could've happened to him. Being in a bad place to be when the scorpion flies attacked, probably paralyzed in an alley somewhere, or in a pile of half-corpses.

We can't wait for him anymore. Humanity's future depends on our survival.

So we decide to head towards the walm, with Nan against our shoulders. She can walk now. Well, it's more of a stagger-wobble, and her head is still drunk with toxins, but she'll pull through in time. Through the miniature ocean cluttered with micro fish and organisms. I wonder if there are water bugs trying to eat the tiny people in the sailboats. I wonder if the tiny people are scared of this new land of giants.

"It must be there," Mort tells me, motioning to a flesh-tangy area up ahead, beings walking (or sometimes oozing) from that direction.

"Here we go," I tell Leaf.

☺

The area is peach-meat sunshine, flowing curly, plastic.

Peculiar shock emotions hit me here, right *here*, emotions that I haven't felt before in my life, wiggling *strong*. Just as strong as love or fear or hate or happiness. Another emotion, never felt by human feelings. So *new* to me, freshly breathing into my system.

Intensities camber and take me over.

I've always figured there could be more emotions out there somewhere, similar to love or sadness, but I never thought they'd be so different, so unexplainable. I feel like the color orange with red dots and a tree branch inside. Then I feel like the tip of a needle and the fabric of a plaid couch. I can't tell if these feelings are beautiful or scary. I can only say that they are extraordinary.

The emotions must be emanating from the walm like sillygo, but I can't see the walm entirely - just a glow of red light.

It's blocked by the people leaving from there. More new people. I see one man attached to a woman, who seems to be his wife. Joined in flesh as well as in marriage.

Another being has a snake's torso, like something from Greek Mythology, but it also seems to be a hermaphrodite with crab-claws for hands. I don't go too near it, especially with my dizzy visions mixing with my dizzy emotions. Who knows what these creatures are capable of?

Mortician is in awe and doesn't speak to me now. I don't speak to him either.

I look towards the red light behind the walm people, over the heads of twelve identical beings.

☺

They're fish-like beings, scaled wings along their arms, and large hook-like skulls that waterfall a salty liquid down their shoulders and into the miniature ocean - the source of ocean water. Dark pools for eyes, staring at me, all twenty-four eyes directly at me.

As they stare at me, I figure out what they are. But I'm not sure if it's my intelligence that comes to this conclusion or if they have subconsciously told me in some way.

I realize: they are the Movac.

The Movac isn't a male or a female, as I earlier believed. It is twelve beings - all with the same mind. They seem to be four males and eight females, an entire race that share a brain. They probably reproduce so that the Movac's conscious thoughts will continue. A race of *one*. A single brain.

"We are not a single brain," says one of the Movac.

I'm surprised to hear it speak, and I'm sure they know that I'm surprised, and I'm sure they knew that I was going to be surprised before he said that.

"We have separate brains, Leaf," says another. "But we lack a sense of individuality, even in our appearance, but we are still individuals."

I think I understand. When you know everything about everything, it's probably hard to be unique from others who know everything. You own every consciousness of every being that is, has been, or ever will be alive. Which makes it irrelevant to have one of your own. It all sounds hideous-depressing to me. But the Movac live for a different purpose than what I live for, so I should stop comparing them to myself. Their purpose is something completely beyond me.

"It is to answer questions," the Movac says, all of them.

"What?" Mort shrugs.

"The purpose of our existing is to answer questions."

"That's it?" I ask.

They all nod.

☺

I feel betrayed and punch my leg. They know *everything* and all that they do is answer questions. What in the hell is that supposed to mean?

"That's why we were created," says the Movac. "We were created because something had to know everything. With us around, nothing will be forgotten. Not a man, not a thought, not anything. You think of us as beings, but don't. Think of us as the record books of *everything*."

"Nobody *else* knows everything?" Mort asks. "What about God? Doesn't He know everything?"

"No, gods created us because they didn't want to know everything. In a way, you give up your individuality to know everything, and the gods refused to give that up. It was necessary for us to exist, for history's sake, and also for the future's."

I ask, "So you are the all-knowing computers of the universe?"

They started nodding before the question came.

☺

I notice that the Movacs have miniature cities inside of their brains. These cities are inhabited by the same miniature people that inhabit the miniature ocean. An entire society physically living inside of a brain city.

They are the brain citizens: physical beings formed from the thoughts of the Movac. The process of knowing everything must be so complex that they need hundreds of brain-workers, functioning together in one society – moving toward one goal - to form a Movac's super-complex brain. And all twelve Movac brains work together to form the all-knowing super computer of the universe. I'm not sure if my theory is correct, but I don't want to know for sure, because theorizing exercises the brain muscles. The Movacs know I am thinking this, so they don't tell me if I'm right or wrong.

The brain citizens build their societies outside of Movac brains too, expanding productivity across the countryside of Punk Land. This entire ocean, which Mort and I are standing in and Nan is lying in, is the overflow of the Movac brain. Ships and villages and animals - all part of the Movac brain, all working together to maintain the knowledge of *everything*.

A female Movac stares at me with a gurgle-leak coursing down her neck. Her brain citizens have built elevators from her chin to her breasts, where they can relax on the soft flesh before taking a shuttle to her toes. Through my swirly eyes, I see her body as an arousing work of architecture. A sky-scraping building that I wouldn't mind laying over a mountain to inject my whale-sized shank through its front entrance, knocking the doorman out of the way and flooding the lobby once I am finished with her.

The Movac woman must've had her dark-pools eyeing into me because she knew I was about to fantasize about her, and wanted to give me a good stare-down before I performed the sex thought, licking some brain citizens from the corner of her white lips to dissolve in thick mouth water. I'm embarrassed, but I shouldn't be, not at all: she's known I was going to do this her entire life. It wasn't a shock in the slightest, I'm sure.

☺

"We're going through the walm," Mortician tells them.

"We know," they say, pig-drippy.

The female, the fantasy building with large vacation breasts and the leaky saltwater entrance, approaches us, stiff-moving with her city built on her insides, trying to keep the brain citizens from falling into the ocean. She glares into my eyes again, her pools gathering hints of purple and silver. Black cave of a mouth . . . shingles for teeth . . . opening with pearl-expression . . .

"Let's go there." She turns and heads to the walm light.

I wonder why *she* is taking us rather than any of the other twelve. Is it because I'm attracted to her? Is she attracted to me as well? Will she take advantage of my weakness to alien women before allowing me to escape through the walm?

I hope so.

☺

She leads the way, through the vapid humanoid crowd emerging from the light. Her walk patterns are mechanical. Her backside is so sensual yet it's like a machine, just how the blue woman's seems to be, but the blue woman is an animal-like machine and this Movac is a machine-like animal. I've never been attracted to mechanical women before. Now I guess it's becoming a trend in my life.

The walm emotions go squirrely here, as do my eyes, running up the tree bark and chirping. Brain liquid drools from the Movac woman's head, and I watch it slowly licking down to her fleshy rounds that are inhabited by the lower class of her body's citizens - the salty odor thickens the air down there - then slipping between the crack to her thighs where it weeps into the miniature ocean world.

I'm paying so much attention to her absorbing body that I don't realize we have reached the source of the light. My head fixes on the lower parts as she stops, then it looks up at the sublime doorway, the walm, eyes fixed without much dizzy-swirling.

☺

The door is a giant vagina. It's lips are spread out wide and emit a green light in all directions. The Movac female statues herself next to it, arms out at diagonals and chin up. Then her muscles go tense and it looks as if she is absorbing energy from the walm, as if she runs on soul-fuel as well, soak-slurping it from the reserve that the walm has collected.

Then the walm door dilates, the green light melting our skin color to lime. It awaits our penetration. On the inside of this thing is our future, our new life. Everything chaotic about this world will be uplifted from our crusty old shoulders. Now the human species still has a fighting chance against extinction.

"I'm not going," I tell Mortician.

"What?" His face goes into shock, or maybe it's disbelief.

"I'm going to wait for Christian."

"You want to wait longer? We can wait for him longer if you want, but I'm not going in there alone."

"You won't be," I say, brushing mud out of Nan's half-conscious eyes.

"Come on, Leaf. Let's go. You know Christian isn't coming."

"You go," I tell him. "Take Nan and the history book and get out of here. If I Christian gets back here I'll . . . Look, I can't just leave him."

"Well, I'm staying too," Mort says.

"No." I shake my head lightly. "I'm willing to risk myself to save Christian, but I'm not willing to risk the future of mankind. Get out of here now before the walm takes anymore of your soul."

"Dickhead." Mortician spits at me. He nods his head and puts the history book of Man in his belt. He takes Nan's arms around his shoulder and she hugs into him, embracing to keep herself from falling and shattering on the ground.

Before he enters the fleshy lips of the walm, he turns back to me and gentle-smiles. Then he tips his pointy head up as a salute. Before I can salute back, he disappears into the walm and its lips press slowly around him, sucking him into another world far away from here.

I'm only giving Christian another hour or two. If he doesn't show, I'm leaving him. Even if he's wounded, another hour is plenty of time to get here. Otherwise, I'll know that he's lost too much soul to make it. He has the ability, but he might not have the will.

I glance back at the walm and realize the light it issues is no longer green, but purple.

"What does that mean?" I ask the Movac.

She turns to me, a cricking of gears in her neck. "The door has opened to a different world."

"You mean I can't go to the world my friends just went to?"

"This world and the world your friends now inhabit will not share a doorway until the cycle is finished," she says.

"How long will that take?"

"Twenty-four hours." She turns away from me and begins to absorb more energy from the walm. She will possibly be absorbing *my* energy from the walm if I stay for too long.

My words come out soft and slightly panicked. "You mean I'm stuck here for another day?"

"Exactly another day."

Scene 26
Ten Commandments

☺

I wait for several moments of time, curled in a ball, soaking in the thick brain sweat of the Movac woman and sometimes rubbing against her fishy leg for erotic purposes, over and over until it becomes droning.

I stare up swirly-visioned at the Movac woman, waiting and waiting for her to say something to me. She has nothing to say. It stands next to me, protecting the walm from my wandering eyes. My head-sickness gets too strong when I look out across Punk Land, so much life-chaos of colors, crowds, all around me. A melting pot far beyond what the United States had been, the melting pot of the universe. And not one of them seem to be human.

"Why has this happened to us?" The words, directed at the building/woman I guess, slip out of me without asking first. The woman was already glancing at me, knew the precise moment to turn her attention. She knows much more about me than I do.

The building/woman answers: "God Hates You."

☺

My eyes wet with brain juice, little brain people crawling through my hair, sometimes sneezing when one approaches a nostril.

The Movac woman speaks to me, "God doesn't want anything to do with you anymore. He hates you."

"I'm sure we all know that," I tell her. "But how can He possibly hate His creation? That's like a mother hating her child."

"Sometimes mothers get sick of their children. Sometimes they steal all the love out of one child and give it to another, a more desirable child."

"That makes God superficial, irresponsible. Maybe even white trash."

"Gods are not the most open-minded of creatures. They are ruled by billions of years of tradition. Tradition closes your mind."

- 201 -

"Religion closes your mind," I say. "It creates a very strong view that is one-sided."

"Closing your mind to religion is no different than the close-mindedness that religions can cause."

"The God of this planet was not worth the religion."

☺

"You speak so negatively about God. You, of all people, should understand Him."

"Why me *of all people*?"

"You combined your soul with God."

My face contorts and before I can ask the Movac to explain, she explains: "Every once in a while God will merge His soul with a human's, to see things out of his eyes, think his thoughts, become that person, for a long period of the person's life. You were such a person. And, in a way, you were God. Or to describe it more accurately, God was you."

I don't believe her, and the Movac knows this.

"God and I are complete opposites," I tell her.

"You know I am right," says the Movac.

I decide not to argue.

"It explains some things," I tell her, gazing over myself and thinking about all of the things that I can do that others can not, all the things I knew that no one else knew.

She tells me: "You have been God for as long as your eyes have been distorted. When God got word that there was a mortal whose vision existed in the rolling world, He had to see it for Himself."

She sits next to me, rubbing her machine body against me and causing an earthquake for her knee citizens.

"You are special, Leaf," she tells me. "God merges with only a small amount of people. And they are usually only the most righteous of men. You were the first low-lifer to ever merge with Him."

"I wouldn't have chosen me," I mumble.

"Yes, God regrets it severely," nodding. "When souls merge together, they do not separate very easily. The process is something that was never meant to be reversed. It was meant for soulmates who wanted to join into one being, to be together forever.

"When your souls were separated, God took some of your lifeforce and you took some of His."

So I am still a part of God.

☺

"Everyone is watching you, Leaf," says the Movac. "Everyone in Heaven. They can read your thoughts. They have been writing down all of your thoughts, all of your actions, as you think them, as you do them.

"They wanted to create a record of the last man who merged with God, the man who is right in the middle of the end of the humanity. Even right now, they are recording the words you hear coming out of my mouth as your brain processes them. Everyone is in your mind."

☺

Behind me, the walm changes color. It turns to a color I have never seen before. Something different than red, blue, yellow, black, white or any of the combinations. It's something totally foreign. My God thoughts tell me it's called *newa*.

"The walm is now a doorway to Heaven," says the Movac woman. "Now that God is a part of you, and you are a part of God, He doesn't want your soul to perish here on Earth. He has made room for one more person to join Him in Heaven. Of all the people on this planet, God has chosen to save you."

My swirling eyes blink hard.

"I don't think I can go," I tell her.

Her face doesn't change expressions. Tiny people marching in and out of her eyeballs and nose.

"I have met a couple people who have been to Heaven and neither of them recommend the place. Perfection is ugly to me. I'd rather take my chances in the walm."

She nods and the walm changes color to a dark blue.

"God respects your decision, but it saddens Him to know your soul will be lost."

"I bet He's only sad for the part of me that belonged to Him."

☺

The Movac eyes me, stretching her face closer to me, so close I can smell the city inside of her brain.

"God wants you to leave Earth as soon as possible. If not to Heaven, then to somewhere else. Just leave right away."

- 203 -

"I need to wait for Christian. We have to all go to the same world. I made a promise to Jesus that we would keep mankind going."

"Christian does not want to come here," says the Movac.

"Where is he? You know where he is, don't you?"

"He is in the trainyard a mile south of here, waiting for his soul to disappear."

"He was supposed to meet us here. Why didn't he come?"

"He lost interest in survival."

"Can I get to him in time?"

"Some soul is still lingering inside of him."

"What will happen if I try to save him?" I ask the Movac woman. "Will he make it, or is it useless? Will I end up losing my soul in the process?"

"We do not speak the future," she tells me. "Knowledge of the future is only for Movac brains."

☺

"I might as well try," I mumble to the brain city. "I have until tomorrow anyway, don't I?"

The Movac woman just glazes me with her shiny black eyes, sniffing the cold crowded air, curling a lip to allow some brain citizens to step inside of her mouth and give themselves over to their monstrous female home as protein.

Scene 27
Sick Train

☺

    The journey to the trainyard slows my vision. My thoughts go limp.

    I am moving very slowly.

    It's not a difficult journey through the streets, even though I'm staggering half-mangled. Not too many people bother to walk anymore; they just sleep in piles along the side of the road. A few walm people flicker to my left, I think. My vision scatters so much I'm not sure if they're real. I don't bother to make sure.

    Emptiness.

    It clots in my head and scabs over all of my fluffy bright-colored emotions.

    The horizon line doesn't seem to make the landscape feel like it goes on forever anymore. The line is more like an ending. It shrinks my path, makes it smaller and smaller, until the path is just a dot. And after the dot, there's nothing.

    Pieces of cars and buildings are curled up in tiny balls next to the street corpses.

    I have brain sickness. I'm drowning.

☺

    The train yard. It has less people in it than the street. The train still moves through its belly. It never stops. It never leaves either. The railroad tracks have been reconstructed into a crooked circle, screaming round and round. It'll keep screaming round and round forever.

    The train has been diagnosed with a dangerous rusting disease; it can't touch other machines or they will go to pieces. The train is quarantined to the rail yard and was told by the rail master that a cure is in its way and to just hold on. But the rail master is walking up the road without any arms or face.

    The sick train paces around the trainyard, shrieking against the track, moving-moving so that it doesn't break into bits.

Some human passengers are aboard. They're speaking casually to one another, waiting patiently to be taken somewhere. Prisoners of the train, these passengers, but they're acting like they're prisoner by choice.

The people are even smiling at each other, and they're shaking hands every few minutes too, oblivious to the outside world and to the sad-sad train that possesses them.

☺

Stepping through a patch of steel weeds.

☺

I trip over an overgrown glass bush, crashing it between my corpse and the ground. My face filets open against the plant shatters.

A watery liquid pours out of my forehead; plastic-clear fluid floats on top of the soil in my face. I'm coughing up knotty ropes of slime into my arms.

Standing. Trying to ignore the large wounds in my flesh. A large section of my body opens up to the piercing gray wind I stagger against.

After stepping a dozen feet I notice the Richard Stein history book has fallen out of my hands. It's lying in the crude pile of mucus that leaked out of my body.

I'll have to get it later. No time to backtrack.

☺

I spot Christian. He's a swirling image but I still recognize his rotten suit. He's sitting in a junk pile made of shriveled up medical equipment that had never been used.

His lungs are still breathing and the way he scratches his leg indicates he still has emotion enough to become physically irritated. Or is he scratching out of habit?

☺

"We were waiting for you," I tell Christian.

He doesn't bother looking up at me. He's staring with deep black-filled eyes at an empty bottle of Gold Rush liquor. Medical ants march in and out of the bottle and gather dry-sticky droplets.

☺

"I guess I couldn't find my way," Christian tells me.

☺

Standing there in silence and staring out at the hills of clutter-architecture, scrambled up in the red landscape.

The clear fluid drips out of me and runs down my legs. Neither my flesh nor the earth will soak in the fluid, allowing it to jiggle and dance on surfaces.

☺

I'm sitting on a hollow respiration machine with my face in my lap.

☺

"Why does there *have* to be life after death anyway?" Christian asks me. "Why can't there just be death."

"You might as well have killed yourself when you were born," I tell him. "Why live at all if everything you did will die with you when you die?"

"We live for the present," Christian says. "The past is always for-gotten eventually. Why try to hold on to it? When our lives end, and we become the past, we won't matter anymore."

"You're suggesting oblivion then," I tell him. "Oblivion is a very ugly place to go to."

☺

"Oblivion is freedom. It's like sleep without dreams, without waking up."

"I would love to sleep forever, but I want to dream. I want to remember."

"To disappear forever is bliss."

"But everything will disappear forever . . ."

☺

"It'll be like nothing ever was."

"Was there ever anything?"

"I think there was something at some point."

☺

The sun goes down and we are still in the trainyard.

"What will we do?" I ask.

"I don't care, do you?"

"I'm pregnant," I tell him.

"How did that happen?"

"The blue woman impregnated me with another blue woman. Maybe I'll raise it."

"Maybe you should abort it."

"I think I should go back to my blue woman and start a family with her. Even though she's a man."

"And only two years old."

"And a cockroach."

"At least you have something to do. I wish I had something to do . . ."

"You have something to do," I tell him. "You're supposed to meet us at the walm."

"I wish there was something else."

"Something else . . ."

"I'm supposed to find my little sister. I promised myself I'd find out whose body she's living in now and protect her from the walm creatures."

"My eyes are all dizzy."

☺

Some medieval ones are battling across the train yard. They're crashing against the rails and making a lot of noise.

The sick train is dying, coughing slowly along the train track, wheezing. There are no longer any people inside . . . as if they were digested within its guttering stomach.

The medieval ones slash each other in our direction, near my face and shoulder, battling and splashing against our corpses.

☺

"Maybe we should go back to the walm and find Mortician and Nan," I say to Christian.

"Yeah, let's go back there."

☺

"Nice fighting," I tell Christian about the medieval ones fighting.

"They go on forever . . . don't they?"

"Forever and ever. Even when they are surrounded by death."

"So violent."

☺

"The sun is coming up and they're still fighting."

"The sun is hardly a sun anymore."

It reflects on a large brick wall ahead of me. A very large brick wall. I'm not sure if it was there before. It's on the path back to the walm. I must have missed it on my way here.

It's so large.

How did I overlook that giant obstruction, a hundred feet in the air?

It's so large.

A sword cuts through Christian's throat. Sounds like the ripping open of a papier-mâché donkey, and his severed head plops into his lap, staring back at himself.

"Has that wall always been there?" I ask Christian.

"My head's fallen off," Christian tells me.

I continue staring at the wall.

"I'm just a head," Christian tells me.

I continue to stare at the wall.

"Why do you keep staring at that wall?" Christian asks.

"I'm trying not to shrug," I tell him.

THE END

ERASERHEAD PRESS BOOKS
www.eraserheadpress.com

Eraserhead Press is a collective publishing organization with a mission to create a new genre for "bizarre" literature. A genre that brings together the neo-surrealists, the post-postmodernists, the literary punks, the magical realists, the masters of grotesque fantasy, the bastards of offbeat horror, and all other rebels of the written word. Together, these authors fight to tear down convention, explode from the underground, and create a new era in alternative literature. All the elements that make independent films "cult" films are displayed twice as wildly in this fiction series. Eraserhead Press strives to be your major source for bizarre/cult fiction.

SOME THINGS ARE BETTER LEFT UNPLUGGED
by Vincent W. Sakowski.
A post-modern fantasy filled with anti-heroes and anti-climaxes. An allegorical tale, the story satirizes many of our everyday obsessions, including: the pursuit of wealth and materialism;the thirst for empty spectacles and violence; and climbing whatever social, political, or economical ladder is before us. Join the man and his Nemesis, the obese tabby, and a host of others for a nightmare roller coaster ride from realm to realm, microcosm to microcosm: The Carnival, The Fray, The Garden of Earthly Delights, and The Court of The Crimson Ey'd King. Pretentious gobbledygook or an unparalleled anti-epic of the surreal and absurd? Read on and find out.
ISBN: 0-9713572-2-6, 156 pages, electronic: $4.95, paperback: $9.95

SZMONHFU
by Hertzan Chimera
Fear the machine - it is changing. The change comes not only from the manner of my life but from the manner of my death. I will die four deaths; the death of the flesh; the death of the soul; the death of myth; the death of reason and all of those deaths will contain the seed of resurrection. This is the time of the stomach. This is the time when we expand as a single cell expands. The flesh grows but the psyche does not grow. That is life.
ISBN: 0-9713572-4-2, 284 pages, electronic $4.95, paperback $15.95

THE KAFKA EFFEKT
by D. Harlan Wilson

A collection of forty-four short stories loosely written in the vein of Franz Kafka, with more than a pinch of William S. Burroughs sprinkled on top. A manic depressive has a baby's bottom grafted onto his face; a hermaphrodite impregnates itself and gives birth to twins; a gaggle of professors find themselves trapped in a port-a-john and struggle to liberate their minds from the prison of reason—these are just a few of the precarious situations that the characters herein are forced to confront. *The Kafka Effekt* is a postmodern scream. Absurd, intelligent, funny and scatological, Wilson turns reality inside out and exposes it as a grotesque, nightmarish machine that is always-already processing the human subject, who struggles to break free from the machine, but who at the same time revels in its subjugation.
ISBN: 0-9713572-1-8, 216 pages, electronic: $4.95, paperback: $13.95

SATAN BURGER
by Carlton Mellick III

A collage of absurd philosophies and dark surrealism, written and directed by Carlton Mellick III, starring a colorful cast of squatter punks on a journey to find their place in a world that doesn't want them anymore. Featuring: a city overrun with peoples from other dimensions, a narrator who sees his body from a third-person perspective, a man whose flesh is dead but his body parts are alive and running amok, an overweight messiah, the personal life of the Grim Reaper, lots of classy sex and violence, and a fast food restaurant owned by the devil himself. 2001, Approx. 236 min., Color, Hi-Fi Stereo, Rated R.
ISBN: 0-9713572-3-4, 236 pages, electronic: $4.95, paperback: $14.95

SHALL WE GATHER AT THE GARDEN?
by Kevin L. Donihe

"It illuminates. It demonizes. It pulls the strings of the puppets controlling the strangest of passion plays within a corporate structure. Everyone, every thing is a target of Mr. Donihe's wit and off-kilter worldview . . . There are shades of Philip K. Dick's wonderfully inventive *The Divine Invasion* (minus the lurid pop singer), trading up Zen Buddhism for unconscious Gnosticism. Malachi manifests where Elijah would stand revealed; and the Roald Dahl-like midgets hold the pink laser beam shining into our hero's mind. Religion is lambasted under the scrutiny of Corporate money-crunchers, and nothing is what it seems." - From the introduction by Jeffrey A. Stadt
ISBN: 0-9713572-5-0, 244 pages, electronic: $4.95, paperback: $14.95

SKIMMING THE GUMBO NUCLEAR
by M.F. Korn
A grand epic wasteland of surreal pandemic plague. Pollution quotient in the southern delta nether regions of the state of Louisiana, the dustbin of the Mississippi river and the nation, whose motto is the "Sportsman's Paradise" but is a paradise of colorful denizens all grappling for a slice of lassez bon temps roule, "let the good times roll", but now all are grappling for their very lives. Nature had to fight back sooner or later, and now what will happen to this tourist state gone amuck with middle-ages plague?
ISBN: 0-9713572-6-9, 292 pages, electronic: $4.95, paperback: $16.95

STRANGEWOOD TALES
edited by Jack Fisher
This anthology is a cure for bland formulaic horror fiction that plagues supermarkets and drugstores. It shames so-called "cutting-edge" publishers who are really just commercial wannabes in disguise. And opens doors to readers who are sick of writers afraid to break out of the mold and do something/anything different. Featuring twenty insane tales that break all rules, push all boundaries. They can only be described as surreal, experimental, postmodern, absurd, avant-garde or perhaps just plain bizarre. Welcome to the dawning of a new era in dark literature. Its birthplace is called STRANGEWOOD. Featuring work by: Kurt Newton, Jeffrey Thomas, Richard Gavin, Charles Anders, Brady Allen, DF Lewis, Carlton Mellick III, Scott Thomas, GW Thomas, Carol MacAllister, Jeff Vandermeer, Monica J. O'Rourke. Gene Michael Higney, Scott Milder, Andy Miller, Forrest Aguirre, Jack Fisher, Eleanor Terese Lohse, Shane Ryan Staley, and Mark McLaughlin.
ISBN: 0-9713572-0-X, 176 pages, electronic: $4.95, paperback: $10.95

COMING SOON:
"Skin Prayer" by Doug Rice, "My Dream Date (Rape) with Kathy Acker" by Michael Hemmingson, and a reprinting of "Electric Jesus Corpse" by Carlton Mellick III

Order these books online at **www.eraserheadpress.com**
or send cash, check, or money order to 16455 E Fairlynn Dr. Fountain Hills, AZ 85268

CHAPBOOKS

Georgie and Her Meat by Joi Brozek $2.50
House of the Rising Sun by Gene O'Neill $2.50
From the Bowels of Birch Street by Kevin L. Donihe $2.50
Ballad of a Slow Poisoner by Andrew Goldfarb $2.50
The Baby Jesus Butt Plug by Carlton Mellick III $2.50
A View from the Shelf by Vincent Collazo $2.50
The Less Fashionable Side of the Galaxy by M. F. Korn, D. F. Lewis, and
Hertzan Chimera (collaborative stories) $2.50
The Hack Chronicles by Vincent W. Sakowski $3.00
Dancing Skinless (anthology) erotic surrealism $3.00
Knock the Dead (anthology) zombie stories $3.00
The Infant Vending Machine by Carlton Mellick III $2.50
Reconfiguring Frankenstein by Jeffrey Little $2.50
The Earwig Flesh Factory #3/4 (anthology) $3.00
I Gave at the Orifice by Mark McLaughlin $2.50
Neurone Fry-up by Hertzan Chimera $2.50
Kafka-Breathing Sock Puppets by D. Harlan Wilson $2.50
Wet Dreams of the Pope by Bart Plantenga and Black Sifichi $3.50
Sick Days by Shane Ryan Staley $3.00
This Year for Christmas by Wiley Wiggins $2.50
The Earwig Flesh Factory #2 (anthology) dark surrealism $3.00
Results of a Preliminary Investigation of Electrochemical Properties of
Some Organic Matrices by David Kopaska-Merkel (*Bram Stoker Award
Nominee*) $2.50
Much Ado About Teeth by Food Fortunata $4.00
Sycophantic Peepshow by Jon Hodges $2.50
The Adventures of You and Me by Aidan Baker $1.50
The Earwig Flesh Factory #1 (anthology) dark surrealism $3.00

Coming Soon:
Uncle River, Simon Logan, Paul Bradshaw, Everette Belle, Eve Rings,
Mark Blickley, Carlton Mellick III, and Vincent Collazo.

For shipping and handling, please include $1 for one book, $2 for two
books, or $3 for three or more books. Purchase chapbooks online at
www.eraserheadpress.com or send cash, check, or money order to 16455
E Fairlynn Dr. Fountain Hills, AZ 85268

Printed in the United States
127679LV00001B/123/A

9 780971 357235